MAZE CHEAT

B.R. COLLINS

LONDON NEW DELHI NEW YORK SYDNEY

Bloomsbury Publishing, London, New Delhi, New York and Sydney

First published in Great Britain in August 2012 by Bloomsbury Publishing Plc
50 Bedford Square, London, WC1B 3DP

A CIP catalogue record for this book is available from the British Library

ISBN 978 1 4088 2760 4

Typeset by Hewer Text UK Ltd, Edinburgh
Printed in Great Britain by Clays Ltd, St Ives Plc, Bungay, Suffolk

1 3 5 7 9 10 8 6 4 2

www.bloomsbury.com

PART I

THE ICE PALACE

He's not dead. But he wishes he was.

He's outside, face down on concrete.

He can smell the smoke in the air, the burnt plastic. There's the stench of melted cloth and something like cooked meat; and below that, even though it's not raining, there's the thick tang of ammonia or acid. It hurts to breathe. He can hear a thin moaning, a trapped, breathless sound like someone dying. He tries to open his eyes, to look round, but nothing moves and the world stays dark. I'm blind, he thinks. Oh, gods, I'm *blind* —

And I can't *move* —

What am I — how did I —

It comes back to him, in a rush. Behind the blood-darkness of his eyelids he can see himself, falling. He can see the explosion that burst through the windows, throwing him out into emptiness; he can see the way it boiled hungrily upwards around him, belching smoke, red and golden. He can see the way the ground flew up towards his eyes, the power-cables that caught him like a net — yes, the cable, he remembers that, thin and fiery as a whip, the unbelievable heat as it seared a line through his shirt, welding it to his skin — and then the fence, Crater's high boundary fence, hooked outwards, that seemed to stretch up to catch him and claw him to pieces, playing with him like an animal as he bounced and fell and bounced again, raked by the wire, and finally dropped him, letting him drop straight to the ground, until —

He's here. On the concrete. Alive.

For a second he's lucid, riding the wave of pain. I got it wrong, he thinks. So much for using the explosion to fake my own death. I've actually killed myself. I may not be dead yet, but I can't see, I can't move —

I can't *move* —

A wave of panic rises through him and he's drowning in it, struggling to breathe, his heart shaking him from inside like it's drilling its way through his chest. Sirens rise and blare, deafening him, but he isn't sure if they're real. Please, he thinks, please just stop this, let it be over, let it be *over* —

And his brain cuts out, mercifully, throwing him into nothing.

Half an hour earlier, Ario had known there was something wrong.

At first she'd thought it was paranoia. The place was a sink of flesh and noise, too loud to think, too rank to breathe. It had been a long time since she'd been here and she wasn't used to it. She leant against a sticky wall, watching the bodies heave and glint in the lights, and wished she was outside again. She was grasping her hood tightly and it was sweating against the skin of her fingertips. The music pounded in her bones, tuneless and too fast. Music on the Richter scale, she thought, and forced herself to inhale. Control yourself. Don't panic. Don't let it get to you. You are not afraid.

You are *not afraid*.

Better. She waited for her eyes to stop smarting, for her nose to get used to the smell.

Oh, she hated this so much. She shouldn't have had to do this. She shouldn't have had to be here — she should have had clients chasing her, faceless, polite, saying *please* and *thank you* and never knowing who she was. It'd been months — no, years — since she'd had to rendez with a client face-to-face. If only she'd — ever since things started to go — *no*.

She clenched her jaw and closed that thought cleanly, like a window on a flatscreen. Concentrate on now. There was a client in here somewhere. A deal. Once she'd got the deal, she could go and work.

OK. Where was he?

She looked round. Her hands were sweating and slippery. No one met her eyes. They're all drunk or flying, she thought, I must stick out like a skyscraper. Come *on*, whoever you are. I want to go home.

And then there was a hand on her elbow, a voice in her ear, and she turned, reflex-fast, electric-fast. Her heart stuttered: he was standing too close, his teeth were glinting in the light. She pulled away, took a deep breath. The voice said, buzzing through the music, 'Hey, you must be Ario.'

'How do you know?' She had to shout.

He was taller than her, but not by much. Rich kid, she thought. Good clothes, latest-generation hood slung trendily across his back. A gamerunner physique, of course: nice, if you liked that sort of thing. He flicked a hand at her eyes and said, 'Spotted you a mile off. You're too focused.'

'Right.'

'Not used to this?'

'It's fine.'

'You look nervous. Maybe you should've taken something. I've got a calmer, if . . . ? Never mind. At least *I* know what I'm doing.'

She tilted her head to one side, hoping her face didn't show what she was thinking. Gods, who did he think he was?

She wanted to say: Don't patronise me. I am the best Cheat in the world. I am the *best*, get it? You're just some jumped-up gamerunner with more money than sense. Instead, she said, 'Just tell me what you want.'

'Let's go somewhere quieter.'

'No,' she said. 'This is safer. Here. I thought you said you knew what you were doing?'

He hesitated, and his smile died. His eyes flicked back and forth across the room. Either he'd taken something itchy, or he was nervous too. So much for trying to pretend he's in control, she thought. He's looking shiftier than I am.

'Right,' he said. 'I'm a gamerunner. I need a cheat code.'

'No kidding.'

'A friend of mine recommended you. Said you were a Cheat.'

She could feel the impatience bubbling up. 'And one and one make two,' she said. 'What do you want, specifically?'

'I — I'm just —' He stopped, his eyes on the doorway opposite. She followed his gaze and there was a man in bright blue staggering through, retching, elegant face slack and shining with vomit. Rich kids, slumming it, Ario thought. They make me sick. 'I — just something easy,' he said, turning back. 'A bot to collect gilt. And other things. You know, so it can do all the boring stuff for me and . . .' He tailed off.

She stared at him. Fingers of resentment plucked at the tendons in her arm. She had to brace herself not to hit him. She swallowed. 'A *bot*?' she said. 'You want — you made me come here so you could commission a *bot*? To collect gilt? You want me to *design* you a *bot*?'

He blinked, twice. Then he said, too quickly, 'Not just a — not a bog-standard, dial-up, 3G bot, I mean a really complicated one, untraceable, one that the surves won't find and disable within a couple of days —'

'It'd be cheaper to keep buying ready-mades,' she said.

'Maybe, but I — I want the best. You're the best, aren't you? Everyone says —'

Not any more, they don't, she thought. But she didn't say it.

'Listen, Ario, maybe — maybe you could do something else for me. What do you recommend? Or maybe one of your — one of the other people you work with — I'm level 74 in the Maze, and I can pay, if one of you had something really good to offer me —'

'Look,' she said, and forced herself to pause. 'Look, I don't know you. Maybe you're a great gamerunner. I'm sure you're a nice guy and you're very rich and most Cheats would be grateful to have you. But you're right, I was the best. I *am* the best. And I am not going to waste my time writing you a bot, or trying to think up something that you might *possibly* want if it's good enough, or introducing you to my friends, or fluttering my eyelashes at you and making small talk. So if that's all —'

'Wait — Ario —'

'And stop using my *name*. You'll get us both into trouble.'

'Yes — just a sec — can't we talk a bit —' His eyes flicked again to the doorway, and back to her.

'You decide on something you want, you contact me online. Securely. Make me a good offer. *Then* maybe we can talk a bit.' She jerked her chin in a kind of nod, turned and left. She had to fight her way out, through a jumping mass of blank-eyed beauty, bare skin leaping and flashing in the lights. He called out again but she didn't turn round. He'd wasted enough of her time.

Is this what I am, now? she thought. Am I a bog-standard, dial-up Cheat? Have I gone from being the best to — well, to *this*, a Cheat you can rendez with in an underground bar, a Cheat who'll jump at anything, who's supposed to be pleased with a commission for a bot . . . ?

She put her gloves on as she went up the stairs, and then her hood. She was determined not to cry. The hood was old and starting to wear out, and any moisture made condensation on the eyepiece. When she logged out of the bar the door-panel flickered before it cleared her handprint, but it was OK, it was just old, and her glove was blurring the print. The door sighed and creaked as it slid open.

She paused in the entrance, breathing in the sour, acrid smell of rainwater. Her eyes stung, and the mist was thick, billowing round her ankles: but the rain itself had stopped, for once, leaving a strange, heavy stillness behind it. When she looked up, every wall and every roof was blurred with vapour. She took a few slow steps and the pitted tarmac crunched and collapsed softly under her feet. One day, she thought, all this will have gone completely. One day the rain will have eaten everything. Tonight, right now, that seemed like a good thing.

There was a noise behind her as the door opened, complaining, and she moved aside automatically. Quick footsteps, the whisper of breathing through a state-of-the-art hood, and there was a bright blue figure in the doorway, looking both ways down the street.

Something made her draw back against the wall, half hidden by the eddies of mist that swirled in the draught from the door.

He paused, looked over his shoulder, and then back. His movements were swift and precise. He called back down the stairs, 'Hurry up —' and cut off. He'd seen her. She'd seen herself reflected in his eyepiece: her thin rainsuit, her sagging hood, her own metallic visor. For a moment all she could think about was their mirrored eyepieces face-to-face, the infinity of it.

It was the man who'd come out of the loos, covered in vomit, glazed-eyed and flying.

Except now he was sober. As sober as she was.

And coming up the stairs behind him, struggling with his hood — as though he wasn't a rich kid after all, as though he'd only borrowed the hood, and actually he was someone else, as if he'd only been pretending —

The client —

Only he wasn't a client. Any more than this bright-blue, streamlined, decisive man was drunk.

Something was flipping over and over in her stomach, humming, as fast as a motor. But her brain couldn't catch up. For a second she was frozen, taking it in, helplessly trying to process the information like a terminal without a motherboard. The rendez wasn't a rendez. The client wasn't a client. It was a set-up. They just wanted to get me here. And this guy in blue followed me out — and —

She ran.

2

At first the panic took over, picking her up and hurling her. She couldn't feel her feet, couldn't feel anything. She ran. She kept running. The fear rumbled in her chest, an explosion that didn't stop, like a petrol engine. The street split and she swung sideways, skidding. Someone shouted behind her. She could hear footsteps, faster than her heart, the echoes scattered by the ground-fog. She didn't know where she was, didn't know where she was going. There were only the flat shadows left and right, milky tunnels of street and mist, currents of sharp-smelling air that sliced through the veils of vapour before they closed again. The fog pushed at her, laughed at her, slowing her down. Her throat hurt. Her eyepiece blurred. I am going to die, she thought. They'll catch me and then they'll kill me.

'Hey!' someone shouted, his hood-voice flat, amplified. 'We won't hurt you. We just want to *ask* —'

Yes, she thought. Ask me where my tankshop is. Which other Cheats live there. Their names. Their usernames. Their account details. The passcode for the door. And *then* you'll hurt me. She tried to speed up, but she was already breathless. Tiny drops of moisture ran down her eyepiece. Her mouth was wet and stinging from acid. What do I do? What do I *do*?

I have to get home. I have to —

No. That was what they were counting on. That she'd lead them home. That was the big prize. That was what they *wanted*. Otherwise they'd have taken her in the bar . . .

She heard the kid's voice in her head: *You must be Ario . . . I need a cheat code . . . one of the other people you work with . . .* They know me, she thought. And they know about the others too — Dion, Spin, Lia . . .

Run.

He was close behind her. His hood whispered and hissed.

She couldn't catch her breath. Her heartbeat was one long roar. She was underwater, drowning, the air thick and dragging her backwards.

A black space gaped on her left. She swerved, desperate. The rain-eaten tarmac sprayed up around her ankles in a gritty splash. One foot sank deeper than the other. She threw her arms out for balance, staggered, and fell sideways. More tarmac disintegrated under her hands in a stinging crunch. Her ankle was burning. The inside of her hood was blank with condensation, monochrome, harsh with the smell of chemicals. She blinked frantically. A few drops rolled down the eyepiece, leaving clear paths. Come on. Get up. Get *up*.

She pushed herself up on one leg, turned awkwardly on her toes, tried to put her other foot down. Her ankle gave way in a blaze of pain. She heard herself cry out. Her ears rang, a high note surging in and out. She thought: I'm going to faint. When I wake up I'll be a prisoner.

If I wake up.

Run. *Run.*

She took a step. Her leg flared sickeningly, all the way to her shoulder. The world sang. She sobbed, tried another step, and fell forward.

Her hands left rough-edged prints on the ground. Groundwater filled them up, fizzing. Part of her brain noticed the vapour rising from her fingers and had time to think: Damn. Soon I'll need new gloves too.

She crawled forward. Down here the air was caustic, chokingly thick with the smell of pollution, making her lungs hurt. Black spirals unrolled in front of her eyes. The sound of someone running rang off the buildings, closer and closer. This is it, she thought. I am going to die.

The footsteps stopped, only a few ems away. Slowly she turned her head to look.

It was the rich kid — or whatever he was, really. The one she'd spoken to. He was staring down at her, his eyepiece unreadable, his shoulders hunched.

She opened her mouth. There was nothing to say. She drew her legs up to her chest, as though that could make her invisible. She waited for him to get out a gun, or shout for the other man. Any moment now —

He reached down to his belt. She felt the breath catch in her throat as he drew his hand back up. He was holding a sed-gun, pointing it straight at her.

She wasn't going to die here and now. They were going to

drug her, take her back to Crater, interrogate her, get the tankshop address, the names —

She opened her mouth, feeling a silent scream push out of her lungs. The barrel of the sed-gun met her gaze, glinting through the mist.

And then everything went gold.

The whole world leapt into colour, as though it had caught fire. The droplets of water that clung to the man's suit flashed suddenly like coins, like tiny flames. The mist shone pale golden, sparkling like a curtain of silk.

And a sun rose in the man's eyepiece, so bright that he must have been half blinded. It opened like a flower, a core of light that boiled outwards and up, dying from gold to amber and red . . . Ario twisted to look, almost forgetting the sed-gun that was still in the man's hand.

The Crater tower. Something had exploded, bursting through the windows in a knot of scarlet and broken glass that glittered like sparks; and now the tongues of fire were licking upwards, flapping great flags of smoke, hell-light dancing on the canopy of fumes.

Then she heard it. The impact drove through her bones, rattled her jaw, pushed her eyeballs backwards into her head like a pair of hostile fingers. A roar rushed past her, sang in her hood, ground its teeth around her. She caught her breath. For a second she was frozen, mesmerised by the fury of the inferno, its glaring beauty, as though someone had trapped a star in the tower . . .

Now.

The voice in her head cut through the fascination, urgent and sharp as a whip. *Now*. He's not looking at you. He's almost lowered the gun. *Now*.

She launched herself to her feet, and ran.

It felt slow — it felt like her limbs were going in different directions, like she was stumbling and scrabbling for footholds in the rain-eaten rubble, like any minute now she'd feel the quick sting of a sed-dart through her suit; but nothing came, only a shout of surprise and outrage. She fell into the shadow of a fallen-down wall, panting, her throat sore and tight. She couldn't go on. Her ankle was agony: one more step and she thought she'd black out from the pain.

Somewhere there was another yell, and a curse, and the quick slide and crunch of footsteps: but they didn't come towards her. And his voice had sounded angry, resigned, like he knew he'd lost.

She listened with every nerve in her body, closing her eyes: nothing. Only faint sirens, screams, the low-level hiss as the inferno sucked at the air. Wait — footsteps . . . She stiffened, feeling her skin crawl as the man walked in her direction. 'Hey,' he called. 'We only want to talk to you. We'll make it to your advantage. Come out, for gods' sake . . .' but he didn't sound like he expected her to believe him. She clenched her fists, willing him to give up. And the footsteps started again, going in another direction now, shuffling in a confused circle. She could hear him swearing; then there was a quick squeak as he rubbed his eyepiece, still cursing. The explosion dazzled him, she thought. That's why he didn't see where I went.

And at last she heard him leave, slowly, turning back and pausing now and then, as though he was peering into the darkness. She didn't dare to move. Her leg drummed and buzzed with pain. She shut her eyes and imagined smooth tentacles of light reaching down her spine, cooling the nerves. It didn't help.

But no one came to kill her.

She waited and waited, until her heart slowed to a manageable pace and the hood was hissing, not wheezing. Moisture slid down her eyepiece, leaving bars of clarity in the condensation. A long way away a gang of streetkids shouted and fought, smashed things, scattered. There were voices nearby as the bar closed, a crowd of rich kids going past — slum tourists, she thought, clenching her jaw — and then silence. The sirens were less frequent now, less strident. And still no one came to kill her.

She looked over her shoulder, keeping her eyes on the fire, as though the Crater tower were a huge beacon, a torch to light her through the night. Slowly the flames died, battled into submission by the Crater firefighters. And the darkness gave way to dark grey, then grey. She didn't sleep, but she let herself drift. Once she heard someone climbing in the rubble a few ems away, and she froze, her heart suddenly leaping into overdrive. But it wasn't either of *them*, the boy or the man in blue. It was only a tiny streetkid, a girl, her face stained and corrugated from the rain, her eyes blank. Ario stayed still, not breathing, but even so the girl seemed to hear her: there was a second of stillness and then she was away, flicking deftly into the deepest shadows like a lizard.

Ario called out, 'Hey –' but it was too late. And what could she do, anyway? Take her home? Give her a hood? After four years of rain, there wasn't much anyone could do. The kid was blind already.

But it shook her. That could have been her, if she hadn't found Dion, if the tankshop hadn't taken her in . . . if Papa hadn't taught her to hack, before he left –

She felt sick. She wanted to go home. She sat up, felt along her leg with her hands. Not a break, just a sprain. That was something. She could walk. Slowly she levered herself up, leaning on a crumbling outcrop of wall, wobbling on one leg. Wisps of vapour rose from the ground, clung to the edges of the ruins like cobwebs. In the daylight the place looked like a warzone. Well, it *is* a warzone, she thought. Us and the streetkids against – everyone . . .

Crater and the government and – *everyone* – out to get us, trying to catch us and take us away, wipe us all out . . .

And me – if it hadn't been for that explosion, whatever it was . . .

Suddenly tiredness hit her, flicking painlessly against her hamstring like a knife, so that she almost collapsed at the knees. She clung to her bit of wall, trying to stay upright. Get home, she thought. Just get home. Don't try to think.

She set off, taking a long route, because she was injured but she wasn't stupid. Every few seconds she glanced behind her, but there was no one there.

She wasn't sure she was safe until she got to the tankshop door. Then she paused, looked round, ducked through the rubbish and the camouflage, put her hand against the comms panel, waited for the retina scan, punched in the code and the counter-code, and then she was in.

Safe.

3

She made it to the tankshop floor, and her station. Then her legs gave way.

She was alone, thank gods; so she let herself cry, ripping off her hood and putting her face in her hands. Her ankle sent flashes of heat up her leg, and her palms and knees stung from grazes, the faint bite of acid where the rain had weakened her suit — but she wasn't crying for that, none of that mattered. She wasn't even crying because she'd thought she was going to die.

You're the best, aren't you? he'd said. *Everyone says.*

And she'd thought: Not any more.

Months ago. It felt like years — but no, she counted on her fingers, calculating roughly, and it was only eight or nine weeks, maybe not even that long. I was the best. *The leetest*, Dion used to say, *my sweet leet Cheat* . . . And I was. Ario, the best. That's not even arrogance.

A couple of months, she thought, and I've gone from being the best to being — *this*. Not even enough of a prize for them to capture me right away. It was worth risking losing me, to try to find the tankshop . . .

How did it happen? My gods, how could I have lost everything so quickly?

But she knew, of course. She knew perfectly well.

And the worst of it was, it hadn't even been her fault. She could remember it exactly, that night: the night everything changed. It sprang out in HD, in technicolor, against her blurred memory of the weeks that had gone before. She'd snatched meals, snatched sleep, gone for days without talking or looking anyone in the eye, dreamt and breathed her flatscreen and lines of code. She'd sensed even then that she was on to something big. The cheat she was working on was the one that was going to change her life. Everyone already said she was the best — but this one would prove it, for ever, to the whole world. After this, she'd be a legend. She would be the Cheat that took on Crater and won. She remembered the day before she completed — while she was checking, running the code obsessively, fine-tuning, second-guessing — Dion had said to her, 'You are going to *own* them, babe.'

'Ye-ep,' she'd said, 'what?' But by the time she'd pulled her eyes from the screen and looked up he was gone.

It was only when the client called that she dragged herself back into the real world; and while she was talking she could still feel the suck of her obsession, distracting her from the conversation. He — probably he, she thought, because of the way he seemed to assume she was male — didn't want to know about the details. All he said was, 'So we're on? All ready?'

Ario took a deep breath, because there were transparent lines of code flowing in front of her eyes. The translation program was slow, and every time there was a pause in the conversation she wanted to reach for her flatscreen, check it over one more time. 'Yes,' she said. 'It's all set up. Transfer the next instalment of the money and then it'll be all stations go.'

'Excuse me?'

'Yes,' she said again, more slowly. 'It's all ready. Transfer the money.'

'Tomorrow?'

'Yes,' she said. Suddenly she was grinning: the light seemed brighter, the surface under her hands more solid. Tomorrow. *Yes*.

And when she hung up, the flare of excitement was still with her, flickering in the roof of her mouth, tingling in her fingertips. She scanned her flatscreen with her eyes. No mistakes. It was going to work.

As Dion said, she was going to *own* them.

But the next day, waiting for the transfer, she'd never been so scared. She sat staring at her screen, almost hoping that it wouldn't come through. When the digits flashed up — wow, she was rich, another couple like this and she could leave Ingland, create a new life somewhere else, and a *legal* one, no less — she clenched her fists and shut her eyes, screwing up the courage to hit **Enter**.

Enter.

There. Done.

And then suddenly she had her life back. She felt time spread out around her, thin and airy and empty, like a desert.

She could eat. She could take a shower. She stood up and noticed how stiff she was, how thin, how her skin had gone a weird silvery colour from too much artificial light. Behind her there was a whistle: good-humoured, mocking. Dion's voice said, 'And has she finished, at last, our little genius?'

She didn't have the energy to come up with something clever. 'Yes,' she said.

'Wow. Congrats. Another week of that and you would literally be dead.'

'Yeah.' She turned and everything swayed around her, as if she was standing at the top of a high building.

'Hey, zombie-girl, don't die now,' he said, and he put his hands on her arms, holding her as though he thought she would fall apart. 'You've got to go and make yourself beautiful, right? Party tonight.'

'Is there?'

''Course there is! We're all going to be watching. You don't think —' He stopped, peering into her face, and then shook his head. 'Hey, Ario. We've been waiting for this. We want to see you beat Crater. Tonight you're going to make history, right? And we want to see it. It's all set up in there.' He pointed to the doorway that led to the tank floor. It was festooned with mini-lights. Ario forced herself to smile. 'Babe, this is your moment of glory. We're going to see these amazing codes in action. So go and get showered. Belle of the ball shouldn't stink the way you do right now. OK?'

They hadn't watched a gamerunner run a cheat code together for a long time; and it had never been like this. When she came out of the shower — none of her clothes were clean, obviously, so she put on what was least dirty — everyone was on the tankfloor, sitting on cushions and blocks, one of Spin's tracks bubbling and ticking on the speakers. They looked round when she came in. Spin waved from the decks. Lia stood up, poured her a drink and put it into her hand. 'Hey, well done, Ario.'

'The code hasn't run yet. It may not work.'

'No, but — well. 'Course it'll work. It'll be great.' Lia smiled, waited for Ario to smile back, shrugged, and went to sit down again.

Dion was branching the tank to a flatscreen that someone had set up on the wall. He winked, finished what he was doing, and then danced over to her. 'Hey hey, Ario, how's it going? Ready for worldwide fame and fortune?' He had a shine in his eyes that made her stomach twist.

'You flying, Dion?'

'Tonight? No! Far too special an occasion.'

'You don't even know what I've been working on.'

'A big fat cheat code that'll shaft Crater.'

She laughed, and tried to pretend she hadn't. 'Well. Sort of.' She wondered whether it was worth explaining that no, she didn't want to *shaft* Crater, because Cheats were parasites and it didn't make sense to kill the host. Beating Crater was one thing, but you didn't want to go *too* far . . . But she couldn't be bothered, and, anyway, Dion knew that. He just liked pretending to be thick. She said, 'It's a cheat that'll get my client into the Roots and to the end. It's a combination — you remember the Ghost cheat? I've adapted it for the Roots and I've created a bug which means he can leave

24

his corpse right there. So he gets in, runs the traps using the Ghost — I hacked a map, so he knows where to go — gets to his corpse, resurrects, and bingo. He's done it.'

'Wow,' Dion said, and whatever he said he *was* flying, she was sure of it. 'The Roots of the Maze. That would be a big deal.'

'Yeah, I'd kind of worked that out myself.'

'Why does he want to beat the Roots, incidentally?'

She stared at him. 'Er . . . because he's a gamerunner, and he wants to win?'

He rolled his eyes. 'Sure. Like all our clients. But the *Roots*?'

'So he wants to win the whole game.'

'But then he won't have anything left to *do*. Endgames are rubbish. That's if the Maze has an endgame at all.'

She went on staring at him. Her eyeballs felt sticky in their sockets, hard to move. '*I* don't know,' she said. 'He wants to beat the hardest part of the Maze, the part no one's ever done before, he wants the kudos or the reputation or whatever. I don't care. He pays me, I write the cheat for him. Why all these existential questions all of a sudden?'

He hunched his shoulders and gave her a big rotten-toothed grin. 'Just out of curiosity. Or overexcitement,' he said. 'Come on, looks like your client was logging on a few minutes ago. You ready?'

No, she wanted to say. No. Everyone leave me alone. I want to watch this on my own, on my flatscreen, through my fingers. She said, 'Yeah, sure.'

The screen on the wall had flashed up a surve's-eye view of her client as he logged in. She hadn't paid much attention to his avatar; she couldn't even remember his name. Now she saw that he was expensive, flashy, clad in gleaming golden armour that didn't strike her as very practical. More money than sense, she thought. No wonder he has to pay for cheats.

The room had gone quiet. She crossed to the nearest block and sat down. The padding creaked and her face went hot. More people were looking at her than at the screen. She stared at her client's avatar without seeing it. Herkules404, she thought. *That's* his name. What a suxor.

You are about to enter the Roots of the Maze. If you die while attempting this quest, your account will be closed. Are you sure you wish to proceed?

Someone made a noise and pointed at the words, huddling into his chair as if this was the opening credits of a film. Everyone turned to stare at the screen. Ario felt it on her face, the relief of not being the centre of attention. She clenched her hands. Go on, then, she thought. Say yes. Let's get this show on the road.

Herkules404 said, **Yes.**

And the Roots of the Maze slid into place around him, the great hall with steps that led down into the darkness, a huge spiral that narrowed and plunged like a well.

There was a murmur; everyone in the room leant forward, sharing an in-breath. No one lasted long in the Roots. Even Ario had only seen a map. She brought her glass to her lips and took a sip. The liquid burnt on her tongue but she was too nervous to taste anything. Dion had crouched down at her side; now he put up his hand and patted her thigh. She looked down at his hand — his wiry, friendly, freckled hand — and for a moment she wanted to hold on to it, grab it like a kid and squeeze. She made herself shift in her seat, moving out of his reach.

Herkules paused where he was: letting his eyes adjust to the dimness, maybe. He moved his head and waved sideways, positioning a map that only he could see. The translation program said, after a second's delay, **Optimise equipment. Load map of Roots of the Maze.**

'Hope he doesn't forget to load the cheat,' Dion said, from the ground.

'He won't.' But he might, she thought. If I'm this wound up, maybe he is too.

Dion said, 'If he junks it —'

'He *won't*.' She sat up straight, stared at the screen and willed him to get on with it. 'He won't. He's paid for the cheat, so he's hardly going to — look. *There!*'

She'd said it too loud, pointing, and a couple of people looked round. But at least she was right: there'd been a flicker, a tiny pause like a split second of crashtime, and then a jump as the game caught up. Herkules had loaded the cheat. It was done.

Now, she thought. If it doesn't work, tough. Now there's nothing I can do. She bit down on the end of her thumbnail, grinding the keratin between her front teeth. Herkules moved forward, looking around. The first trap will show us, one way or another, she thought. Go on, find a trap. I can't take much more of this. Find a —

He took another step. There was a click.

A tiny pause. Everything was frozen, even her heart.

Then a blade swung out of the shadows, clean as a whip, catching the light as it came. She was so intent on the screen that she almost screamed: but she couldn't move, couldn't open her mouth, couldn't breathe.

Zing.

She shut her eyes.

When she opened them again, someone was laughing softly. Dion. He said, 'Who's the best, then? Who's *uber*leet?'

And in front of her, on the screen, Herkules was jumping from foot to foot in a kind of jig, pummelling the air with his fists. The blade had gone through him, and he was still there. The Ghost was working, then.

'No, wait,' Ario heard herself say. She kept her eyes on the corner of the screen, staring at the Surveillance ikon. If they notice, she thought. If they ask themselves what a ghost is doing in the Roots . . . if I haven't cloaked it well enough . . . but the little eye stayed green, steady. She breathed out, slowly, until her lungs were completely empty. 'It's the cloaking that makes the Ghost code illegal,' she said. 'Anyone can be a ghost wherever they want, as long as they're not doing anything else wrong. It's just that the surves would cotton on to it, and wonder what was going on, and then they'd sweep for cheats . . . it's the corpse that's really bending the rules, this is just a way to get to it, past all the traps . . . I just had to make sure he didn't attract their attention . . .' She was burbling — Dion knew all that, he was almost as leet as she was, after all — but every second that the eye stayed green added to her relief, and she couldn't stop herself. The stealth part was working. So far so good. As long as Herkules ran sensibly, so his patterns weren't picked up automatically . . .

And the corpse. That was what *really* mattered.

Her back had started to ache. She rolled her shoulders, loosening the muscles, and stood up. 'I'm just —'

'Hey, babe, wait, where are you —'

'— going to check the corpse —'

'— no, Ario, come on, you can't leave your party, use a terminal here and split-screen it, we want to see too.' He said it loudly, and Spin looked round and nodded, flicking his hands in the way that meant, *Yes, I agree*.

She would've ignored Dion, but Spin was different. She didn't want to check in front of everyone — but she wanted to know *now*, and it would be the quickest way, everything was set up . . . She went to the terminal branched into the tank, and tried to ignore the flatscreen above her. On the terminal's screen a smaller Herkules was dancing his way past smaller traps, jumping and laughing and punching the air as though it was *his* skill that was taking him through. Little suxor, she thought again, and tried not to let him distract her. She split-screened, found the map — her own, beautiful, adapted map, elegant and clear — and zoomed in on the target, the hidden portal that not even the Maze's own maps would show. There. The space in front of it, the little magic square where she'd put the corpse, that corpse that she'd worked on for months, and — if it had worked, if when Herkules activated it, if, if, if —

It was there.

She closed her eyes, opened them, looked again.

Yes.

Yes.

She heard Dion whoop behind her, break into a joyous chant, 'Woot! Woot! Woot!'

Her face was burning. She wanted to cry. She was smiling so hard it hurt. I've done it, she thought. As long as he gets there — and what's going to stop him now? — as long as he gets there, I've done it . . .

She looked up. Herkules went on down the passages, through fire-nets and cross-blades and nests of spyders, through a cave of shadows, past a long wall of creeping mould that moved towards him and then hesitated, confused. She watched him go, and it didn't matter that he was just a spoilt rich kid, because he was running her codes, hers, and together they were going to *win*.

4

She'd never been so proud, or pleased, or excited about anything. It took hours, but she didn't mind that: watching Herkules go deeper and deeper into the Roots, flicking her eyes to the Surve ikon every few minutes, laughing because it was still green. Beside her Dion was drinking his way through a bottle of water; every so often he'd say, 'Hey, babe, why don't you have some? Real vintage stuff, doesn't taste of anything, it's *crazy*,' and she'd shake her head, not wanting to look away from the screen, not even for a second. The others were still there, but they hadn't realised it was going to take so long, and now they'd lost interest; they'd plugged in their iThings, or they were chatting, or half asleep. Spin had put on another track, a sound that washed and sang around them like the blood in their veins. She thought, I could be dreaming. This is so good it can't really be happening.

But when Herkules started to get close she blinked and sat up, and the sharp twinge in her neck reminded her that she was awake. The split-screen was still up, and her map was glowing blue and lovely in the other half. She could see the dot that was Herkules, only a little way away from the portal. Her heart sped up. Go on, Herkules. Go on. Make me proud. You're almost there . . .

'Who's the other one?' Dion said.

She thought she'd misheard. 'What?'

'The other player.' He gestured to the screen, and for the first time she noticed another dot, working its way past a network of time-traps, only a few hundred ems from Herkules. The dot paused in a wide hall, surrounded by sucker bats; then stepped on to a plate-trap. But the dot stayed alive: the trap was silvery, when it should have been blank white. Disabled.

'Ario,' Dion said, with a new note in his voice, 'what's going on with the *other* gamerunner?'

'I — don't — know,' Ario said. Another gamerunner — and that trap, disabled, when it shouldn't have been, when *she* certainly hadn't touched it . . . A cold bubble formed at the bottom of her stomach and pushed upwards, expanding. Someone else in the Roots? *Now?*

'He's not anything to do with —?' Dion stopped. She felt him shift in his seat to look up at her.

'It's fine,' she said. 'Just another gamerunner, I expect. And they can't fight Herkules because he's a ghost. He just needs to get to his body, resurrect and get through the portal before whoever-it-is has a chance to challenge him.'

'Right,' Dion said. They sat still, watching the two dots converge.

In the silence, Ario said again, 'It's *fine*.'

*　　*　　*

And it might have been fine, even then.

Herkules ran the last passage, vaulting and twirling extravagantly. The last gallery, the last few traps. And then he was at the hidden portal — a dead end, apparently, only Ario's map showed what it really was — and his corpse was slumped against the wall. Ario's ribs jerked painfully, and she coughed and exhaled. She'd been holding her breath. Come on. Nearly there. She wished she'd written code for a ventrillo — she needed to warn him about the other gamerunner, he hadn't noticed, she needed to *talk* to him — or even some kind of override . . . if she could just have reached out now and taken over, made sure he didn't do anything wrong —

Look, she shouted in her head, *look*, there's another gamerunner behind you, can't you *see* —

Herkules stood where he was, stretching, rolling his shoulders. He tilted his head, checked the map one last time, and smiled at his corpse. For a moment Ario felt the triumph surge again, like hunger; then she glanced at the map, and it faded. The other gamerunner was right there. Waiting, a few ems away. As if he — no, wait, she — knew . . .

Herkules touched his corpse.

A blue swarm of stars burst open, surrounding him. It spun, shining, and cleared. The corpse dissolved into smoke.

And Herkules wasn't a ghost any more. He was solid and alive. At the end of the Roots, ready to run the portal.

Ready to *win*.

There was a crackling, electric silence in the room. Then someone said, 'Wow, Ario, it *worked*, you are a *genius*!' A ripple of applause spread out — irregular and sporadic as

33

people woke up, unbranched their iThings, realised something interesting had happened — but applause, real applause. For an instant Ario felt the warmth of it, and she almost smiled.

Then the other gamerunner came into view. And the screen said, **PvP mode is enabled. Athene Glaukos is in range and wants to engage you.**

Dion looked up. He said, 'Ario . . . ?'

She put her hands over her face, so that her fingers were like bars across her vision. She forced herself to breathe. Herkules, don't engage her, she thought. Please just run the portal. Please don't let her —

Herkules turned round, slowly.

No, she thought. No, please. Just *run the port*—

'But it's OK, isn't it?' Dion said. 'He's got fight cheats as well, upgraded weaponry and all that, even if he does take her on it'll be OK, right, Ario?'

She didn't answer. On-screen they were talking — that pointless gamerunner I'm-going-to-kill-you small talk — but the words didn't register. Dion was right. Herkules had won all the fights he'd had. It would still be OK, even if —

Herkules turned away. Don't turn your back on her! Ario wanted to shout. Please don't —

And swung back, so fast the flatscreen showed a glowing trace where he'd moved. He went for Athene, followed her down when she dropped and rolled, stamped with one foot. Athene blocked it, but only just. Ario bit down hard on her fingernail and tasted blood; beside her Dion said, 'He's pretty impressive, right? Quick as broadband. Nothing to worry about.'

34

It didn't last long. Athene was on her feet again, her daggers trembling in her hands, but she hadn't got time to get her balance back before Herkules went for her again. He smashed his sword down on her hand, punched, dodged her counter-punch, and slid the sword smoothly into place below her chin. Athene froze, her eyes flickering. The blade stayed still, poised just above her larynx. He'd got her.

Ario breathed out. A long way away, Dion said, 'See?'

'Kill her, then,' she said, as if Herkules could hear her. 'Get on with it.'

But he didn't. He said, **How come you got this far? Who's your Cheat?**

Dion muttered, 'Good question.'

'She can't have a Cheat,' Ario said, and anger made her voice crack. 'No one could get her this far into the Roots. No one's as good as I am. We'd *know*.' Please just kill her, she thought. Please just do it. She's not even real.

Athene said, **Daedalus.**

There was a silence; the room rippled with something that was between amusement and confusion. Ario glanced at Dion and he was frowning. He mouthed, *Daedalus?* and rolled his eyes. When he saw Ario was watching him he sketched a square in the air with his fingers and made a jumping motion with his hands: mad as a box of frogs. 'Yeah, right,' he said aloud, to the whole room. 'And *my* Cheat is the Delphic mucking Oracle.'

Ario wanted to laugh; but she couldn't. The way Athene had said it — and the way Herkules was listening . . . even though he said, sharply, **Daedalus isn't *real*, you silly girl . . .**

I'm from Crater, Athene said. **Daedalus is a friend of mine, one of the designers. Whoever your Cheat is, Daedalus is better.**

From Crater? She couldn't be. Ario felt a stab of panic, as if *she* was there with Herkules' sword at her throat; but it wasn't true, it wasn't possible. Crater didn't work like that. Crater would've found the cheat codes and disabled them; they wouldn't have sent in some kid to take Herkules out like this. And if Athene were from Crater ... well. She wouldn't have lost the fight.

And Daedalus *wasn't real*. Everyone knew that. The Maze hadn't been created by one man; it was unthinkable. The Maze was huge, it was a whole world. No, Daedalus was just a convenient myth, a generic name for the design team. It was like saying *Crater* was your Cheat. It didn't make sense.

Ario was afraid of things that didn't make sense.

She wanted this to be over, now. She just wanted Herkules to finish it.

But he went on asking questions, and Athene went on answering them, her stance shifting infinitesimally with every second that passed. Ario couldn't look away from the screen, but she couldn't take in the words: all she could hear was the rushing sound of Spin's track — unless it was the blood in her ears, roaring and fading in waves. She brought her hands down from her face, pressing them together to stop them shaking. *Look*, she wanted to scream. Look at the way she's standing. She's trying to distract you. You have to kill her *now*. Or —

The tip of Herkules' sword dipped, wavered, slid absently to one side. The tension in Herkules' hand relaxed. He said, **And how do I know this isn't a —**

And Athene punched upwards, dagger blade straight into his windpipe.

Herkules' body went straight down, dropping cleanly to the ground. His ghost stayed where he'd been standing, staring at Athene in disbelief. He said . . . **a trick?**

There was a pause. It must only have been five seconds; but Ario thought she could feel herself getting older, the creeping growth of her nails and hair. Her heartbeat rang hollow and flabby in her ears.

The corpse evaporated smoothly. Herkules' ghost turned to watch it go. His transparent fists clenched. He started to say, **Muck you, little female dog, muck you —** and then he was gone too, snapped neatly out of sight like a light. Half the split-screen filled with writing: **I am sorry. You have died in the Roots. Your account is now closed.**

Silence.

Dion shifted suddenly in his seat, as though he'd started to move and thought better of it. He said, too loudly, 'How lame is that translation program? We really need to patch that,' but no one laughed or even reacted.

Ario felt people turning to look at her, the air so thick and heavy that every movement made ripples in it. Her eyes stung. She couldn't focus. In front of her, on the other side of the screen, Athene opened her inventory, seeing what she'd won. Herkules' armour, his weapons and flashy

37

accessories and hundreds of gilt . . . But all Ario could think of was her beautiful map, her lovely blue map — and the hidden portal. Don't you dare, she thought. Don't even think about it.

Please . . .

Athene took her time, staring up at the map, gesturing as though she was comparing it to another version. Then she laughed, made her way back down the passage to get a clear run-up, put her arms up to shield her head, and ran at the wall.

And it opened for her.

For a moment Ario was frozen, staring at the screen. The End of the Roots. A garden, a glowing garden, beautiful, full of a golden, shimmering haze. **Welcome to the endgame.**

Athene's done it, she thought. She's *won*.

And Herkules is gone, dead, account closed. He's dead.

I'm dead.

She was out of the door, running, blind with rage and shame, her stomach heaving. She ducked into the nearest cube, retching, and her mouth flooded with bile. She hadn't eaten enough to throw up properly, but she couldn't stop shaking and the nausea didn't go away.

She stayed in the loo for hours, ignoring Dion when he knocked on the door. She knew she'd remember that toilet all her life: the smell of it, the clammy warmth of the seat where she rested her forehead on the plastic, the smears on the wall behind. And Dion's voice: 'Hey, babe, it's OK, it wasn't your fault, you're still the best, you're uberleet, you're a total roxor, you know that . . .' Until he ran out of things to say and they both just sat there, either side of the locked door, knowing that she was finished, junked, that whatever he said no one would take her seriously ever again. Getting a client's account closed? That was suicide. Even if it wasn't her fault.

At last, when she couldn't bear it any more, she said, 'Go fy, Dion.'

'Right.' She heard him stand up, hesitate, and leave.

And then she put her hands over her eyes, and cried.

5

That had been months ago. And nothing had got better.

Right now, staring at her blank flatscreen, her ankle full of fire and her eyes still smarting from the rain-fumes, she would have given anything to go back and do it differently. But differently how? She still didn't know what had gone wrong. She still didn't know why Athene had turned up like that, just at the wrong moment; she still didn't know how those traps had been disabled. And I should know, she thought. I should've known *then*. If there was another Cheat that good, working on codes for the Roots . . . it's a small world. Someone would've told me.

Unless — Daedalus —

But that was mad. Daedalus wasn't a real person. She shut her eyes and rested the heels of her hands against her eyelids, letting automatic tears wash the sting away. Athene, Daedalus . . . Their names echoed in her dreams, calling down tunnels, their voices unravelling like threads as she tried to follow, losing her way.

But what did it matter? She had to get on with her life, didn't she? And if her life had gone from one she loved — because yes, she'd loved it, being a Cheat, being the best

— to what it was now . . . well, tough. If she had to create bots for a living, then that was what she'd do.

Not right now, though.

The tankshop was very quiet. She pushed back the block she'd been sitting on, and stood up. She should have been tired, but the night had left her with an uncomfortable, fizzing kind of energy. Where was everyone? Asleep, probably — being a Cheat wasn't nine-to-five, after all — but suddenly she felt lonely. She stood still, listening. There was a shuffle and a thump from the doorway that led to the tankfloor, and she went to look. Spin was there, moving hardware. When he saw her he smiled, but his arms were full and he could only waggle his fingers in greeting.

'Hey, Spin,' she said. 'Where is everyone?'

He tilted his head and shrugged. Then he set his box down, beckoned to her and nodded at the corner of the floor. She followed his look. Her heart twitched, as though someone had squeezed it. She felt her mouth open a little, her chapped lips peeling stickily apart.

She knew what it was; but for a second she couldn't take it in, and all she saw was something very beautiful.

It was like it had grown there: halfway between a cylinder and a huge curved bud, pale and gleaming. It was so smooth the light seemed to fall into it, leaving a silvery halo that clung to the edges like dust. Only the tangle of wires at its foot hinted at its purpose.

'The iTank,' Ario said. 'Wow. We got one. It only launched yesterday.'

Spin grinned.

She took a few steps towards it, and ran her hand down the side. The skin was so silky she could hardly feel it on her fingertips. If the new version of the Maze matches the new hardware, she thought, this is going to be impressive. 'Is it branched yet?'

Spin shook his head, and raised a rueful eyebrow at the mess of cables. One of his hands sketched a gesture: *We need more wiring*.

'Oh, right.' That was where the others were, then: on a supplies mission. It had never been her scene — she was brains, not brawn — but she felt a little pulse of hurt that no one had even told her they were going. 'I don't know, though. I reckon we could do it with what we've got here,' she said. 'What do you think?'

Spin met her eyes, and the corner of his mouth twitched.

'Yeah, OK,' she said, 'I'm being impatient. I can't wait to see what it's like. But the faster we get it running, the faster we can start working on new codes . . . I wonder how transferable they'll be . . .' She turned on her heel and glanced at the old tank, looking back and forth, comparing them. 'And there's the new Maze expansion too, of course . . .' But the Maze expansion would be — well, just more of the Maze. It was the iTank that fascinated her. She knelt down and started to look at the connections, and Spin put down a box of spare parts next to her. Soon she was absorbed in the problem: it wasn't the same as writing codes, but it was satisfying in its own way, and after a few minutes she could see that they *could* branch it with the stuff they had. Stupid boy, Dion, she thought. All that danger and pollution exposure, for nothing

. . . She shuffled into a more comfortable position, cross-legged and leaning against the wall. The rumble of the generators soothed her, and she closed her eyes. I'm just visualising the circuitry, she said to herself, I'm just getting it all clear in my head . . .

She fell asleep.

When she woke, she didn't know what time it was — or, for a moment, where she was, or who. She was alone, the mess of wires still spread out in front of her, although Spin had wrapped her in a crackly luminium blanket. She sat up, groaning, rubbing her eyes. Her face was still sore from her leaking hood.

In the outer room there were voices, low and urgent; and then a different, strident note rose out of the blur, a new voice cutting through the others. It was Lia. 'Dion,' she shouted, 'this is *not OK*! Are you crazy? What the hell were you thinking?'

Ario stood up, walked to the doorway, and peered through.

There was a cluster of people at the far end of the tank-shop, as though they'd shut the outside door behind them and started arguing before they had time to take another step into the room. Spin was hovering a few ems away from the group, twisting a length of wire-sheath between his fingers, his face grave. Dion was — where was Dion? She caught sight of him kneeling on the ground, half obscured by Lia's legs. What's he doing down there? she thought.

Lia shook her head and turned away, kicking the leg of a table as she went, so that the whole counter shuddered.

'You are so irresponsible! Were you flying or what? You're putting us all in danger, for what? For *nothing*!' She paused, looking over her shoulder as if she was waiting for some kind of answer; but Dion was staring down, intent on something, and there was only silence. Someone shuffled their feet and coughed. At last she said, 'Go fy, Dion. Seriously. Go *fy*.'

She went straight past Ario and into the corridor that led to the cubes, smacking the comms panel so hard that at first it beeped and wouldn't read her print.

When the door shut behind her it seemed to break the spell, and the voices rose again, quieter this time but with the same urgent tone. Ario caught phrases here and there: 'What do we — do we have a spare cube — what if Crater —? Are you sure, Dion — who is —'

Dion said, from his position on the floor, 'He can have my cube. The code's $C_8H_{10}N_4O_2$. Someone go and get my bedbag.'

'Why —'

'We need to carry him. I don't think dragging him by the arms is the best strategy, do you? In the state he's in?' Dion's voice was clear, sharp. Ario thought: This is serious, then, if he's talking like that.

Someone — when they turned Ario saw it was Java — said, 'OK, Dion . . .' and half ran towards the cubes, the way Lia had gone. Where she'd been there was a gap, and Ario could see through to what Dion was looking at, what was on the floor.

A body. The face was scarlet and swollen, the nostrils

leaking blood. The eyes were closed. The clothes were shredded, too flimsy to wear outside, and they were burnt away in places, burnt right into the skin. She could see one bare hand and it was crimson, peeling and singed, the nails blackened shards.

Ario's breathing stopped and started again, as though her brain had crashed and recovered. What —? she thought. What has Dion *done*?

She thought he — she? — it — the body — was dead. It had to be, surely, if it looked like that . . . But it moaned, spitting and slurring, and she saw a bubble of saliva slide from the corner of its mouth. The froth was red.

'Java! Get the medikit too,' Dion called. 'Painkillers. Morphine.'

'Morphine? But, Dion, we hardly have —'

'Just *get it*.'

Java paused, and the others looked round at her, then back at Dion. Dion held her look, unblinking. She bit her lip, and went through the door. It seemed only a second before she was back, the medikit in her arms and Dion's bedbag over her shoulder, the end dragging along the floor. It left a shiny trail in the dust and sent tiny LX components spinning towards the walls.

'Put it on the floor. Now help me put him on it.' Ario admired the way he said it: as if it didn't even occur to him that he might not be obeyed, obeyed *right now*. And it worked. They bent down, picked the body up as if it was a sack and dumped it on the bedbag. It cried out, a short jagged sound that made Ario wince.

'OK,' Dion said. 'Good.' He opened the medikit, fumbling with the catch. His voice had been so calm; but Ario thought she could see his fingers shaking. He loaded a hypo, flicked a few drops from the needle, and jammed it into the body's leg, through the clothes. Another cry, but it died into a choke almost as soon as it had started. No one moved; Ario saw those blackened, oozing fingers relax, and realised she could breathe more easily.

'Yes,' Dion said, and coughed, as though he was trying to cover a crack in his voice. 'Right. Let's go. I'll try and set up something a bit more permanent when we've got him installed.'

He bent his head, so that Ario could see the vertebrae leading to his skull like steps. 'Come on. Let's go.' A couple of people crouched on either side of the body, and with an awkward, stumbling movement they picked up the bedbag and its sagging load. Someone grunted, but no one said anything as they staggered towards the door. Ario watched them go past. Dion flicked a look at her, but she couldn't read his expression.

The door opened and closed behind them. Spin had stepped aside to let them pass. Now he tossed his bit of wire-sheath into the shadows and met her gaze.

'What the hell is going on?' she said.

He shrugged, and raised his hand as if to gesture. Then he stopped, sighed and walked past her with a jerk of his shoulders.

Yes, that's about right, Ario thought, staring after him. I haven't got a clue, either.

*   *   *

The corridor outside the cubes was packed. When Ario opened the door Java nodded at her and Nax, sitting against the wall, said, 'Hey, Ario, you look like completely oom. Better get some sleep before you crash out.'

'What's going on?'

Java swapped a glance with Nax, and said, 'Better ask Dion.'

'Who's the — the body?'

Nax fiddled with the toe of his runner, pulling off bits of corroded rubber and flicking them at the wall. 'Better ask Dion,' he said, echoing Java exactly.

'But —'

'He'll tell *you*. Then maybe you can tell us.'

'Right.' Ario could feel the hostility in the air. This isn't fair, she wanted to say, just because Dion likes me, you all blame me when he does something weird . . . but the tank-shop was like that. You couldn't live with twenty-odd other Cheats without having cliques and allies. 'What's he doing right now?'

'Setting up an IV. So that he can give all our morphine to that kid.'

'Where did the kid come from?'

'We found him. Well, Dion found him.' Nax glared up at her, as if it was her fault. 'And we didn't even get the supplies we were after. The new Maze expansion is live, and we haven't even got a working iTank. By the time we're up and running everyone else will have already started writing cheats. They'll trash us. Our tankshop is going to get totally owned.'

'Oh . . .' Dammit, she thought, I didn't finish branching the iTank . . . She hovered for a moment, torn between curiosity and pride; then pride won, and she added, 'That's OK, I've worked out a way to branch it with the stuff we've got.'

'That's great,' Java said, with the hint of a smile. But it wasn't what Ario had been hoping for. It wasn't what she would have said, before Herkules and the Roots . . . 'Probably worth getting on with it, so we can have a look at the new Maze ASAP.'

It was an order. But Ario didn't have to take orders from anyone. Who the hell did Java think she was? What had *she* ever done?

'Yeah, probably,' Ario said, hating herself. 'I'll go and do it now, then.'

She backed out of the door. When Dion emerged she'd ask him face-to-face. Whatever was going on, she'd find out eventually; and she didn't want to fight her way down the corridor, anyway. All those people, that tense silence, the smell of rain-fumes clinging to them. And that body, in Dion's bedbag . . . She wasn't squeamish, but those swollen eyes, that limp scarlet hand, the carbonised stumps of his fingernails —

She went back to the iTank. No one else was on the tank-shop floor, and it was good to be alone. At last she got it branched, turned it on and loaded the demo. It seemed to work; she was no gamerunner, but she'd branched her terminal and the flatscreen gave her a clear picture. The graphics were flattish and clunky — but then, the iTank worked with two-way feedback, direct to and from the gamerunner's brain, so it made sense that her software wouldn't work as well as it had on the old gametanks. OK. Good. She peered at the image — a ruined palace or something, trees with drifting leaves, yeah yeah, so far so meh — and rubbed her eyes. She was knackered. She didn't know what time it was, or how long she'd slept for.

She heard something behind her, and turned round.

Dion. He gave her a wide, wide smile, and sauntered over, every joint loose. Flying.

'Hey, babesauce,' he said. 'How's it going?'

'Branched.'

'Cool. Woot. You tried it yet?'

'I don't run games, Dion. I sit on the outside and write code. Gamerunners are suxors, remember?'

'S'posed to rock, the iTank.'

'Yeah, who says? Crater? You don't reckon they might be trying to sell something?'

He laughed, throwing his head back. One of his incisors was pitted at the top, coming away from the gum. 'Just saying . . . so you got it branched?'

'Dion . . .' He was boring when he flew; he repeated everything. 'What was going on . . . earlier, with that — whoever it was . . . ?'

'Whoever who was?'

'You brought someone in. Nax said you found him. What's that about?'

'Oh yeah. Yeah. He escaped from the Crater complex. Place blew up. Did I not mention that? Most amazing thing, actually,' he said, and the grin came back and crept across his face like mould. 'Must've been twenty storeys up. Some kind of explosion.'

'I know. I saw it,' she said. 'It saved my life.'

But he didn't seem to hear her. 'And this kid — shoots straight out, on to the power cables, falls and hits the fence, he's still alive when we get to him . . . I mean, what are the odds? Plus it's not raining. So we bring him in. *I* bring him in.'

She said, '*Why?*'

'He came from Crater,' Dion said, as if that was an answer.

'But —'

'When was the last time anyone got decent insider info from Crater? It doesn't happen. The only time anyone leaves that complex is to go to the airport. And this kid was just — just lying there. He could be anyone. What have we got to lose?'

Everything, she wanted to say. What were you thinking? If Crater want him back . . . if they come looking . . . Lia's right. Dion's crazy. She said, 'Dion —'

'Also, he needed help.'

She looked at him, and through the drug-haze she thought she saw the determination she'd heard in his voice when he was giving orders; and the softness, hidden and unexpected, that had made his hands tremble when he prepared the hypo. She clenched her teeth, and thought: He took me in. I was as almost helpless as that boy, after Papa disappeared.

I could react like Lia. Or I could take a chance.

And in the back of her mind, irrational and comforting, she could still see the Crater tower: burning like a torch, keeping her company in the dark.

'OK,' she said. 'I'm on your side.'

'Love you for ever,' he said. 'You rock, roxor.'

'But if something goes wrong, you're sorting it, OK? You're in charge of him. He eats out of your budget. And if he dies, you're on disposal duty.'

'Hey, Ario, you're so kind and caring.'

'I just —'

'Like you would ever help me with that, anyway.' He grinned, and there was a sudden moment of silence. 'H and K, sweetie. See you later.'

He got up to leave, but he paused in the doorway. 'Nothing'll go wrong,' he said.

Ario kept her eyes on her terminal. 'Sure,' she said.

'Really. Trust me.'

'Sure,' she said again. For a second she thought she might have started a loop: but there was no answer, and when she looked up he'd gone.

She played around with the iTank for longer than she realised. When she finally got up and stretched she was stiff and sore all over, and starving. She felt as if someone had rubbed the insides of her eyelids with sand. There was the faraway scratching of someone's iThing on speaker; it sounded like something eating through the wall.

In the outer room, the lights were off, and there was only the faint glow of sleep LEDs from the terminals. She navigated her way carefully towards the door to the cubes, trailing one hand against the wall so she didn't fall over anything. She could hear a strange sibilant murmur, hissing and pausing in a constant rhythm like bands of blue noise. After a few seconds she realised it came from the corner, where a dark shape was huddled underneath a counter. Ah. Dion was snoring.

She made her way down the corridor, past the sounds that came from each cube: Lia's iThing, amplified, something old with a pounding beat; Spin's iThing, playing a liquid, bubbling track; the creak of Nax's bed and Java's voice, wordless and so uninhibited Ario wanted to put her fingers in her ears as she went past; and then Dion's cube, and silence.

Or not quite silence. Ario stopped where she was, and she thought she could hear the ticking of an IV, and the murmur of someone too weak to call out. Was he on his own, in there, the kid? Had Dion just plugged him into the drip and left him? She heard Dion's voice, *you're so kind and caring*, and made herself walk past, speeding up as she went. Dion's problem, not mine, she thought. Whoever this kid is, he's nothing to do with me.

She got to her own cube, logged in, watched the door slide open, turned on her heel and went back down the corridor.

Ario put her hand on Dion's comms panel and said, 'Listen, if you can hear me . . .'

He couldn't. Of course not. Not with all that morphine inside him.

But the comms panel said, **Welcome, authorised person-nel**, and let her in. For a moment she hesitated. Weird, how long have I been authorised for Dion's door? she thought. And why didn't he tell me? But she didn't want to stay in the corridor. She took one step into the cube, and stopped, staring at the body in the bedbag. Her stomach contracted. He was even worse, now that she had time to look at him, than she'd realised. His eyes were closed and swollen, and his lips were flaky, the colour of blood but scabbed and dry. The hand that the drip ran into was like a creased red glove — and those nails, burnt and ripped off as though the explosion had had teeth . . . But at least he was still, and still breathing.

She stood, watching him. There was no way to tell what he'd looked like before. He was thin, she could see that, and lightish-skinned; but his hair had gone, and his eyebrows. She was glad most of him was hidden by the bedbag.

But — Dion said *twenty storeys*. And he's alive. He must be tough.

Then his eyelids flickered. He opened his eyes.

She heard a gasp and jumped back, stumbling, before she realised it had been her own voice.

Only a slit of his eyeballs showed. The whites of his eyes were red. He looked like a nightmare.

'Dead . . .' he said, the word so low and slurred she wasn't sure whether she'd really heard it. 'Dead . . . please . . .'

'No, you're not dead,' she said, too sharply, because she was afraid. Oh, hell. What if he *did* die on her, right now?

'*Dead*,' he repeated, and she thought she saw a flash of something in those blood-webbed eyes — anger, or fear . . . 'Poor dead . . . poor Athene . . . dead, in the Roots, I'm sorry . . .'

'It's OK,' she said, and then heard what he'd said. '*What?*'

But it was a coincidence; it had to be. This kid was nothing to do with her.

'It's OK,' she said again, backing away, reaching behind her back for the comms panel to let her out. 'Calm down. You're alive. You're safe. You're on morphine, it's probably making you a bit . . .'

'Crater,' he said, and this time the word was clear. He was looking at her, and she could have sworn that he knew what he was saying.

'You're safe,' she said again. 'This isn't Crater. This is a tankshop —' She cut herself off. Stupid. She'd said too much. If the kid was from Crater, he was dangerous. Oh, Dion, she thought, you're crazy, bringing him here . . .

'Not Crater,' he said.

'Not Crater.'

'Good.' His face was too damaged to smile, but she thought she saw a tiny spasm at the corner of one eye, as though he'd tried. 'Dead,' he said, his voice fading. 'Please, find dead . . .'

She opened her mouth, but there was no use: the drugs had swallowed him again.

She was shaking. She felt the comms panel against her palm and pressed, suddenly desperate to be out again, to be back in her own cube, to pretend this hadn't happened.

But when she was in her bedbag, eyes open in the dark, she thought she could still hear that scraping, painful voice. It said, *dead*, over and over; and something niggled at her, telling her that she was missing something, something she ought to understand.

He's dreaming.

He's dreaming about the old days, and it's beautiful. He's in the Maze, running easily. He's surrounded by traps, his ears full of the zing of rotating blades, and the **enemy in range** signal burning on the back of his neck; but he's good, he's the best, and he knows he's going to win.

He flips, lands on his feet, the air singing in his ears. In front of him there's a door, outlined in golden light. A long time ago — the first time he ran this quest — he died, just before he got there: but this time he knows he can do it. *Zing*, he hears, *zing*. He rolls, reaches out, and his hand is touching the door. It flickers, dissolves in front of him, and he follows through on his somersault. He falls through the archway, laughing.

Only it isn't what he expected. No glittering prize; no daylight, no **Congratulations! You have completed this quest.** No, there's only a bare room with high windows, old-fashioned, wooden-floored.

Wait. He remembers that this is the loading room for the new Maze; and suddenly things come back to him in a confused, panicky wave. He's trying to escape from Crater

— no, from the Maze — and Daed — Daed, his father, his father, Daed —

Daed, he thinks, is dead.

I remember. I was at the launch party for the iTank. Daed told me to stay there, but when he left I followed him. I found him in an iTank, and there'd been some kind of malfunction, and he was dead.

And I went into the Maze to find out what had happened. And I was in this room, the loading space, and he came in — a copy of him, I mean, not real, but I spoke to him, he spoke to me —

He runs towards the door in the opposite wall. He wants to wrench it open — to get out, or just to see what's waiting beyond it, he doesn't know — but the floor slides away underneath him and he doesn't make any headway. And somehow he knows what's going to happen before it does. He knows that the door is going to open inwards — disobey-ing every rule, making something stutter in his head — and Daed is going to come through it, the way he did before. Daed, who is dead, but had been somehow still there, in the Maze: a computer-constructed Daed who talked as if he *knew* he was dead, who was his own sarcastic, distant, infu-riating self, who made jokes about the Turing test as if he didn't really care what anyone thought of him. No one could write a non-player character like that — but that was what he'd been — was, is . . . Just an NPC, dead and stuck inside the Maze for ever . . .

Why would you do that? Was it just a kind of signature, so no one would forget him, Daedalus, the great designer? So that he'd become even more of a legend than he already was?

Or was it something else, something . . .

But the idea he's got slips away from him, slick as soap between the fingers of his mind. Because Daed does come through the door, raises one eyebrow at him, and says, 'Fine mess you've got yourself into . . .'

He knows he's dreaming. He knows that this time it *isn't* Daed. But a great tsunami of anger and loss bashes into him, so hard it leaves him breathless.

'Silly boy,' Daed says. 'I set everything up for you. All you had to do was stay where you were. You'd have had an easy life. But now . . .'

'Now *what*?' he says. He forces himself to stay where he is, because if he tried to touch Daed he knows that the world would slide away again, cheating, and he'd only waste energy.

'Now — well, look at you,' Daed says.

'I'm OK.' But something changes as he says it. He looks down, and instead of his old gamerunning clothes, he's wearing the black slim-cut suit he wore to the launch party — the one he was still wearing when he lit the fire in his room, when he ran from it, when it spat him through the window in a flare of broken glass and flames, when he fell —

And as he stares, he sees that it's torn and singed, melted into his skin. There are dull carbonised patches, bubbled and corrugated, and he doesn't know if he's looking at the clothes or his body. His hands are scarlet, the nails half torn away. It doesn't hurt; but it horrifies him. What have I done? he thinks. Am I going to die?

'You're not going to die,' Daed says, as if he's heard his thought. 'But you're not exactly looking good, are you? Why couldn't you just take what I gave you?'

'I'm sorry.' And he is. Daed's always been right, and he's right now.

'You're going to have a tough time, here.'

'Here? Where am I?'

But Daed doesn't answer. 'You watch out. Don't let them use you.'

It's a dream — so is that what Daed would really say, he wonders, or is it my subconscious? Who cares? It's good advice. 'Yes, Daed.'

'That girl. Don't let her get too close.'

Which girl? But as soon as he thinks it, he knows the answer. He can see her face, like a dream within a dream, dark skin and eyes, but something in her expression that seemed familiar . . . Wherever he was, the last time he opened his eyes, she was there too. He shuts his eyes and tries to remember when he saw her, what she has to do with him; but there's nothing, only her steady black gaze and a strange ticking, a sound that should mean something but doesn't. I don't know where I am. I remember falling — but after that . . . He says, 'Daed? Tell me what's happening. Please. I need to know.'

But Daed only laughs. 'How am I supposed to know, if you don't? I'm only a dream.'

'Are you sure?'

''Fraid so. If you really want to see me again, come into the Maze.'

'I can't. You barred me, remember? You said the Maze would recognise my brainprint and not let me in. You said there was a malfunction, and you were protecting me.'

Daed tilts his head thoughtfully and smiles. 'Oh, yes. So I did. Sounds like dreams are the only place for us to spend quality time together, then.'

'Except that you just said you're not really here.'

'Hmm. Well, I am dead, after all.' He laughs.

And disappears.

There's nothing, no trace, not even the echo of his voice. There's no way to be sure he was there at all.

'Daed — come back —'

But it's no good. His voice cracks. The wave of anger washes forward and over him and leaves him behind, shaking and abandoned. He tries to call out again but his throat closes on itself. He's alone in the loading space, and when he starts to run nothing moves, nothing changes, and he's still in the middle of the room. His eyes are hurting, and the inside of his lungs feels raw, acid-eaten. There's a pain in his hands as though something is gnawing through his fingers. The ticking he heard before is louder now, like something counting down.

I'm going to wake up, he thinks. The idea fills him with sadness — a dull, dreary, grey kind of sadness — and then fear. He doesn't know what's waiting for him on the other side of consciousness. He can feel himself surfacing now.

Pain hooks into him, jerking him upwards, and there's nothing he can do to resist.

The last thing he sees, before the dream breaks, is that girl's face; and he hears Daed's voice again: *Don't let her get too close*.

6

Ario slept badly, but when she got up, gritty-eyed and tired of turning over and over in her bedbag, Dion was already at his terminal, his face bathed in pale blue light. He was working. She stood in the corner of the room looking at him, and he didn't even register her presence. For a moment she felt calmer, just watching him: there was something about his concentration, his unswerving gaze on his flatscreen, that made her think that everything was OK. Sometimes she thought she liked him best when he thought he was on his own.

He finished a line of code, leant back and stretched his hands above his head, cracking the knuckles. She winced, and he caught sight of her. 'Hey.'

'Hey.'

'What's up?'

'Couldn't sleep,' she said. 'The kid you brought in —' She stopped.

'What about him?'

'Nothing.'

He held her look, as if he was waiting for her expression to give something away; but she shrugged and tried to untangle her hair, picking at the knots with her nails, and after a second she heard the murmur of his fingers running over his flatscreen again. 'By the way,' he said, the rhythm of his words staccato, as if he was only thinking about his code, 'how did the client meeting go? Get a commission out of it?'

'No,' Ario said. 'It was a trap.'

But he must have been listening, because he jerked his head up to look at her. '*Ario*,' he said. 'You should have said! What happened? How d'you get away?'

'I was lucky.' She could have told him about the explosion, the way that sudden sun had saved her, blazing from the Crater tower like a beacon; but it was all mixed up in her head with the kid in Dion's cube, and she didn't want to think about it.

'No one followed you back?'

'No, Dion, I'm not totally clueless.'

He flashed her a grin, but it only lasted a split second before he turned back to his screen. He was doing things too fast: flying, as usual, Ario thought. He could dismiss the danger as easily as clicking his fingers, now it was over. And they all had to live with it, anyway, didn't they? You couldn't worry all the time . . .

'So no job, then.'

'Nope.'

'How's your account looking?'

'Haven't you checked?'

He hunched a shoulder, smiling at his flatscreen. 'Ario, babe, your account is the only one I *can't* hack.'

She tugged at the most stubborn knot in her hair, and tried not to smile. It was probably just flattery, but she couldn't help letting it go to her head, a little rush of pleasure like a drug. Then she thought about the question, and it faded. 'It's looking pretty bad, actually,' she said. 'I was doing OK, but now I'm running out. It's been a long time.'

'Anything you can vendor?'

'No.' All she had were her clothes, her terminal, her bedbag: the basics. She didn't need anything else, but she didn't have anything spare, either. 'You're not going to chuck me out, are you? I don't think I'm cut out for dealing or the Other Game.' She thought she meant it as a joke, but from the way it came out she realised that it wasn't.

''Course not,' Dion said, but he didn't look at her. 'We need you. With the iTank, and the new Maze expansion and everything. You're our best asset . . . it's just that you're not getting any contracts. Your reputation is a bit — well, it got nerfed, didn't it? Not to put too fine a point on it.'

'Thanks,' she said, although it was true. 'So you want me to start accepting commissions for any old spam, do you? Or do you want me to shave my head and become a gamerunner? I wouldn't be much good, but I suppose I could farm and collect gilt all day, if you want. Until I die of boredom —'

'Ario, thicksauce,' he said, and held up his hand, rolling his eyes. 'Shut up and listen to me, will you? I'm just about to offer you a job.'

'Oh. Right.' There was a pause, and then he looked round at her and they both laughed. But there was something in his eyes: a spark of wariness, as though he was holding something back.

'OK, uberleet, listen up. I've got a client who's a bit special. She was a realrunner — a streetkid — and she managed to get a couple of hours in a tank on the black. She found a Hephaestian sword, and now . . . well, you can imagine how much *that* was worth. And now she's a gamerunner, and she's pretty good, but it's started to get serious. You with me so far?'

'Yep.' It didn't happen much, but it wasn't unheard-of: someone ran the Maze for money, got the money and then spent it all on running the Maze . . .

'So she wants her own personal Cheat. She wants to be the first to win the new Maze expansion, with the iTank.'

'What, win it *all*?'

Dion wiped a hand over his flatscreen, rolling his code into a flag of shadow that curled down into a corner. 'Well, no,' he said. 'Just the big one. It's always the way, isn't it . . . ? They all want to win the Roots.'

She swallowed. She could hear someone moving on the tankfloor, and then the faint mesmeric surge of one of Spin's tracks. 'The Roots?' she said, trying to keep her voice light. 'Yeah, sure, 'cause I've got such a great record on that.'

'If you can't do it, no one can.'

'Dion, that's really nice of you, but the Roots — and especially with the new software, the iTank, all that — I'm not sure — I'm really not — I don't think —'

'No,' he said. He turned round, got up, and walked towards her — and she had to tell herself he was flying, he definitely

64

was, because otherwise the look in his eyes would've been scary. 'You don't have a choice on this one, Ario. You take the contract and you do it well. Otherwise it's the end. You understand?'

She gritted her teeth. What was *wrong* with her? She was being cowardly. A year ago she loved getting new contracts, especially the ones that seemed impossible. I can do it, she thought. The harder it is, the more glory there'll be, when I manage it . . .

Except that if she failed again —

But she didn't have a choice. That was what Dion was saying.

'OK,' she said, pitching her voice low and steady. 'I understand.'

'If you need any insider knowledge, you can ask the kid I brought in.' Dion said it smoothly, turning on his heel and going back to his flatscreen. 'That's what he's here for, after all.'

I am not going anywhere *near* that kid, she said. But her mouth closed itself on the words, and they didn't come out. She'd never seen Dion in this mood — so certain, so unamused — and she didn't want to push her luck. She just nodded.

'Here. I'm sending you her details. You'd better start work straight away. She wants to be the *first*, OK?'

Ario nodded, although he wasn't looking at her. She went to her terminal and booted up, her eyes feeling suddenly dusty and dry. As soon as she'd logged on Dion's file was there, and she skimmed it, taking in the gist. A high-scale commission: *services to be agreed, consultation between both parties, salary + bonus according to success* . . . Her stomach bubbled with anxiety, and she shook her head. Gods, maybe you *should* start writing bots, she thought. Bots and add-ons. Spam. That's all you're good for.

But if you think I'm going to pump your mysterious burnt-out kid for information, Dion, you've got another think coming. He freaks me out.

I'm not going *near* him.

She put her head down, and got to work. And when Dion got up, and she knew he was going to check the morphine drip and see whether the kid had woken up, she kept her eyes on her screen, telling herself that all she needed to do was keep working.

7

The new client was called Pir. For the first time in ages Ario wished their terminals were branched to the worldnet, so that she could have googled her; but they weren't, of course, and she gritted her teeth and told herself that security was much more important. Anyway, Dion had uploaded a file on to her iThing, and that was something. The first things that came up were news stories: *RAGS TO RICHES, REALRUNNER HITS THE JACKPOT!* And there were pictures, hundreds of them — which wasn't surprising, Ario thought, because Pir was beautiful. She smiled out of image after image, lovely, with bone-pale skin and narrow eyes, a sharp little chin and eyebrows as black as her pupils. The photos must have been digitally enhanced — no ex-streetkid had skin that smooth, or white teeth — but all the same Ario found herself staring at them, wishing that this new client could be faceless, the way Herkules404 had been. That much beauty made her uncomfortable.

Dion said, from behind her, 'How's the iTank looking?'

'Not as good as my new client,' she said, without turning round. 'Is she GM'd or what?'

'Obviously not. I told you, she was a streetkid.'

'Yeah, I know, I was . . . never mind. I'm just looking at her Maze stats. She's pretty good. Her reputation's even better. Looks like she's good at avoiding fights when she has to. I like that.'

'After Herkules-what's-his-face, I'm not surprised.' He gave her a wide grin. 'Hey, babe, just kidding.'

'Gag off, Dion.' She put her iThing aside, logged into her terminal and started the connection to the iTank. It was going to take time to work out what had changed, and how to adapt her code; she didn't have time for Dion's needling. It felt good, actually, having something else to think about.

'The Crater kid looks a bit better,' Dion said, in a tone that sounded like it was meant to be casual. 'Wonder how soon he'll be up to answering questions.'

She didn't answer.

'You seem to have made an impression on him, anyway.'

'What?' She'd resolved not to be drawn, but that took her by surprise, and she found herself twisting in her chair.

'He kept saying, the dark girl, the dark girl.'

'How do you know he meant me?' she said, refusing to let him see her shock. 'That could mean lots of us.'

'He definitely meant you.' Dion held her look, and cracked a smile. 'Not sure if he wanted to see you or wanted *not* to. Reckon you might have made a friend. Or an enemy.'

'Well, that's fine, because he's got nothing to do with me. He's *your* problem, Dion. I'm not going to go there.' She cracked a smile straight back at him. 'And BTW, since when have I been authorised on your comms panel? And why didn't you tell me?'

'Didn't want you taking advantage,' he said, and laughed.

'Frankly,' she said, 'I think I'm more likely to take advantage now that your overcooked morphine zombie is in your bedbag.'

'Ouch.'

'Leave me alone, will you, Dion? I'm trying to work. You told me this contract was important, remember?'

He didn't respond, and when she looked up he was at his own terminal, already withdrawn into the world of his flatscreen. She went back to her own programming, smiling. That was the thing about the other Cheats: even when they were annoying, they understood the feeling of writing code, the way it could take you over.

And, slowly, it did take her over. She sank into it happily, rocked and comforted by the complexity, the predictability of it. It was hard but not impossible, and as she analysed, checked, rechecked, she felt like a kid, playing with the biggest toy in the world. She was a Cheat, but you couldn't cheat with code: it obeyed the rules, it did what you told it to do, there was nothing random or dangerous about it. No people, she thought, no emotions or stupidity, only cold, lovely logic.

She blocked out all thoughts of Pir, or Dion, or the kid in Dion's cube, and the world was reduced to lines of code on her flatscreen, and Spin's track in her ears like the surge of blood, keeping her alive.

She lost track of time. She ate when people gave her food — although she never really knew if they were people, they might have been disembodied hands that slipped P&V bars on to the desk in front of her and dematerialised as soon as they'd done it . . . Once Dion — it must have been, she remembered recognising his clever fingers, while his voice blurbed at her, a long way away — slipped a little papery fold of a square into her hand, and the next few hours were extra sharp and the code came like water, pouring down her flat-screen in lines of glinting silver. After that, she went to her cube and fell into a sticky, itchy sort of sleep, while ants ran across the inside of her eyelids. She didn't know how long it was before she was up again, logging on; and she didn't care, either, because all that mattered was her work. She was starting to get an idea of how the new stuff fitted. And slowly she felt the excitement bubbling up, because the iTank was brilliant, the new Maze was brilliant, she had nothing but admiration for the Crater developers — but she could do it, she was sure of that now, she could find a way to crack it.

It must have been a day, two days, three days . . . time stretched out and squashed up like a wave, and Ario didn't pay attention. It was only when she finished a loophole she'd been trying to create that at last she took a deep breath, sat up straight and looked around. It was day, probably: there was no natural light in the tankshop, but more terminals were filled than were empty. She rolled her shoulders and grunted with pain. Dion looked up, met her eyes, and grinned. 'The Kraken wakes,' he said.

'What?'

'Come back to us, have you? You look ganked out.'

'I'm fine,' she said. Suddenly a yawn took over, as irresistible as if someone had grabbed her jaw and forced it apart with their hands. Her whole body was aching and numb at the same time. She was used to working long hours, but she wasn't sure she'd ever been this tired.

'Go to bed.'

'Yeah, I will, I just want to —' Another yawn swelled in her throat like a balloon.

'Come on,' Dion said. 'Don't worry about that. I'll log out for you.' He stood up, came over to her and grabbed her by the arm, pulling her up off her block. She staggered into him, letting him take her weight. He grunted, 'Wow, you're not taking any prisoners . . .' but he was surprisingly strong. 'OK, good girl, let's go . . .' The others were staring as he walked her towards the door, but she didn't care. 'That's right, one foot in front of the other . . . good girl . . .'

'Stop calling me *good girl*, Dion. Go fy.' But she was slurring her words, and even if he understood he pretended not to.

'When did you last sleep, babe? A week ago? Ten days?'

'It hasn't been that long,' she said, forcing the consonants into place like components that didn't quite fit. 'Has it?'

'Since you went under? A week, easy. No wonder you're wiped. Come on —' He navigated her through the door, wedging it open with his foot as she stumbled. 'Let's go. You're doing really well. That's good . . .'

'Stop encouraging me,' she said, and felt a sharp edge of amusement cutting through the mush of fatigue. 'I know you. You're trying to get in my good box so you can wheedle my codes out of me . . .'

'Yep. Nearly there.' He had to take his arm away to push her down the corridor in front of him. She blinked and focused on walking straight. The walls seemed to sway and press inwards. They went past Lia's cube, Spin's, Nax's . . .

Dion's. She stopped, involuntarily. There was a noise — a voice, low and intense, a rhythm of stops and starts as though it was one half of a conversation. She said, 'Dion?'

'It's OK,' he said, from behind her, one hand tightening on her shoulder. 'It's just the kid. He talks to himself. It's the morphine.'

'What does he say?'

'Not much. Give it a few days, we should be able to decrease the dose, get some real answers.' He pushed her forward. Part of her wanted to go with the pressure; but the other part of her stayed rooted to the spot, swaying.

'He's creepy,' she said.

'Right. Having half your body burnt off probably has that effect. Come on, not far now.'

But she still didn't move. 'How come he's talking? He couldn't, before.'

'He's getting better. I thought you didn't care?' There was a silence, and she felt Dion put his other hand on her other shoulder. 'Hey, babesauce, he's GM'd to the hilt. Even with what's happened to him, he'll be on his feet pretty soon. Hopefully,' he added, with an ironic note in his voice, 'looking less *creepy*.'

It isn't how he looks, Ario wanted to say. It isn't that. It's the way he looks at me . . . and he makes me think of myself, how *I* needed to be rescued too . . .

'Good news, isn't it,' Dion said, and this time she let him push her down the corridor, away from his door. 'Good to know he'll be around to help us.'

'Do you have something specific in mind?' She turned, and for a second the curtain of tiredness flickered, letting through a sudden light of clarity. 'Dion . . . why did you take him? He might not be anyone, we might be wasting our morphine — our food, everything . . . or he might put us in danger. If he *is* someone —'

'He *is* someone. I know he is.' Dion shook his head, looking past her as if he was talking to someone else. 'I don't know, Ario. I don't know why I took him. It was a hunch. Just a — I don't know. But he *is* someone. He's special. The way you are. I knew with you, and I know with him. And I am *sure*, sure and certain, that somehow it will pay off. Trust me.'

She looked up at him. His eyes were tinged with red, but his gaze was steady and she could tell he wasn't flying. She felt the tendons in her knees flutter, as though her legs were going to give way and pitch her forward. She reached out and took hold of his arm, steadying herself. She was going to say something — argue, disagree, she wasn't sure what.

Then the moment passed, and she turned away and stumbled to her cube.

And she didn't remember anything else until she woke up in her bedbag, sweaty and fully clothed, and it was time to go back to work.

8

Time went on: days, weeks, possibly months. Ario didn't care enough to measure it, except by hunger and tiredness, food and sleep, the sudden moments when she would move and be taken aback by the stiffness in her joints, or catch a breath of her own unwashed armpits. There was the date, of course, changing every so often at the corner of her flat-screen: but it seemed to update so erratically and so quickly that she didn't quite believe it was real. Dion left cups of water on her desk, P&V bars, once sent a chat that said, **u need 2 showr, I cn smell u frm here**. She caught his eye over their flatscreens and stuck out her tongue, but he was right. She managed to wrench herself away from her code for ten minutes, walking in a preoccupied daze to the shower cube and coming back with her hair still claggy with soap suds. She heard sounds from Dion's cube as she went past — the kid was getting better, moving around, weaning himself off the IV — but she didn't stop to listen. After all, she told herself, the kid wasn't important, not compared to her work.

Then there was the day that Pir came into the tankshop to see her. It was raining heavily, so that the hiss of it reached them inside; when the door slid open and Pir came in, the air that swirled in and clung to her out-clothes stank of ammonia. For a second, when Ario saw the anonymous figure in the doorway, a shock of fear kicked at her heart; but it was OK, she could see Dion standing up and beckoning. He must have buzzed her in . . . Then she took off her hood, shaking sharp-smelling drops on to the floor, and it was Pir. Everyone in the tankshop looked round at her. 'Hey,' she said. Her voice was low and husky — rain-damaged, Ario guessed, from when she'd been a streetkid — but her face was surprisingly smooth and her eyes were very clear. That was what came from being able to afford a decent hood. 'I'm here to see Ario . . . ?'

Dion stood up and pointed over the desks. 'That one there,' he said, 'looking screen-drunk. Ario, your client's here. *Ario*.'

'Yes,' she managed to say. She'd known Pir was coming, of course, but she was in the middle of an enticing experiment and she had difficulty not sounding annoyed. 'Sure. Just coming.'

'Don't let me distract you,' Pir said, and for the first time Ario met her eyes. There was a glint of humour that she hadn't expected: rich kids always took themselves too seriously, and treated Ario like a servant. But, then, Pir didn't have your average rich-kid profile . . . 'Want me to come back later?'

'No, now is good. Let me just . . .' and she went back to her code, trying to finish it off quickly. After a while she heard Dion cough, and realised she'd completely forgotten they were there. 'Sorry. Just coming. Really.'

'It's OK,' Pir said, 'I can come back another time. Really,' she added, with a sly flicker of her eyelashes that wasn't quite a wink.

'No,' Ario said, with an effort. 'No, I want to see you run. That way I can work out what you need most.'

'Great.' She tilted her head and ran a hand over the fuzz of hair on her scalp. Of course, Ario thought, for the iTank you don't have to wear a gamecap . . . She realised she was staring and looked away. There was something about Pir that made her — not *uneasy*, exactly, but . . .

She said, 'Let's go, then,' and stood up.

Dion said, 'Er . . . Pir, can I get you anything? Glass of water? We've got a couple of vintage 2019s, if that's your sort of —'

Ario said, 'Let's just get on with it, shall we?'

Dion gave her a steady look, face neutral, holding it for just too long to be comfortable. Then he shot Pir a big grin, and said, 'Well, have fun — anything you need, just let me know, we're not all as socially inept as my charming colleague here . . .'

Pir nodded. 'Thanks.' Then she followed Ario to the doorway. She moved like a gamerunner: precise, economical, leaving the tiniest space possible between her body and anything in her path.

'This is the tankfloor,' Ario said, gesturing. It didn't need saying, really, but if Dion wanted her to be polite, she'd be polite. And politeness was all about saying things you didn't need to, wasn't it? 'That's our iTank, over there.' Someone was in it: the outside was opalescent, wave after wave of milk-drowned colour washing over it. She caught sight of movement from the flatscreen — the terminal was still branched to the iTank — and forced her eyes away. Polite. Be polite. 'Don't worry, they'll be out in a sec, it's probably one of the kids farming for a bit of pocket money . . . We're Cheats, obviously, but sometimes people like to do something mindless — something a bot could do — just to relax. Anyway, those are old gametanks over there, we're keeping them for a bit because obviously not everyone's upgraded yet, there's still a market for all that stuff . . . That's our spare components store, that big pile in the corner, it's actually much more organised than it looks.' There was a silence. She couldn't stop herself adding, 'And those are the walls and that's the ceiling.'

Pir laughed. It caught Ario by surprise, so that she turned to look at her. Pir held her gaze, smiling straight into her eyes. 'It's OK,' she said.

'What is?'

'You don't have to be . . .' She shrugged, and ran her hand over her skull again, ruffling the short hair with her fingers as if she was still getting used to the feeling. 'Look, your mate — Dion, is it? — he thinks you've got to give me all this bee-ess, be nice to me and make me feel like I'm in charge, and you know what? I actually don't care. You can be rude to me, that's fine. I'm not paying you to be my friend. You're supposed to be the best Cheat there is. You were a *legend* when I was a realrunner. So if you're rubbish with people, if you think people are pointless and pathetic and your cheat codes are more important than anything human — well. That's *fine*. Really.'

There was another silence; and it felt like someone had let the plug out of Ario's head, so the slopping bath of cheat codes and ideas drained away. Pir's voice resonated round the shiny emptiness of her skull. She opened her mouth, but all that came out was, 'Oh.'

'So let's get on with it, shall we?'

'Yes.' She felt sick and shaky: for the first time she felt her own body, heard what it was saying to her, and a big lump of nausea and fatigue bumped against her ribs, making it hard to breathe. As if she'd been flying, and suddenly Pir's words had sobered her up, brought her horribly back to earth. 'Yes. I'll just get —' she gestured at the slick-glimmering iTank, unable to finish her sentence. She went to the terminal and sat down. The flatscreen swam in and out of focus.

Behind her, Pir said, 'Look, I didn't mean to be harsh.'

Ario didn't answer. She stared at the moving colours in front of her and willed her eyes to work properly.

'I meant — honestly, I mean it's *OK*. However you want to be. Even if you're a complete frea— oh gods, I — look, I'm only a gamerunner, *I*'m no good at talking to people, either. I just mean . . . Don't worry about trying to do all this cust-serve stuff. What matters is that you're a Cheat, a really good one.' She moved closer, so that Ario smelt a hint of something chemical, the dizzying perfume of rain. 'That's all I was trying to say.'

Ario opened her mouth to answer; but at last her eyes managed to follow what was happening on-screen, and it blocked out everything she was feeling in a wave of fascination. For a second everything else stopped existing and her whole world was taken up by the stuttering graphics, the figure in the centre . . .

'OK, well, let's just forget I — wow. Who is *that*?'

Ario shook her head, wordless. She felt Pir bend forward to look over her shoulder, and a part of her mind noticed that smooth cheek a few centi-ems from her own; but the rest of her was absorbed, following the images on the flatscreen with frozen, uncomprehending attention. Who *was* it? She didn't know.

Whoever it was, they were —

'*Amazing*,' Pir said, and the admiration in her voice was so mixed with incredulity and envy that it made Ario want to laugh. 'Wow. I didn't know you had real gamerunners here. I thought you were all haxors and geeks . . .'

'We are,' Ario said.

Pir didn't answer: she was leaning forward even more, as if the screen was exerting some kind of magnetism. 'Wow,' she said again.

There was a pause: and together they stared at the slideshowing flatscreen, fascinated.

It was only the iTank demo, not the Maze itself; but that didn't matter. It was as complicated, as beautiful — even relayed through the struggling terminal — as anything Ario had seen in the Maze. In the centre of the shot there was a gamerunner fighting a shadow warrior. They were outside — on a wide flat floor of moss-mortared brick, surrounded by trees that dropped slow golden leaves, swayed in a gentle breeze and threw nets of dying sunlight over the fighters. And the fight itself was beautiful, both figures ducking and spinning and sliding blade against blade, so quick and elegant that it was hard to follow. The shadow warrior was all in black, hard to see, with a strange inhuman rhythm; but the gamerunner, whoever he was, gods, the *gamerunner* —

Ario had never seen anything like it. Not even Herkules404 had been as good, without Ario's cheats to help him. He was a scrawny, sinewy boy — or young man, rather, youth, whatever, Ario's age, not quite an adult — with an odd jerkiness to his movement that wasn't anything to do with the graphics. His spine wasn't flexible enough, so that more of his movement came from his limbs than his centre. But he was so quick, and his reflexes were so fast, that he was keeping the shadow warrior at bay, and his awkwardness had a kind of contradictory grace. The fight had a driven, electric feel to it, like music.

Ario laughed, out of admiration, out of delight. She knew what it was like to be the best, she knew the best when she saw it . . .

But who was he? Pir was right, this was no haxor or geek. Not one of us, Ario thought. So —

It was over in a blink, between two screenshots.

The gamerunner stumbled. The shadow warrior slid his sword forward in a swift stab, striking a spark of gold sunlight; and the gamerunner twisted to avoid it, staggered and caught his breath. His free hand went to his side, clutching as though the sword had found its mark; but there was nothing showing, no change in his health bar . . . It only took a split second — then he recovered, jumped away, put his sword up in a wild parry — but it was too late. The shadow warrior slipped the blade smoothly into the muscle above his kidneys.

Game over.

The screen paled and blurred. **Try again?**

Pir breathed out, a long hiss through her teeth that seemed to last for an eternity. Then she said, 'What happened? What's wrong with him? Did he sprain something?'

Ario shrugged. It was stupid, but she felt shattered, almost tearful. She could have gone on watching that fight for ever. 'I don't know,' she said.

There was a pause. Ario would have liked to say something — anything — to the runner in the tank, whoever it was; but they were still having problems setting up a ventrillo, and she didn't want to activate the emergency logout . . . She stood up, put her hand on the side of the iTank — as though it could feel her there — and watched emerald and silver swirl around her fingers. **Sorry, this iTank is already occupied**, it said, but the message sank suddenly into the cloudy white of the shell, and the door hummed and slid open before she could finish. The coloured lustre died.

And through the doorway, stumbling a little, came the boy Dion had brought in: scarred and sweating, trembling with exhaustion, but with the same stiff, unexpected grace as his avatar.

When he saw them he stopped dead, swaying. He reached out with one hand to steady himself against the iTank, his gaze wary, flicking between them. Of course, Ario thought, he didn't know we were there, watching him . . . But she still couldn't get over how he had moved — and how he was standing there now, back straight, hands and face still webbed with burns, but on his feet and in good shape . . . Brilliant shape, in fact, she thought, for someone who'd fallen twenty storeys not too long ago. Dion had said he was getting better — but fighting like *that*?

'That was pretty good,' Pir said. 'What happened to you at the end?'

He blinked, looking from Ario to Pir and back again. At last he said, 'Thanks.' His voice was still husky and burnt out, as if his vocal cords had been half eaten away. His eyes were bright blue against the sharp red of his scars.

'I didn't know you were a gamerunner,' Ario said. It came out like an accusation.

'I'm — not, really. Not any more,' he said, and the shiny skin around his mouth creased and smoothed out again as if he had started to grimace.

'Who are you?' Pir said. 'You look like — I mean, were you a realrunner, before . . . ?'

'I'm —' he said again, and his eyes slid to Ario. She wasn't sure; but she had the impression that if she hadn't been there, he would have spoken more readily. 'I'm no one,' he said. 'Listen, I'm sorry, Dion said I could use the iTank if no one else was . . . Sorry.' He started to walk away, twisting his shoulders away as if he was afraid of touching them.

'But you were great,' Pir said. 'How long have you been gamerunning?'

He stopped, and looked back at them. For a moment his face was utterly blank: as if the light had gone out behind his eyes, or as if he didn't understand the words. Then those tiny creases came and went at the corners of his lips. 'For ever,' he said.

'I meant —' Pir said; but he'd already gone.

There was a silence, thick and heavy, as if the inside of Ario's ears had been corroded. She looked at the screen in front of her, trying to make sense of what she'd seen. The way he'd moved, the way he'd run the iTank demo . . . *No one*, he'd said. *I'm no one*.

'Gods,' Pir said at last. 'I feel pretty inadequate now. Not sure I want to run the Maze any more . . .'

'Just get on with it,' Ario said. Her voice was sharp, as if someone else had taken control of her larynx. She didn't know what had happened to her. Why was she so shaken? Loads of people were gamerunners . . . loads of people could fight shadow warriors . . . and he'd *lost*, hadn't he? He couldn't be that special, if he'd lost . . .

Pir shifted a little, as if Ario's tone had surprised her; but she crossed to the iTank and went in without another word. The door slid shut, and those hypnotic colours started again, gleaming and rippling over the white.

Ario gritted her teeth and frowned hard, forcing herself to pay attention to the terminal's shuddering graphics. Pir was standing still in the loading space, ready and poised. The high windows threw clear rectangular shadows on the wooden floor, the varnish shining. She's beautiful, Ario thought, the room's lovely, she's lovely in it . . . But she could still see the boy, the gamerunner, his shrug, the creases in the scarred skin at the corner of his lips. Stop it, she thought. He's not that special. *Concentrate*.

Pir's Guildhall came up — the Silver Shield — and she walked on to the practice floor, strolling to the weapons rack and saying aloud, 'Demo fight partner, please.'

Ario gritted her teeth. She leant forward, squeezing her temples with her hands. The screen was giving her a headache. Pir was fighting now, ducking and weaving, her sword swinging, and the image was jumping badly. She smacked her hand down on the terminal but it didn't help.

But it wasn't the terminal that was bothering her, not really. It was Pir. Lovely Pir, fluid and beautiful, fighting like a demon: who seemed — somehow, in spite of everything — lacklustre, only just competent, as though something were missing.

9

Afterwards Ario let Pir see herself out, and went to her cube, forcing herself to walk straight past Dion's door without pausing. She didn't want to think about the boy, the game-runner . . . Something about him nudged at her heart, exciting and uneasy, something she didn't like to examine more closely. She didn't tell Dion what they'd seen.

She slept deeply, for hours. She had the impression that she was dreaming, but when she woke up all she could remember was Pir — Pir's voice saying, *you're rubbish with people, you think people are pointless and pathetic*. I'm not, she wanted to say. I don't. But there was no one to say it to: and she knew that she hadn't managed to say it in her dream, either.

She sat up. Everything was quiet. Too quiet; she couldn't hear anything, not even the low drone of the generators. She said, 'Lights,' and nothing happened. The power had gone down; it must have been the stillness that had woken her.

She reached for her iThing — it still had some battery left, although not much, because it was old and had already lived longer than it was designed to — and it lit up at her touch, throwing wintry blue light over the walls of her cube. The light reflected off the lifeless comms panel next to the door. For a second she felt her heart squeeze, and she found herself on her feet, scrabbling at the door: but it was OK, the power loss had switched it to manual mode, and it slid open stiffly under her fingers. Outside the corridor was pitch-black, and silent. The time on her iThing said *0349*. Maybe no one else had noticed the power dying.

She took a deep breath, and smelt the stale, slightly chemical scent of air that hadn't been purified. There was no need to panic — the generators went down every so often, it was normal, everyone knew how to get them going again — but all the same she felt a shiver down her spine. Without the generators they'd die, slowly. And it was so dark, so still: as though she was the only person in the world. An impulse to shout caught her by the throat, but she swallowed it back. Calm down, she thought. Get a grip. Don't embarrass yourself.

She walked slowly down the corridor, holding her iThing in front of her to light the way. The trapdoor down to the generators was on the tankshop floor, behind the old gametanks; she had to cross the main hall to get there. She dragged the door open, and stood in the doorway, looking at the rows of terminals, the shadowy shapes of counters and boxes and mess, just visible in the dimness. There were little LEDs here and there, keeping vigil as back-up power drained away and batteries ran down. They watched her like eyes. She gritted her teeth, taking another long breath of unfil-tered air. The sting of ammonia flared in her nostrils. She swallowed, grateful for the noise it made. The blanket of silence made her feel like she'd gone deaf.

She was afraid. She admitted it to herself, and then pushed it to one side. She wasn't going to let it stop her, so what was the use in thinking about it? Gods, scared of the dark like a kid . . .

She inched her way carefully across the room, her hands out in front of her at the height of the counters, in case she bashed into something. If she knocked something over — broke a terminal — that would be a catastrophe. She bounced gently off a wall and then let her fingers trail along it, to keep her steady. Her fingertips glanced over a comms panel, and then the door was there, under her hand. She pulled at it until it gave and slid open wide enough for her to get through.

Inside there were a couple of battery-powered emergency lights to mark the first-aid kit and the trapdoor, so that instead of blackness it was all shadows and shades of grey. There was a huge empty space in front of her, curtained in darkness. The tanks lurked against the wall, their contours grainy and blurred; the heap of components in the corner glinted like coal. She stepped forward, her heart pounding in her ears. There was something wrong. She felt a tiny movement of air on her face, heard a little shuffle or scratch from somewhere in the darkness.

There was someone here.

She opened her mouth to call out — it might be Dion, Spin, Lia, anyone, there was no reason to be scared — but something stopped her. Slowly she pushed one foot forward,

87

transferred her weight. Her eyes were adapting, slowly, and now she could see more — different depths of blackness, something moving . . .

Her hands were tingling. She didn't know what to do. If someone was here to steal the iTank . . . Stupid, she thought, don't be ridiculous, how would they get it out? No, maybe it's just some streetkid who's broken in for the shelter —

Then she saw him.

For a second she wasn't sure what he was doing. He was moving purposefully through the shadows, turning and stepping. The fear flared and she froze, not sure whether to stay where she was or slip out again through the door. If only she could *see* . . .

His movements brought him into the centre of the floor, and she saw that he was kicking in slow-motion, twisting, blocking, punching, as though he were underwater. The slow-fight form. Ario knew what it was, but she'd never seen it performed; and especially never like this, in the dark, in silence, the boy spinning the blackness between his hands like thread. She found herself holding her breath. She couldn't see his face, or his scars — only his eyes, glinting half closed, and the deeper shadow of his clothes against the dimness. He swung an arm slowly round as though he were pushing the heel of his hand into someone's face; but the gesture was fluid, bleeding smoothly into something else without a pause, and there was no violence in it, only grace. At last he folded the air around himself like a sheet, bringing his arms down, and stood still.

Ario exhaled. It felt as though she'd been holding her breath for hours.

Who *is* he? she thought. Why is he here, alone, in the dark?

And then, as he rolled his shoulders, gasping a little as though the muscles were tight — or no, it must be his skin, those dreadful scars, even though he was better they'd never heal completely — she thought she understood. It was a strange, clear moment — as though everything had combined, the power cut, the silence, the faint smell of rain, especially to bring her here, with him.

She thought: He's no one. He *wants* to be no one.

I know how that feels.

She felt something strange happening to her face. Her heart was still bumping hard in her chest, but she wasn't afraid any more.

She opened her mouth, and this time she was definitely going to call out. But there was a flicker from the ceiling, and suddenly the generators coughed and droned back into life. The lights hummed, flashed and settled into a steadyish glow. Her eyes stung with the sudden brightness, and she blinked furiously. When she could see again the boy was standing still, staring at her.

'Sorry,' she said, and she was: although she didn't know for what, exactly.

He shook his head. His face was expressionless — because of his burns, she supposed — but there was a glint of something in his eyes like wariness or hostility. He said, 'I wasn't hurting anything.'

'I know. I just came to look at the generators.' She wanted to say something else, but nothing came.

'I sleep here now,' he said, and pointed to the far corner of the room. There was an old bedbag trailing from behind a makeshift screen. 'Dion wanted his cube back.'

She nodded. He didn't want her there, that was clear. And the strange closeness she'd felt to him had left her, as though it had never been. He was just a freaky, scarred kid, a game-runner, not anyone she cared about . . . She shrugged and started to leave. But something took hold of her, and she turned back on a sudden impulse. She said, 'Why are you still here?'

His eyes widened. 'Here?'

She gestured widely. 'In the tankshop. Why are we still feeding you? Giving you somewhere to sleep? You look like you're better. Shouldn't you be gone by now?'

He held her gaze, his eyes very steady, and there was something there she couldn't read. He licked his lips, and she heard him breathe. At last he said, 'Where else would I go?'

She almost said, *Back wherever you came from*. 'Look, you're a gamerunner,' she said. 'And you're amazing. You don't need to stay here, you could earn a living easily. You don't have to stay with us Cheats, you could find somewhere less dangerous. Find a tankshop where they farm all day — except that you wouldn't need to farm, you could do better stuff, you could . . .' She heard her voice running like a tap that hadn't been turned off, and made an effort to shut her mouth.

'No, I couldn't.'

'Why not?'

'I've been barred from the Maze. I can run the iTank demo, but not the Maze. The iTank recognises my brainprint and won't let me in.'

'You mean your *account* was closed. We could cheat that, easi—'

'No. It recognises *me*.'

'But — how can you have been — you —' She shook her head. She didn't believe him. Sure, OK, the iTank could probably do that, but they'd found him burnt half to death the night it was released, he hadn't had *time* to get barred . . . And yet somehow, after all, she did believe him.

'So I'm not a gamerunner. Not any mo—' He stopped, took a deep breath, stared into the corner of the room at his wrinkled bedbag. 'I'm no one. I don't know why Dion is letting me stay, but I don't have anywhere else to go. He should have let me die.'

'He thinks you'll come in useful,' Ario said.

'He's wrong.'

There was a silence. She looked at him, not wanting to say the wrong thing. *He should have let me die . . .*

'Sorry,' she said. 'I'm so sorry.'

It came out of nowhere, catching her unawares; but she meant it. She felt a warm, sick rush of something, bubbling up in her throat, prickling in her eyelashes. It was so unfamiliar that it took her a moment to realise that it was pity.

He narrowed his eyes, but his gaze was level, not exactly hostile, and the skin at the corner of his mouth creased. 'Thanks,' he said.

They looked at each other in silence, taking their time, as if they'd never seen each other before.

I wish I could help you, Ario thought, amazed at the strength of it. I wish I could do something. I wish I could —

'I'm Rick,' he said, so quickly she could hear the effort it had taken him to say it.

'I'm Ario,' she said, and found herself reaching out, stretching her hand towards him as though she expected him to take hold of it.

Dion's voice said, 'Hey, having a party? Without me? Ario, I'm hurt.'

For a second she was so angry she could hardly speak. Go away, she thought. Go away and leave us in peace. Then the irrational blaze of it died, and she turned round. Dion was there in the doorway, an odd, guarded look on his face. Ario said, 'Not a party, the generators cut out, I was going to fix them. And . . .' But she didn't mention the slow-fight form. It wasn't a secret, exactly, but part of her didn't want to put it into words — not for Dion, not even for herself. It had been too strange, too intimate; it was uncomfortable, better forgotten . . .

'They're working now, the generators,' Dion said.

'Yes, they came back on.'

'Goodnight,' Rick said. He turned and made his way to his bedbag, lay down on it and shut his eyes. The conversation was over. He was dismissing them.

Ario swallowed the rush of disappointment, and turned away too. 'I'm going back to bed,' she said to Dion. 'Why don't you check the generators?'

And she left him there before he had time to protest. She crossed the hall and went down the corridor to her cube, wondering if she'd dreamt the whole thing. Tomorrow there'd be no way of telling whether it had really happened; nothing would have changed, except her own memory. She paused and shut her eyes, trying to see it again: the darkness, the slow figure in the dimness, a fight with nothing, so stylised it was beautiful. Her heart sped up. If only Dion hadn't come in . . . What's happened? she thought. Why do I feel like this?

But there was no answer. She let herself into her cube, got into her bedbag, laid down and turned the light off; but her eyes watched the shadows for a long time, until her mind danced her to sleep.

10

Time went by. The code grew in Ario's system, like a monstrous plant. Work was broken up by food and showers and sleep that was full of dreams — shadows fighting with nothing, images that left her bewildered and work-blunt, until she dosed herself with caffeine. She didn't see Rick again: or rather, she saw him coming and going, running errands, dripping rain on the floor in a fizz of acid, and she ignored him. She didn't look at him, even, so she didn't know if he was looking at her. She rather suspected he was avoiding her gaze too. Not that it mattered. Not that she cared.

Pir came and went, gave advice and suggestions and encouragement until she realised that Ario was hardly hearing her, anyway. Then — that last time — she shook her head, laughed, scribbled a note on Ario's iThing, and left. The writing sat there, glowing, until Dion came over to put a P&V shake down on the counter next to her terminal. 'Hey, Ario,' he said, 'you know your client was here just a moment ago, trying to talk to — oh.' He bent over to peer at the iThing. '"See you when it's done." Right. She's got more patience than I would have.'

'Dion, I'm working.' She'd said it so many times it was on autopilot, and it was like the voice came from somewhere over her shoulder.

'You'll be finished soon, right?'

'I'm working. Go away.'

'In a sec. How soon will you be finished?'

'Dion, I'm wor—'

Suddenly there was a hand over her screen, and she blinked. Her back ached, and she was starving. The fingers over her terminal flexed, came closer to her face and started to wave in front of her eyes. She flapped the hand away and shut her eyes, feeling them sting. 'OK, OK,' she said. 'You've made me lose my concentration now. What do you want?'

'First you should have a drink,' he said, and she felt him push the plastic cup into her hand. 'Drink. You look completely oom. I swear you've lost about half your body weight since you took on this commission.'

'Yeah . . .' She opened her eyes again, looked at the cup of brown sludge, and put it back on the counter. Dion picked it up and pushed it back at her, without a word. This time she took it and balanced it on her lap.

'And more importantly, when are you going to finish? She might be patient, but I'm not. If someone else runs the Roots before her, you're looking at massive reductions to your bonus.'

'Soon,' she said, without thinking, because that was what she said every time. 'I just have to check —' She stopped. The screen in front of her sparkled and glowed.

She'd been lost in her work, so lost that she hadn't thought — hadn't even —

Dion said something, but she didn't hear the words. She was staring at her screen, a wave of cold going up and down her backbone, making her shiver. Yes, she just had to check a few things — *re*check them, because for the last few days that was all she'd been doing, just checking and rechecking obsessively — the programming itself was —

She started to shake. The cup of P&V sludge fell on to the floor. The contents began to ooze very slowly towards the lip of the cup, like something geological.

'Hey, you OK? Babesauce?'

'Fine,' she said, and she was impressed at the way the word came out, because the rest of her was freezing and trembling. There were big gulps of air forcing themselves in and out of her lungs. 'Fine, I'm, yes. Just have to check again, a couple of, check — it's, most of it, it's —'

'What? Is there a problem? Ario? Come on, you can tell me. What's up?'

She took a deep breath and put her hands over her face. Her fingers were cold. She breathed in the unwashed, sticky smell of her skin.

'Hey — Ario — listen, it's OK, whatever's happened, we can —' He petered out, and she heard the uncertainty in his voice. There were things you couldn't fix: and Dion knew it.

She brought her hands down again, spread them on the counter in front of her terminal, and said, 'It's done.'

'What?'

'I've done it. I've finished. The last couple of days I've just been checking it was going to work. I think it will.'

'You've —? Wow, Ario, wow . . . *woot!* Wow, have you told Pir yet? You are such a roxor! That is —'

'It's done,' she said again. And then she leant forward, rested her forehead on the counter between her hands, and started to cry.

It was exhaustion, mainly. She knew that; they all did. After months of intense work *everyone* collapsed, in different ways: Lia left the tankshop for days, coming back with her hood half eaten through and no answers; Spin branched himself into his iThing and didn't unplug himself; Nax made things with his hands, talking all the time in a continuous burble of nonsense; and Dion — well, Dion flew, of course. It was just that Ario had always been different. She'd always prided herself on holding it together, getting on to the next commission straight away, not even giving herself a day off. It was only now that she thought maybe that was just as weird, in its own way.

And this time she didn't have anything else to work on. So she fell apart.

She slept, and dreamt of lines of code, with figures duck-ing and running through them, as though they were traps; she woke to find food and drink on the block beside her bed. She spilt the shake on her bedbag as she tried to drink, but she fell asleep again immediately, and when she woke up there was a dried crust of P&V sludge on her collarbone and shoulder. She stared up at her ceiling and felt water roll out of her eyes and down her neck; but she didn't feel anything, not even pride. Later — when Pir ran her cheats — she'd feel good about it; but right now it seemed a long way away, as if it had been someone else.

She didn't know how long it lasted. Time stretched and hummed like elastic, until suddenly it pinged back into place. She jerked out of a dream — not knowing whether she'd been awake or asleep — and heard the comms panel buzz. She sat up. 'No,' she said.

The buzzing went on. **An unknown person is requesting entrance.**

'*No*,' she said, and flopped backwards on to the bed. 'Go away.'

'Are you sure?' Pir's voice came through the door with a laugh in it. 'I thought we could celebrate.'

Ario sat up again so quickly her head spun. What —? How does she know —? *Dion*, she thought, damn him. Because *I* didn't contact her . . . She meant to say *Go away* again, but instead something took over and she got to her feet and pressed the comms panel so that the door slid open. Pir grinned and made a little mocking bow.

Ario said, her mouth twisting the words suspiciously as though they tasted strange, 'Celebrate how?'

But Pir didn't answer. She just took her by the shoulders and pushed her along the corridor to the shower.

In the scratched blur of the mirror Ario saw the thick crust of dried P&V shake on her collarbone, spikes of her hair pointing towards the ceiling. She stood under the water — it smelt of the outside, and stung her nostrils — and felt it

wash the dirt off her skin, out of her eyes and her brain. She
would have liked to sink to a crouch and stay under the warm
flow for ever; but Pir was waiting. She was surprised to realise that made a difference. In the end she turned off the
water and came out of the cube to find that Pir — presuma-
bly — had left her a pile of clothes. Clean shirt, trousers,
underwear . . . and out-clothes, new ones, much better than
her own. She paused, half dressed, her hair dripping over
her forehead, and ran her finger over the fabric. Not mine,
she thought. Where did they come from?

Pir said, from the other side of the door, 'Come on. What's
taking so long?'

She opened the door, but she stayed inside, holding the
gap open with her foot. 'These out-clothes,' she said. 'Whose
are they?'

'Yours,' Pir said. A faint smile touched the edge of her
eyes without moving her mouth.

'I've got some.'

'Not as good as those.'

'No, but —' Ario shook her head. 'Thanks, but I don't need
them.'

'Yes, you do.'

'No, really, I —'

'Yes, Ario, you *do*,' she said, cutting her off cleanly. Now
the smile had spread to the corners of her lips. 'You really
do. Because you're coming with me. Outside. Didn't you
hear? We're celebrating.'

'But —' Ario stared at her, and the silence seemed to churn
inside her: until at last something snapped, and she put her

hands up to her face and started to laugh. 'OK,' she said, through her fingers. 'OK. Whatever you say. Thanks for the out-clothes.'

'Great. You can keep them, after. Let's go.' Pir reached out and took her hand. Ario started to pull away, but Pir didn't let go, and after a second Ario gave up trying. It was strange, the warm skin against hers, the shape of Pir's fingers on the back of her hand. She didn't mind it, actually.

As they went out through the hall Ario saw Dion look up from his computer with a glint in his eye. Ah, she thought, it *was* you . . . but she couldn't muster any annoyance. She was almost — well, grateful. She caught his eye and he waved. 'Going out?' he called.

'Looks like it,' she said. She could feel a silly sort of grin on her face. 'We're going to celebrate.'

'Cool. You want something to fly on?'

She shook her head; but by that time Pir had already dragged her past Dion's desk. They paused in front of the door, and she started to put on her out-clothes, automatically. Then she stopped. She looked up and Pir was watching her, her head tilted to one side. 'What's up, Ario?'

'Don't you want to — I mean — the code, don't you want to check —?'

'Dion said you'd finished.'

'Yes, but — don't you want to have a look, before we go anywhere?'

Pir shook her head, and then laughed, as though Ario's expression was funny. 'Hey, I'm excited about it. But let's savour the moment, yeah? Sometimes it's fun, you know. Like before you open a present.'

'I haven't ever had a present,' Ario said, and bit her tongue. 'I mean —'

'What, never?' Pir blinked; her eyes were wide and bright, too beautiful to look at. 'Ario, really?'

She's feeling sorry for me, Ario thought. How dare she? She's just some streetkid who struck it rich, and now she's standing there *pitying* —

'I'm fine,' she said. 'I don't want presents, anyway. It's all junk, all that stuff. It's stupid.'

'All that stuff? You mean, like friends?' She was almost teasing; almost, but not quite. 'Having people who care about you?'

'Dion cares about me.' She hated herself for getting drawn in. She should've shrugged, let Pir think what she liked . . . but somehow she couldn't, and the words came out wrong, childish and defensive.

'Sure he does,' Pir said. 'But you do your best to stop him, don't you?'

'What's that supposed to —' Her voice cracked, and she looked away. She was exhausted, still; that was why the moisture rose into her eyes, prickling against her lashes. 'Forget it,' she said.

There was a pause. Ario heard the rustle of Pir's out-clothes as she put on her hood, and smelt the faint breath of chemicals that clung to the fabric. Then there was a hand on her shoulder — Pir's hand, gloved, warm — and Pir said, very gently, 'Hey. Sorry. I'm an idiot.'

Ario shook her head silently. The floor rippled as the tears swelled and spilt; then it was clear again, in focus, and the pain in her throat eased.

'Come on. There's somewhere I want to take you. Somewhere special. Put your out-clothes on.'

She obeyed, without saying anything. Why am I doing this? she thought. She's just a client, and I've finished her commission. I don't even know her . . . But she did it anyway. The hood fitted perfectly; when she took a deep breath she could smell the cleanness of the air. It made her want to keep inhaling, for ever.

'OK?'

'OK.'

'Let's go.'

Where are we going? Ario wanted to say. But something stopped her. Maybe this was what Pir had meant: the excitement of not knowing, of trusting someone else, of letting things happen without controlling them . . . Or maybe I just can't be bothered to talk through the hood, she thought. Stop *thinking*.

They went out through the door into the rain.

He watches them go, from the shadows in the tankshop. This is how he survives now: slipping from darkness to darkness, avoiding people's looks, taking the dregs of abandoned P&V shakes so that he doesn't have to ask for food. Otherwise, sooner or later, someone will realise he's no use, that they're feeding him for nothing. He has to be invisible; to be no one. Only every so often, in the dead of night, he goes into the iTank demo. Then — for a few moments, just a few moments — he remembers who he is.

And when he sees Ario. Then, too.

There's something about her . . . Her eyes, her expression, the way the Maze is the only thing that matters to her. He knows how that feels. She reminds him of his old life. It hurts, like hunger, but he wants to stay near to her. That unease, that soreness in his gut, that ache . . . it's all he has. It's the only thing that makes him feel *anything*.

So he watches her, when he can. He's watching her now. She's beautiful, the other girl — the client, whatever she's called — but he hardly notices; his eyes are on Ario. He follows her with his gaze, not moving his head, as they stand together next to the door, putting on their out-clothes. They haven't seen him. He wishes he could hear what they're saying, but he can't get closer. If he moves into the light someone might notice him.

But he takes one more step towards them, in spite of himself. It's as though he's drawn by a magnet. He can't help it.

The client says something, and Ario answers, raising her voice. He catches a word — three, four — *Dion cares about me* — and he looks down, his skin suddenly warm and prickling with resentment. She sounds like she's on the edge of tears. Who does the client think she is, making Ario cry? But then, who does he think *he* is, eavesdropping? And what does he care, if Ario says *Dion* with such emphasis?

For a second he feels nothing but a wave of misery, homesickness so strong it's as if he's overflowing with it. Then he draws back into the corner of the hall, feeling the shadow fall across his face again.

He waits, willing Ario to turn, to look at him just once before she leaves; but they go through the door without looking back, and there's nothing but the sharp, acrid smell of the outside air.

11

It was cold. The rain gleamed and flashed on the eyepiece of Ario's hood; there were glints of moonlight between the clouds and it outlined every drop in silver. Pir had slipped her hand into Ario's, and she could feel the warmth through the gloves, making her nerves tingle. She slid a glance sideways, but Pir was looking straight ahead, her expression unreadable through her visor. She let Pir lead her down the street, round a corner, down another street . . .

The last time I was outside, she thought, it was the night of the explosion, the night I was chased . . . But she wasn't afraid. She knew Pir could defend her — gamerunners were useful in a fight — but it wasn't that. There was a kind of magic in the air, like a note too high to be audible, and it told her she was safe, that nothing bad could happen to her tonight. She knew it was irrational but she let it take hold of her, and under her breathing panel she felt herself grin.

She would have looked up, to know where they were going, but she had to watch her feet. The pavement was less fragile than it had been, when it had crumbled every time she took a step: now it was frozen, still blurred by vapour but holding together under her sole, creaking. Tiny needles of ice flared around her feet as she crossed a frozen puddle. She was so punch-drunk with tiredness that everything was too bright, too focused: it was like she was flying, she wanted to stay where she was, taking in every detail. Pir glanced at her, and said, her voice hissing through her breathing panel, 'OK?'

'Yes.' Ario shook her head, trying to clear it. ''Course. Just coming.'

They walked together through the dark streets, drawing back into alleys when they heard voices. Once there was screaming, quite near, and Ario's heart jumped and started to pound. Pir's grip tightened on her wrist; then she leant closer and said, with the hint of a laugh, 'Don't worry. It's a recording. To clear the streets.'

'What?' She couldn't help clutching Pir's hand.

'They play recordings to clear the streets. Everyone runs away when they hear screaming, so . . .' She shrugged, as though it was nothing unusual. 'But you get to hear the difference, after a while. They always use really short loops.'

'Oh.' It still felt wrong, to walk towards the cries; but Pir didn't let go of her, and she took deep breaths and forced herself to relax. And when they got close, she could hear the difference too: the cries were tinny, with odd accents, like rich kids pretending to be streetkids. But all the same she was grateful when they turned a corner, away from the sound.

At first she'd recognised the streets — she didn't go out much, but she'd lived in Undone all her life, after all — but as Pir led her further and further from the tankshop the streets were narrower, darker, full of banks of debris and makeshift barricades where gangs had fought. The air was thick with freezing mist and silence. Something crunched under Ario's shoe, and when she looked down she saw shards of broken glass that were already frosted and eroded by the rain.

Pir looked round. 'Quietly,' she said, and pointed to one side of the street. A block of blackness seemed to stand out from the walls, sharp-edged as a flatscreen. She held her finger to her lips, and moved towards it, beckoning to Ario to follow. They stepped softly past the coastline of rain-eaten rubble, past a doorway — ah, that's why we need to be quiet, Ario thought, it must be a gang HQ — and towards the rectangle of darkness.

It was the entrance to an alleyway. Ario's heart squeezed uncomfortably, as though she'd swallowed something that was still alive and battering to get out; but she followed Pir into the dark.

Pir leant towards her, and said, 'Follow me.'

And disappeared.

It took a second for Ario to understand, and then it was only because she'd stretched out her hand. Her fingers found a wall, rough and cold, even through her glove. 'Pir?'

And then, as she slid her hand sideways, there was a blunt corner — a wide vertical crack, a fissure the width of a chimney — and through it, nothing. She reached deeper into the shadow. Still nothing. '*Pir!*'

'I'm here. Come on.'

Oh no, she thought. No. I'm not getting into that. 'I — Pir, I —'

'Don't be scared. It's narrow but you're easily thin enough, don't worry.' There was a silence. Ario could hear the hissing of Pir's hood, just the other side of the wall. It should have reassured her, but it didn't. 'Hey, we've come this far,' Pir said, and there was a strange note in her voice, not quite a laugh. 'Come on. Trust me.'

I don't trust you, she wanted to say. Why should I? I hardly know you.

She said, slowly, 'OK.' Then, breathing out in a long slow sigh to stop herself panicking, she turned sideways and pushed her body through the gap.

The scrape of the walls against her suit seemed to go on and on; but after a few seconds the sound of her breathing panel changed, as though there was more space surrounding her. She felt in front of her face, and the darkness was empty. 'Pir?'

'I'm here. Follow me.' There was a click, and a faint veil of silver snagged on the rough brickwork in front of her face. She looked round, and the contours of Pir's suit were outlined in the same pale gleam, like moonlight. Pir raised her hand: there was a small bright sphere between her fingers. 'Ready?'

Ario took in a long breath and crept forward. Her suit wasn't touching the walls any more, but she could feel them pressing in on her, smell the grains of ice clinging to the brickwork. 'Are there more — narrow places —?'

But Pir had already moved deeper into the shadows. The walls were close around her, sparkling with frozen moisture.

A drip fell from the ceiling, flashed in a vertical stripe of white light and clicked against the ground, leaving a tiny circle of vapour. Then the silence came back, filled with the hiss of their hoods.

Ario gritted her teeth, and followed.

The passages went on and on: never as narrow as that first gap, but still so small that if Ario had spread her arms she could have grazed both sides with her elbows. Pir was a silhouette in front, blacker than black, like a person-shaped hole in the world. They turned a corner, another, clambered over a half-fallen archway, went up a flight of rough steps, around another corner, along another long irregular passage-way ... until time seemed to stop, and Ario could have sworn that Pir was leading her in circles, through the same shadows again and again. This will go on for ever, she thought. We can walk and walk but we'll never arrive. Even through her hood she could smell the damp and the odd burnt odour of corroded stone. The silence and cold sank into her bones.

Pir stopped.

Ario was so numb and frozen — her mind as well as her limbs — that she almost stumbled into her. She pulled up short, and felt Pir touch her shoulder gently, steadying her.

It was a dead end.

The wall rose straight up in front of them, glittering with tiny crystals of ice, the brickwork eaten away into lace. Pir's hand moved and blackness jumped and trembled in every tiny hole. In the enclosed space the whisper of her breathing was very loud; but from far away Ario thought she heard a limping footstep, hurrying towards them. She said, 'Pir?'

'We're here.' Perhaps, on the other side of Pir's visor, there was the faint shine of teeth; but Ario wasn't sure.

Are we? Where's *here*? But she couldn't say it. The footsteps were sprinting now, thudding in her ears, and she realised it was her pulse. Her hood wasn't letting in enough air: she was breathless, the inside of her lungs prickling with horror. She stood still, looking at the wall, and the acid-eaten bricks crawled with worms of shadow.

I understand, she thought.

Pir's brought me here, to a dead end. And no one, no one in the world knows where we are.

I am such a *fool*.

She knew she should run. She had a chance, maybe.

Or maybe not. Even if Pir didn't catch up with her there was still this maze of passages, the cold and the dark. Without Pir I'll never get out, she thought, I'm lost . . . And she knew — with a cold, dead feeling, as though the numbness had spread to her heart — that she wasn't going to run anywhere.

If this is how it's going to happen, she thought, then it'll happen. She took a deep breath and closed her eyes. Come on, then. Just do it quickly.

'Ario? Are you OK?'

Her eyelids flicked open, in spite of herself.

'It's not as hard as it looks,' Pir said. 'Seriously. Do you want to go first?'

She was pointing towards the top of the wall. Ario followed her finger, but there wasn't enough light to see clearly:

everything was lost in a blur of shadow.

'What?' Her voice trembled a little as she said it. There was a faint, struggling flame of hope in her gut; she was afraid to speak too loudly in case it went out.

'There,' Pir said. 'See it?' And she held up her sphere of light, stretching on tiptoes. At the top of the wall, where it met the ceiling, there was a flat hole, just wide enough for a person. 'It's not as scary as it looks. Seriously, are you sure you're OK? You look a bit . . .'

'I'm fine.' The fire of relief blazed up inside her, flickering up through her ribcage, tickling her larynx. She felt the beginnings of hysteria and forced herself to swallow a laugh. I'm not going to die, she thought, and it was wonderful, marvellous, absurd. 'Don't worry about me.'

'So . . .' Pir gave her a long look. 'Watch. It's easy.'

She turned to the wall, reaching up with her hands. In a second — too fast for Ario to see how she'd done it — she'd swung and clambered upwards, one foot scrabbling for purchase and dislodging a fine rain of ice and stone that pattered against Ario's eyepiece. Then, like a reptile, she disappeared into the crack. For a moment Ario was left alone in the pitch-black, her eyes inventing swirls of colour, fiery wheels that spun like traps in front of her face. The fear rose again, irresistible — but then there was a wriggle and muffled swearing from above her, and the little globe of silver rolled out of the fissure and bounced down to her feet with a sharp clatter. Pir called, 'You can leave it there if you want. There's light this side.'

OK. I can do this, she thought. I can. I may not be a game-runner, but I can climb a wall.

She reached up, the way Pir had. She was shorter than Pir, but one of her hands found a knot of irregular brick. It felt crunchy and fragile under her fingers, but if she was quick . . . She brought her foot up, pressing her toe into a gap where the mortar had worn away, and took a deep breath. One big push, and the momentum would carry her upwards. The crack wasn't far above her — only an em or so, nothing impossible.

Pir's voice said, faintly, 'Are you coming or what? Don't tell me you're stuck.'

'No.' She didn't like the word *stuck*; it made the walls edge towards her, sly and menacing. 'Just a sec.'

Without giving herself time to think, she bent her knees, gripped the outcrops of rotten stone, and dragged herself up. For a moment she was lost, her feet swinging ridiculously at the end of her legs, her arms aching with the effort; then, unbelievably, she found the strength to heave her body upwards. Her hands found the edge of the crack and she dug at the wall with her toes, pushing until her chin was level with the hole and she could slide one elbow on to the flat surface. If it hadn't been for the fire in her muscles, she would have paused before she slid herself into that dark space; but she didn't have time, and the fissure swallowed her like a black toothless mouth.

It was tight. The stone touched her suit all the way down her body. She tried not to move sideways — not to arch her back, or flex her feet — because she didn't want to feel the cold pressing on every side of her. She crawled forward, her hands trapped close to her body, and the bumps and bulges in the surface hurt her knees. She took a long breath, and said to herself: By the time I breathe out I'll be on the other side. But her lungs filled up until they were jerking uncomfortably, bloated with air, and she was still on her stomach, still crawling.

One more breath. And one more.

There was a blue space in front of her, ragged at the edges. It opened like a flower as she moved towards it. She tilted her head to see more clearly, but her visor was squashed and the curve of the panel blurred the contours of everything. She scrabbled against the walls, hurrying to get out, bruising her shoulder, her elbow, but it didn't matter, she was so relieved to see the light.

'Hey — careful —' Pir said, and she was there, at the end of the tunnel, waiting with her arms spread, ready to help Ario down. 'Can you — never mind, I can hold you — wriggle forward, that's right —' She gripped Ario's shoulders, and her hands were warm through the gloves, and strong. 'Well done, just a bit more, it's OK, I've got you —'

Ario nodded, slithered the last few centi-ems, twisted and dropped awkwardly, letting Pir take her weight. Together they reeled giddily; then she found her feet and stepped away. She found that she was laughing with relief — and with embarrassment, because of the way Pir had held on to her, because of that clumsy scuffling waltz in each other's arms. 'Thanks,' she said. She looked round. 'So is this — where are —'

She stopped speaking, because her heart somersaulted in her chest.

12

They were high up, surrounded by space. Above them there was the night sky, fraying clouds outlined in a blaze of moonlight and a prickle of stars, framed by the edges of a roof and stumps of old rusting beams. A great broken arch pushed itself out into emptiness like the prow of a ship. Everything gleamed and shimmered with ice.

And below them —

They were on a kind of ledge. To both sides there were rain-eaten walls, with high, gaping gaps; curved sections of stone were dropped here and there like bones, hinting at fallen-down arches. In front, two bumpy, pitted slopes ran down to meet each other, as though they had once been stairs. Another staircase, a bigger one, led down at right angles to — no, stopped dead, broke off. Where the floor should have been there was a huge chasm, dark as water, bottomless as the sky. The walls went down and down: below the useless staircase there were more arches, more pillars and windows, more stairs, more crumbling stone . . . As far down as she could see, there was nothing, only space and snapped columns, the last remnants of another ceiling; and beyond that, deep in the depths, something flashed and shone like a bright coin.

The moon.

She heard herself laugh, as she realised what she was looking at.

A huge expanse of ice, smooth as a dance floor, a mirror, the blade of a knife. The building around her was reflected with such clarity that even now, looking down, she felt a kind of vertigo, as if gravity could drag her down into that fathomless sky.

And everything around her was coated in crystal, twinkling, and she'd never seen anything so lovely.

She didn't know how long she stood there, perfectly still; it was only when Pir shifted her weight that she realised that she was uncomfortable, stiff and cold, and that she was gripping Pir's hand so hard that she'd cut off the blood flow to her own fingers. She relaxed her grip. 'Sorry.'

'Do you like it?'

'It's — yes,' she said, and that irresistible laugh pushed up again into her throat, chirruping there like a bird. 'Yes, I do. Where are we?'

'I'm not sure,' Pir said. She jumped down from the ledge, landing lightly, and stretched out her hand to help Ario down. She took her weight easily and swung her to the floor. Then they stood leaning against the balustrade, bowing their heads to look into the huge mirror that stretched out in front of them. The moon guttered and died as a cloud swept across it, and in the sudden darkness all Ario could see was the glint of stars, a long, long way down. Then suddenly it flared again, and the world was dazzling silver. Everything is priceless, she thought, this is a king's ransom, riches beyond the dreams of avarice . . .

'No one comes here,' Pir said. 'It's too dangerous. And why should they? There's nothing here.'

'Nothing?' Ario turned to look at her, and their eyes met.

Pir smiled. She turned to look at the arches hung with diamonds, the silver-woven brick, the stone faces poxed with brilliance. 'Nothing,' she repeated, and it was like a password. 'A special kind of nothing. A nothing you can't eat, or burn, or do anything with. You couldn't stay here.'

'Is it old?'

'I think so. It looks like it. Maybe it was a church . . . but the river came in, and the foundations went — look.' She pointed towards the nearest pillar, and Ario saw that it was out of the vertical, as though the whole building had lurched to one side, lifted up on a frozen wave.

There was silence. Tiny storms of ice-dust lifted around Ario's feet and danced for a second before the breeze let them drop.

'Why is it so smooth?' she said at last. 'Why doesn't the rain eat the ice away?'

'I don't know. I think maybe it's to do with the chemicals in the water — if it's just on the point of freezing, tiny variations in temperature might make it melt and refreeze so it's always smooth. Dunno, though. I'm not a scientist.'

'It doesn't matter, anyway.'

'No,' Pir said. 'It doesn't, does it?' She grinned, and Ario found herself grinning back.

There was another silence. Ario turned away and sat down on the steps, wrapping her arms around her knees. It was cold, but she didn't want to leave, ever. She tilted her head back and looked up at the moon flying between trailing swatches of cloud. She thought she could feel the earth spinning. Or — no, it's as if I'm in outer space, she thought. Like this is a spaceship, and my old life is falling away behind me so quickly it's already the size of an atom. Pir and I are the only people alive. And we're free.

Pir sat down next to her, without saying anything. Ario was grateful for that: right now she didn't want to talk. More than anything she would have liked to take her hood off and feel the cold wind on her face; but she couldn't, of course. Instead, surprising herself, she reached across and took Pir's hand.

After a while Pir shifted her weight a little, and said, 'You don't think I'm an idiot, to bring you all this way?'

'It's worth it.'

'Good.'

Another pause. Ario noticed, without surprise, that she wasn't tired any more. There was a strange kind of space in her head, a lack of curiosity, a lack of desire . . . But it wasn't boredom or fatigue. She stared through the balustrade into the ice-reflections, wondering what it was, the feeling. It wasn't bad, just unfamiliar . . .

Happiness, she thought.

I'm *happy*.

She started to giggle. Pir turned to stare at her; and then, as if it was contagious, she joined in. The sound echoed off the stones, ringing out as though they were at the centre of a bell of ice.

'You're really odd, Ario,' Pir said at last, shaking her head.

'I know.'

Pir took a breath. She said, 'I don't know anything about you . . . How did you get to be working in a tankshop?'

'I just —' She started the sentence automatically, ready to push the question away unanswered. But she stopped, and the reflected moon caught her eye and winked at her. She looked at Pir's gloved hand in her own, and shrugged slowly. 'I had to,' she said. 'I wasn't very old, and it was the only thing I could do. Well — that or the Other Game, I guess . . .'

Pir was watching her, the way she'd done before: alert, ready to catch her if she fell.

'My papa was . . . I don't know who he was. We had loads of Maze stuff, a really high-tech terminal and a gametank, back when hardly anyone did. Only rich people, I mean, and we weren't rich. And he was always a bit scared, I think. He used to talk about Crater as if they were people he knew . . . He taught me to write code. And then one day he went out and didn't come back. I waited for a long time, I really — I did wait for him, but in the end —' Her voice was strung taut, threatening to break, like a cable. She swallowed, easing the tension away. It was so long since she'd let herself remember; even longer, since she'd told anyone . . . But it wasn't as hard as it might have been. She glanced at Pir, taking in her gaze, her steady grip on Ario's hand. 'In the end I had to find somewhere else to go. And then I met Dion, and he let me into his tankshop.'

'How long ago was that?'

'I don't know.' She saw Pir raise her eyebrows, and shrugged. 'I really don't. I could probably work it out, if I had to. It was . . . before the second-generation gametanks. Five years ago? Four?'

Pir nodded slowly. 'So the only person you had . . . he just *left*, and you don't know what happened to him.'

'Yes.'

'That explains a lot.' But her voice softened the words, blunting their edge until they were almost kind. 'Listen . . . I don't know if you remember — I *hope* you don't remember — when I said you were — well, I was a bit harsh, the first time I met you, and I said —'

'You said I was rubbish with people, that I thought they were pointless and pathetic and that my cheat codes were more important than anything human.' She smiled. Somehow it didn't hurt any more.

'Oh. Guess you *do* remember, then.'

'Don't worry.'

'I just wanted to say —'

'It's OK, Pir.'

'But I —'

'It's *OK*.'

There was a pause. Pir nodded. She was smiling ruefully, her mouth turned down at the corners. 'Right. Well . . . good.'

'You know I said I'd never had a present?'

'Yes.'

'Well, I was wrong, wasn't I? You gave me these out-clothes.'

'So I did.'

'And —' She hesitated, and then spread her hand out in front of her, so that the fabric of her glove gleamed. Above her the stars burnt, sharp and steady. 'And all this. You brought me here. You didn't have to.'

They sat still, watching the moon slide imperceptibly across the floor until it was swallowed by a billowing cloud. The light from the sky was pale, diffuse. The glints in the brickwork died. Gently the rain started again, and faint traces of vapour rose from the stone. Now it was a palace of dim fog and shadows, full of the sibilance of the rain.

The tiredness started to seep back into Ario's body. She yawned, tasting the faintest trace of ammonia, and leant her head on Pir's shoulder. She was grateful for the warmth coming through her suit where it touched Pir's.

'Are you asleep?' Pir said.

'Not entirely.'

'It's too cold to sleep, you might never wake up. We'd better go back.'

'Just a few more minutes,' Ario said.

'A few more minutes, then,' Pir agreed. They sat together watching the rain as it washed the building slowly — imperceptibly slowly — into dust.

The way home seemed shorter. Maybe it was because Ario was lost in dreams — even as she walked through the dark, freezing passages, lit by the frail glow from Pir's globe, her mind was back in the deserted hall. If she'd closed her eyes she would have seen broken, glittering arches and stars drowned in ice; but she didn't, because the floor was rough and pitted and she needed to concentrate.

It seemed like hardly any time at all before they were making their way through the streets. It was a little warmer now, and raining hard: that made it safer, because the gangs would be inside, but it filled the air with mist and the stink of bleach. Ario gritted her teeth and followed Pir, glad that at last they were coming to a crossroads that she recognised. They turned the corner, and there — behind the rubbish and camouflage, of course — was the door of the tankshop. She slipped in front of Pir for the retina scan, and punched in the codes. She realised, too late, that she hadn't shielded her hand from Pir's gaze; but when she glanced over her shoulder Pir was looking tactfully away.

The door slid open, and they went through. Ario reached for the fastening of her hood, and took it off: her first breath was thick with the stench of ammonia coming off her suit, but when the coughing had died down and her eyes had stopped streaming she could smell the familiar stale, comforting air of the tankshop.

'You OK?' Pir, sensibly, had waited for the chemicals to evaporate a little before she took her hood off. Now she was taking off her gloves, running her hands over her head.

'Yes. I'm not used to — I don't go out much.'

'No kidding,' Pir said, with a glint of mockery in her eyes. Then she smiled, swinging her hood from her hand. 'Well. At least I got you home safe.'

'Yes. Thanks.' Ario wiped the last moisture from her cheeks. Inside the tankshop the noise of the rain was muffled, and the hum of the terminals was hardly audible. The silence pressed uncomfortably into her ears like fingers. Was there something she should say? 'Thanks,' she repeated.

'I should go, I guess. From the way you looked this afternoon when I woke you up, you need your sleep.'

'Yes.' She felt wooden, useless. Why wouldn't the words come?

'Goodnight, then. I'll come back tomorrow. For my cheat codes.'

'Yes. OK. Of course.'

There was another pause, as if they'd both forgotten their lines. Then Pir smiled again and started to put her gloves back on. The rustle of the fabric was very loud; it rang in Ario's ears as though it was echoing off the walls.

'Wait,' she said. 'I'm not tired. If you want — um, do you want — there's no one else awake, if you want to look at the cheat codes now — if you want to try them out, in our iTank —'

Pir paused. 'Really?' she said. Her voice was casual, non-committal; but her eyes had narrowed. 'That's nice of you, but you don't have to. Tomorrow will be fine.'

'I mean —' Ario said, and spread her hands helplessly. 'Only if you want to.'

Pir held her gaze. Then suddenly she cracked into a smile, and started to take off her gloves again. 'Well, come on, then,' she said. 'Don't you need to turn on your terminal? What are you waiting for?'

Ario lugged her terminal into the tank room while Pir warmed up. For a moment she looked round for Rick; but tonight he wasn't in his corner. She stared at his empty bedbag with a feeling that wasn't quite relief, and then forced herself to turn her attention back to her code. There were a couple of new ideas she'd stuck in, but when she started to say, 'Hey, Pir, I came up with a couple of extra add-ons that I thought you might like —' Pir only grinned and made a gesture with her hand as if she was waving the words out of the way.

'You can give me the full rundown tomorrow,' she said, breathlessly, swinging her arms. 'Right now I just want to get into the Roots and see how far I can get.'

'To the end, I hope,' Ario said. The words sent a little thrill to her stomach. The end . . . no one knew what happened then. Did the Maze have an endgame? It must do, she thought, the Maze, the greatest game ever, it must have *something* . . . But it was secret, untouchable, like the heart of a labyrinth — and it *was* the heart of a labyrinth, the last quest, the last portal hidden in the vast knot of the Roots. Where Pir was going to go . . . She gritted her teeth, forcing herself to focus on her flat-screen. Everything was ready. And it was good. Stop worrying.

Pir flopped over in a final stretch, then stood up and grinned. 'OK. You all set?'

'Yes. I just need to send this to your account, and then we'll be live.'

There was a flicker in Pir's face. 'Do you want me to pay you first? I know it's not usual for you to transfer the code before —'

'I trust you,' Ario said, grinned back, and added, 'and, anyway, Dion would come and hunt you down.'

'Great. That's reassuring.'

Ario took one last look at her flatscreen. Then, without giving herself time to think too much, she hit **Enter**. There. Done.

'OK,' she said. 'When you're ready. Once you're in, the codeword's "Helios", to load the cheats.'

They looked at each other, and for a moment it was as if they were two halves of the same person, strung together by the same excitement. Pir nodded and walked towards the iTank. 'Did you manage to branch it properly? Last time, when that kid was running the demo, your flatscreen was really struggling.'

'Don't worry, Spin sorted it out. The other terminals too, but with the direct connection you can get player's-eye view. I'll be able to see every move. And I've — if you want, I can run a ventrillo . . .' She shrugged. 'Normally clients don't want me breathing down their necks, giving them orders —'

'I don't mind. I like it when you're all masterful . . .' Pir grinned.

'Yes, well . . . I want to see whether my codes work,' Ario said. 'If they do, you've got infinite health, so you can walk straight through the traps. And I've tweaked the timing when you fight so you'll have a speed advantage, as well as the health. Basically I wouldn't worry too much.'

'I hope you haven't made it *too* easy . . .' Pir winked. Then she slid her hand along the side of the iTank. It rippled with light — it made Ario think of a cat arching its back, wanting to be stroked — and opened for her. 'Wish me luck.'

'If I've done my job properly you won't need it.'

'Please,' she said, pouting absurdly, and fluttered her eyelashes.

Ario rolled her eyes and said, 'Good luck.'

'Thanks,' Pir said. She swept one hand to her breastbone, and bowed. 'If I win through, it's because of you.' She was smiling, but there was something steady in her eyes: something more than gratitude.

Ario looked at her, then down at her screen. It was blank, but she thought she could see the shadow of the ice-hall, the faintest glitter of stars. It was fatigue, probably, but tiny crystals seemed to sparkle in the corners of her vision, as though part of her was still sitting on those steps, watching the rain. An hour ago she'd been so happy; and now, feeling Pir's eyes on her face, she wanted to be back there, not here in the tankshop. The happiness had changed into something less comfortable, excitement and pleasure and . . . No, she thought. It's simpler than that. I'm afraid.

For a strange, heretical moment she didn't want Pir to run the Maze. She wanted this instant to go on for ever, Pir frozen and smiling, with her hand on her heart.

If I say I've made a mistake — or just say her name — stretch out my hand, tell her —

'Just get on with it,' she said. There was a silence, but she didn't look up.

At last she heard Pir get into the iTank and the door close behind her. For a second — half a second, a fraction of a second — Ario almost called her back.

But she waited too long. The screen flashed into life, showing the loading space, and the excitement took over.

13

Pir looked different on-screen to how she was in real life. She was stockier, with dark shadows under her eyes and longer hair. It took Ario aback — she still wasn't used to the iTank, the way it showed the players' own ideas of how they looked — and it gave her a strange pang, to see that Pir didn't know how beautiful she was.

You are about to enter the Roots of the Maze. If you die while attempting this quest, your account will be closed. Are you sure you wish to proceed?

She took a deep breath. Just seeing the words made her spine crackle at the top like static electricity. But Pir didn't wait. She said, **Yes.** Without looking round, she raised one hand in a jaunty little wave. **Ready, Ario?**

She nodded; then rolled her eyes at herself, because of course Pir couldn't see her. Hurriedly she reached for her mic and said, 'Yep. Go ahead.'

Her flatscreen flickered — the graphics still weren't perfect, but at least it didn't slideshow like it did before — and the Roots of the Maze were suddenly there: the great hall with steps that led down into the darkness, a huge spiral that narrowed and plunged like a well. Pir did a little dance, jumping from foot to foot, pantomiming her excitement. Then she stood still, putting on her concentration like a cloak. **OK, Ario. Let's go.**

Ario took a deep breath. She sat up straight, fiercely glad that this time there was no big screen, that the other Cheats were safely asleep. 'OK.' She couldn't say anything else, her throat was too tight.

Well then. *Helios*.

The screen jumped. It was so slight Ario wouldn't have seen it, if she hadn't been watching for it; but the movement seemed to sing along her nerves to her spine, sending a fizz of anticipation to her fingertips. That was it. The moment of truth.

Hope that worked.

Ario laughed aloud and dragged her block closer to her flatscreen. She said, to the familiar-strange figure on-screen, 'You know what? It did work. Now *go*.'

Pir nodded a little, took a deep breath, and began to run.

The Roots were strange, like a dream of the old version: the same and yet not the same, winding dark passages that danced in the light of torches, full of traps that slid out like tongues, seductive and dangerous . . . but somehow Ario thought she could sense Pir's mind reacting to the iTank: there were glitters in the walls that reminded her of the ice sparkling in the tunnels below the hall, a faint mist in the air as though the rain had trickled down from the real world into the Maze. It was impossible to know which of the details came from the designers, which from Pir herself. That was what the iTank did: fed on the unconscious input from the player, fleshing out every detail so that the gameworld was perfect. Ario shook her head, admiring the mastery of it. If I wasn't a Cheat, she thought, I would have liked to work for Crater . . .

But she was a Cheat; and proud of it. So the envy only lasted a minute, and then the thought of her codes came back to her with a jolt. She didn't know yet if they worked: or rather she did know — they *would* work, of course, she was good, she was the best — but she just wanted to be sure . . .

And Pir . . . She was sure Pir was doing it deliberately, running the traps as though she didn't have any cheats at all, flipping easily over and under the blades, showing off. It was a kind of challenge: as though she was saying, *Sure, Ario, you're good, but look, so am I*. Or teasing her, playing . . . Ario knew suddenly that Pir was laughing, that she knew exactly how Ario felt. 'OK,' she said, laughing back; and even though Pir didn't reply, Ario saw the shiver of amusement, the fractional hesitation as she heard her. Then she sat back and crossed her arms, forced herself to yawn. 'I can wait. In your own time.'

Then —

She never knew if Pir had taken pity on her, or if she'd simply made a mistake; but it didn't matter. Halfway through a flip Pir landed, went to tumble again but caught her foot on an irregularity in the floor. The impact twisted her ankle to the side, throwing her off-balance, and she swore and landed on her hands, falling through the wicked sword that spun just above the ground.

The codes worked.

Yes. Ario clenched her fists. She felt a surge of triumph, pure and powerful as a drug; and then an aftershock of relief. She'd done it.

Oh. That tickles.

Pir was lying on the floor. The blade flicked into her ribcage and out again. Her health-bar flickered each time, but the health bar stayed on 100. Ario nodded to herself, grinning as though she was acknowledging a round of applause. It wasn't the Ghost cheat: it was better than that, cleaner. Infinite health. It sounded simple, but it wasn't. Hey, Crater, she thought. I *own* you.

And she'd made Pir invisible, so the surves wouldn't notice.

She took a long breath and hissed it out through her teeth. There was a strange sort of melting feeling in her stomach, as though someone had untied a hard, painful knot that had been there for so long she'd stopped noticing it. It was OK. She was still Ario, the Cheat. She *was* the best, after all. She was . . .

Thank you, she thought, leaning forward, saying it in her head like a prayer: to the Maze itself, to the designers, her brothers and sisters at Crater, to the whole world. Thank you.

Then she sat back, propped her chin on one palm, and settled down to watch Pir run deeper and deeper into the Roots.

She drifted into a kind of dream. She was so tired that her eyelids prickled and closed on their own. She jolted awake to find that Pir was in a pillared shadowy hall, fighting a many-headed monster that wove its necks in and out with a fluid, dangerous ease. But although Pir was breathing hard with the effort — her face was wet with sweat, catching the torchlight with a metallic gleam — her health bar was still full, even when the edge of the monster's teeth grazed her shoulder, dripping venom. Ario blinked and rubbed her eyes, glancing at the time. It was early in the morning — the deadest time in the tankshop — and Pir had been going for hours.

But she didn't look like she was going to stop any time soon. Ario knew how she felt: that total absorption, total concentration so that nothing else mattered, not fatigue or hunger or the demands of anything else. It was risky, losing yourself like that — Cheats collapsed or started to hallucinate, gamerunners got injured if the Maze didn't beat them first — but the thrill, the haze of it, when you were in the zone . . . that was what they all went after. It was like flying. Ario stood up to ease the stiffness in her legs and shoulders and said, 'Hey, Pir, be careful.' But she'd be OK. After all, she didn't have to fight too hard, with the cheat codes on her side.

Ario was hungry. It was so long since she'd really been *hungry* . . . For a second it was almost pleasant to feel the pangs, to remember that her body was there and working. Then it started to gnaw at her stomach like a pair of jaws and she knew she had to eat, right now. 'Back in a sec, just taking a comfort break . . .'

What? Yep. OK. Pir didn't pause.

When she came back to the tankshop with a P&V shake and a plate of home-grown protein mush, forking it into her mouth with as much relish as if it tasted of something, Pir had got past the hydra-headed snake and was stalking down a passage of pressure-traps. It made Ario grin, seeing her make all that effort when it didn't matter. But that was the thing about gamerunners and cheat codes — they wanted them, but they wanted to run the Maze themselves too. The cheats were there just to make it possible. Only Cheats wanted cheat codes to be *perfect*.

She flicked up a map of the Roots. Pir was doing well: she'd penetrated right to the heart of the labyrinth. But there was no centre to it any more . . . She noticed suddenly that there were hidden portals everywhere, at the end of every passage, after every boss fight. So which one's the big one? *Is* there a big one? Ario thought. But there had to be. That was how the Maze worked. The quests got bigger and bigger. There was always one at the top.

So. All those dots of red, those portal ikons . . . Which one should Pir go for?

She shook her head suddenly, swallowing her mouthful of protein. What was she thinking? Pir didn't need to run the big one, not tonight. She was just trying out the codes.

But she was a gamerunner, wasn't she? And gamerunners could never resist . . .

And Ario wanted to see it. She didn't want Pir to save her game and log out — not now, not ever. She flipped her flat-screen to player's-eye view. Pir had brought up the map too, and the camera followed her eyes as she looked at it. Ario could guess what she was thinking, just from that movement: she was comparing different routes, wondering which fight she was in the mood for. A swarm of small-fry monsters, or a boss? 'Go on, go for a boss,' Ario said; and she thought that maybe Pir's eyes lingered just slightly longer on the route that led down to a single dot in a wide space. Then Pir waved the map away and set off, down a flight of trap-scattered stairs, and Ario was sure. 'Woot,' Ario said, and her own voice made her laugh. She sounded like Dion.

Pir hurried down the steps, running straight through the traps without bothering to flip or dodge. She was tired, Ario thought. She must know herself that she'd soon be too wiped out to win a fight. Infinite health would help, of course, and the speed cheats, but all the same Pir would have to do *something* to win against a boss . . . It didn't matter how long you could last, if you couldn't finish off the enemy. 'Go on,' Ario said again. 'Then we can log out and go to bed.'

Pir ducked and rolled through the low gap under a half-collapsed doorway. Then she stood up, looking round at the space in front of her. It was a cave, vaulted by shadows and stalactites, lit by a glowing green fog that boiled around her feet. Through the lurid fog-light, dark depths seemed to come and go in the cave floor.

So where's the monster? Ario thought.

Where are you . . . ? Pir said, but she wasn't talking to Ario. **Come out, wherever you are . . .**

Far above, in the age-sculpted arch of the roof, a slow ripple of stars spread out, twinkling as green as the fog. Pir

looked up, and Ario saw it through her eyes: like phosphorescence, tiny flowers of light. It was unlikely, almost comic, like a field coming into bloom; but suddenly it made Ario uneasy. Pir went on staring at it, but Ario flipped back to surve's-eye view so that she could see what was going on at Pir's feet, the tendrils of lurid mist snagging around her ankles. She wasn't a gamerunner — didn't have a gamerunner's instincts — but all the same she had a sense that something was wrong, that they were missing something . . .
'Come on, Pir . . .'

So *where* . . . ? Pir murmured again.

Eyes.

They were *eyes*.

Ario leant forward, clenching her hands together. The stars were opening everywhere, covering every irregularity, every fold in the cave walls. They were reflecting the mist, like sequins.

The monster was everywhere.

'Hey, Pir,' she said. 'Better get ready to fight.' She felt a tightness behind her breastbone, but she didn't mind; Pir might not win, but she wasn't going to lose. She watched as Pir glanced around, following the contagion of light, and shifted her weight on to her toes.

A single star detached itself from the highest vault of the ceiling and sank slowly towards the floor, swinging slightly as though on a thread. It came down and down, so that for a moment it was eye to eye with Pir. Her eyes were steady and dark, with a reflected green glint in the pupils. She stood staring at it, knees bent, alert.

Then it struck, like a snake.

Pir threw up her arm to block the attack and stepped back. She was hissing with surprise, but she kept her balance with the grace of a gamerunner, reaching for her weapons. She'd told Ario she fought with net and blade, like a gladiator, but now both hands held daggers as though she'd already decided that a net was no use. She swung both hands round, and both blades connected with the eye. The first one blinded it; the second one sent it flying in a splash of shiny liquid towards the far wall of the cave. Yes.

It was a challenge. Immediately there was a kind of swell and bulge in the stars above, and they were dropping like rain. Some stayed hanging where they were, like another layer of fog, sparkling and blinking; others dropped straight to the ground and slid straight towards her.

Pir stepped forward, her arms poised, a grin on her face. **Come on then, suxors.**

Ario laughed. Then her gaze went to the floor, and something cut off her breath, neatly, like a switch in her windpipe.

It was a series of bridges, islands linked by irregular isthmuses of rock; and below —

The darkness she'd seen beneath the fog was the darkness of a void. Nothingness.

If Pir took a wrong step —

'Pir,' she said, her voice creaky and thick. '*Pir*. The floor. Careful . . .'

She won't die, Ario thought, saying it to herself over and over. She won't die. She *can't* die. I've given her infinite health . . . If she falls, she logs out, that's all. It's not the end of the world. Not like before, with Herkules . . .

But all the same she dug her hands into her forehead, watching through her fingers as Pir stepped forward and back, dancing with the monster eyes, twirling in a murderous, elegant waltz.

Come on. Come *on* . . .

Pir was stabbing now, picking off the eyes one by one in a line, a flick of the wrist for each as though she were shooting darts. Her other hand swung around in a fluid shielding movement, almost absent-mindedly. A few times an eye swooped in, flashed open like a mouth and struck at Pir's face; but she brushed it away impatiently and her health bar didn't change. And when Ario looked up at the ceiling, she could see that there were fewer lights. Or she thought so, anyway. 'Go on, Pir,' she said. 'Go for it. Don't let them zerg you.'

Her feet were placing themselves beautifully, steady and flat, the toes curling into the rock. Her knees were bent, and her back was straight. She won't fall, Ario thought. She won't.

And the fight went on. Every time Pir moved, Ario could feel her heart in her mouth, flipping over and over, almost choking her: but the blades swung, the feet clung to the ground, Pir's eyes stayed steady. The stars died, one after another. If Pir hadn't had infinite health, she would have been dead a long time ago; but as it was, Ario admired her for still being on her feet, fighting. That stamina had to be *real*. Maybe she'll get too tired to carry on, she thought. She bit her lip, and kept her eyes on Pir's shoes, following every step, turn, shuffle. Go on. I want you to win.

Now the cave was darker. The mist had rippled and washed towards the edge of the cave, worn into wisps and trails around the space where Pir was fighting; the ceiling was nearly empty, and the bare, dark talons of stalactites seemed to reach down towards the light. But now that the eyes were spread out they had more room to swing away from Pir's weapons, tempting her towards them. They gaped at her in flat flashes of green, darted in and away, so that Pir had to spin and lunge to get to them. Every time her dagger punctured one there was the wet squelch of its blood hitting the floor; but it was taking longer and longer, and every move took her further into the cave.

But her luck held. The fight went on and on. Ario checked the time, flicking her eyes to it and back so quickly she hardly took it in, and she saw that it had lasted ten minutes already. Ten minutes was *long*, for a fight like this. Surely Pir would have to give up soon. Any moment now . . .

But she didn't give up. Fifteen minutes. Twenty.

And then there was only one eye left, swinging from the highest, darkest arch of the ceiling.

It had swollen until it was the size of Pir's head: and now, close up, Ario could see the teeth, the grotesque mixture of gums and eyelashes dripping with poisonous tears. A biting eye, blank and malevolent . . .

Pir flinched as it came closer, and hesitated. One hand went to her weapon belt, while the other stayed where it was to guard her face. The blade she'd been holding flicked neatly out of existence, replaced instantly by a net of fine silver that caught the light. You could see the weight of it, from the tension in her shoulder: but that was why she'd chosen it, Ario thought. It would catch the eye and slow it down.

The eye was gaping open like a lurid wound. The long thread that held it to the ceiling bobbed and lengthened like mucus; but there must have been muscles in the string, because it was rippling from side to side. It was going to strike.

Pir swayed with it, mimicking the movement like a snake charmer. **Come on, then,** she said. **Come on, beautiful.**

There was no way of telling whether it could hear her, or understand; but something must have enraged it. Suddenly — too quickly to see properly, at least on Ario's flatscreen with its bodged connection — it threw itself forward, darting with such strength behind it that even though Pir leapt back the teeth swung past her ear with micro-ems to spare.

Ouf . . . that's right, my lovely. Come on . . .

It was a new kind of dance now. It was even harder to watch than the massacre had been: this slow circling, like a mating ritual, the tension between them like a bowstring. Once Pir flashed into a lunge, swinging the net; but the eye was too fast for her, and immediately they were back where they had been, an arm's length apart, circling again. Ario didn't know which was prey and which predator: they were both so fast, so tense, so fierce . . .

The circling went on and on, graceful, neither opponent gaining an advantage. Ario was frozen, mesmerised, in front of her screen; it felt as if it was going to go on for ever.

And then, like lightning, it was over.

Pir must have sensed the stalemate. She was a gamerunner, after all, and a good one. She must have realised that they could go on like that all night, circle, lunge, block . . .

She swung her sword. But not towards the eye. She swung it sideways, into her own body.

The angle was awkward, but the blade swung through her. It should have killed her — *would* have killed her, if it wasn't for Ario's cheat.

The eye followed the movement, and drew back a little, trembling on its string with vile satisfaction. The lashes drew together, letting a thin slice of eye shine through like a silver smirk. Then it closed entirely in a momentary blink.

And in the split second of stillness, while the eye smiled between its fanged lashes, she threw the net.

Gotcha.

Ario was on her feet, her hands at her mouth, hardly breathing, as Pir tugged the eye towards her, carried the sword round in the same fluid swing, and sliced the eye neatly through its equator. *Yes*.

Jelly the colour of sulphur splattered over the floor of the cave. And Pir stood still, laughing.

14

Ario stood in front of her terminal, laughing with relief and pride. She was burbling: 'Pir, gods, Pir, I was sure you were going to fall, I was terrified, wow, Pir, well done, Pir . . .' She heard her own voice and clenched her jaw to force herself to stop. Then she dropped back into her chair.

She put her hands over her face, shaking her head, giggling. The rush of euphoria was like being drunk, as though every tendon in her body had dissolved into mush. She took deep breaths, trying to pull herself together. Honestly, Ario, it's only a *game*.

When she looked at her flatscreen, Pir was looking up at where the surve's-eye view camera was. **Hey, Ario,** she said, grinning. **Have you seen this floor? It's got *holes* in it.**

'No kidding,' Ario said, and the giggles surged again, picking her up and shaking her like an animal.

Well. Anyway. I'm knackered. Pir paused, looked around and shook her head. **I guess it shows.**

She waved the map into place above her and looked up at it. There were no enemies within range; only the long twisting paths that led away, towards the other knots and nests that filled the Roots.

But on the other side of the cave, hidden, there was a portal. And there was nothing to stop her getting to it now. Ario saw Pir's balance shift, her shoulders straighten as the desire overcame the fatigue, saw her give in to temptation. She laughed, and Pir must have heard her, because she threw a grin over her shoulder and said, **Well, OK, maybe not** *that* **knackered** . . . And she sheathed her weapons slowly, and set off towards the portal.

The mist slid over her ankles, veiling the depths, playing with her; but she knew that the holes were there, and so every step was careful and slow. It took a long time for her to cross. Ario wondered every moment whether Pir would lose patience or balance, step too far or too fast . . . But she didn't. Her feet took her safely to the other side; and then she was standing on a wide ledge in front of where the portal should be, nodding a little to herself.

Ario hated portals — hated the thought of them, although she'd never run one herself, of course. Portals were tough. They opened if you hit them hard enough, running at full pelt: but if you didn't get enough speed, they were just a wall. And walls were real, in a gametank. They hit you as hard as they would in real life. She'd seen gamerunners with broken noses and broken jaws from trying to run portals — or trying to run walls that they thought were portals. And iTanks would hurt as much, even if the physical damage wasn't the same . . . The thought of it made Ario flinch. She could imagine someone at Crater — one of the devs, one day — and how they must have said, 'Hey, guys, how about we invent this thing that makes people run into walls?'

the codes were stubborn too. She'd spent a whole
.n once trying to find a cheat code for portals, and she'd
never come up with anything that worked the way she
wanted it to. But Pir hadn't asked for any portal cheats.
That's good, Ario thought, that must mean she can do them,
no problem. She took a deep breath, watching. She didn't
want to see Pir get hurt.

Pir glanced behind her, calculating how much space she
had for a run-up. She checked the map one more time, stepping forward and back to make sure that she was right in
front of the portal. Then she waved it away and shuffled
back to the very edge of the precipice.

Ario heard herself say, 'Careful, Pir, be careful . . .'

**Is this the way to the endgame, Ario? Have you really
got me to the endgame?**

'Just be careful.'

Dion's right, you know. You are *brilliant*. Pir grinned,
swung her arms around to loosen the shoulders, and then
shook herself into readiness, her feet jumping and weaving
a few centi-ems from the abyss. Then she got to her knees
and slid herself into a sprint-start. The sole of her runner
scraped against the floor and a little trail of dust wafted
down into the shadows.

'Gods, Pir, be *carefu—*'

But Pir had already moved, launching herself forward like
a cannon.

Ario held her breath.

Pir went straight at the wall, her arms crossed over her
head. For a moment it was blank rock; then, just before Pir hit

it, it flashed into a golden filigreed arch. There was a dazzling glow, filling all of the flatscreen, a veil of rosy light like dawn.

The endgame, Ario thought. This has to be it.

But when the light cleared, she couldn't believe her eyes.

It was the loading space.

A quiet, light space, with high windows. Rectangles of daylight fell across wooden floorboards. The walls were the colour of cream, but not as smooth.

Pir said, looking round, **What the —?**

Was it the endgame? But there was nothing here. Nothing but —

There was a figure at the other end of the room, waiting under the windows, half illuminated by the shafts of light. He was tracing patterns on the floor with one foot, while glints of dust fell through the beams of sunlight like rain. He looked up, and smiled.

He was tall and slight, with a strange beauty in his face that made Ario lean towards her flatscreen and then check herself, uneasy. What was going on? She reached automatically for a map to find out whether he was an enemy or an NPC — but there wasn't a map, of course. They'd gone beyond the mappable world.

Hello, Pir, he said.

How do you know my real name?

I have my sources. He smiled, and stepped forward. There was something menacing about him: although it wasn't in his face, or his voice. Ario took a deep breath, watching him.

Who are you?

'Yes, who are you?' Ario echoed.

But he only smiled. **The last hurdle,** he said. **I'm the last hurdle.**

'Get out,' Ario said, surprising herself. 'Pir, get *out*.' Something felt wrong; she didn't know what, but the back of her neck was running with little cold shivers. It wasn't nervousness, like before, when she'd just wanted Pir to win; now it was something colder, more urgent. Serious.

But Pir ignored her. **You're the last boss fight? Something like that.**

Pir looked him up and down, and her eyebrows came together. **You? Are you** *sure*? she said, and the disbelief in her voice made Ario smile a little, in spite of everything.

He laughed. **Yes.**

Ario felt the smile die, and stared. The trickles of ice intensified, spread to the top of her spine, making her catch her breath. He shouldn't have laughed. An NPC wouldn't have laughed. The way he was reacting — it was as if he was really *there* . . . Another player. He had to be another player. But how had he got there? What was he doing?

This doesn't make sense, she thought. This is all wrong. 'Pir, log out *now*.'

But Pir only waved her hand as if Ario was an annoying fly, buzzing in her ear. She was a gamerunner; she wasn't going to turn down a fight.

How did you get this far? the man asked, watching her. There was a hint of tension at the corner of his mouth that could have been a smile. **Did you have cheat codes? No.**

Really. He didn't believe her; but somehow it was almost as though he was pleased.

Pir shrugged and gave him a little smug smile. **Tell the surves to have a look at my account,** she said. **It's clean. Anyway — who are you? What am I doing here?**

Well . . . it's complicated. Let's just say this isn't exactly the Maze.

The endgame? Is this the endgame?

In a manner of speaking. The quirk of his mouth broadened into a grin. *I'm the endgame.* **Fight me.**

Another player, Ario thought. It *is* another player. It has to be. I'm sure of it. Her stomach was full of sick slush. 'Log out,' she said again, helplessly. 'Log out, please . . .'

The emergency logout, she said to herself. Maybe now — but she didn't know if this was still the Roots. If the portal was a save point, and this was something new, then maybe . . . but then it wouldn't matter if Pir lost. And the emergency logout killed the avatar — if this *was* still the Roots, then Pir's account might get closed. And it wasn't her choice, it was Pir's . . . No. She couldn't risk it. She dragged her hands over her skull, scraping at the scalp with her fingernails. There was nothing she could do.

And she could see already that Pir was going to fight. She had that calculating, amused look in her eye — the look of a gamerunner who didn't believe she could lose. And she *couldn't*, with infinite health. Of course she'll win, Ario thought. There's nothing to be afraid of.

So why am I afraid?

When you're ready, the man said. He was standing very

straight, watching Pir with a steady, interested gaze. Ario shook her head, chewing her bottom lip. No, she thought. He *isn't* a gamerunner. He can't be. He's not standing like someone who knows how to fight. And he's . . .

Untouchable.

She shook her head again, trying to clear it. But — yes. Untouchable. Distant. Like whatever happened, he knew he was going to win.

So, she said to herself sternly, suppose he's a clueless, rubbish gamerunner, with a brilliant Cheat. And Pir's a wonderful, amazing gamerunner, who *also* has a brilliant Cheat. Relax, Ario. Who would you bet on? But it was no good; she couldn't swallow the unease.

I'm ready, Pir said. **If *you* are.**

Always. There was a silence, and he stepped further into the centre of the room.

Then the walls blurred and dissolved and the floor disappeared, so they were standing opposite each other in a cloud of nothingness. Ario blinked and instinctively wiped her hand over her flatscreen; but the fog was inside the iTank, not the terminal. What . . . ?

Use whatever you want, the man said.

What does that mean? Pir said. There was a new note in her voice, and her hands were clenched.

The man smiled, and held out his hands. **Think of what you want. And use it.**

I . . . Right. Pir stepped back, half laughing. **Look, mate . . .** For a split second Ario was sure she was going to change her mind and log out.

Think of the best way to fight me. And then do it.

Pir looked at him. He looked at her. And the mist grew and swirled around them, thickening and thickening until Ario's screen was white. The sounds faded too, as though the veil had wrapped itself into every space, muffling the resonance, until there was silence.

What the —? Ario leant forward, rubbing her hand uselessly against the flatscreen, disbelieving. She was locked out. 'Pir. Pir! Answer me, something's happened — something — can you hear me? What's happened? Answer me!' But there was nothing. Whatever was happening to Pir in the iTank —

Her eyes stung. The little nerves in her fingers started to buzz. This was wrong. This was mad. What was happening? She flipped her screen to player's-eye view — back to surve's-eye view — back to player's —

Nothing. Only that dense, hostile page of white. And silence: as if Pir's voice had been erased too.

Come on. *Come on* . . . think. She flipped to her coding interface, running her eyes quickly down the screen, trying to take it in. It must be some program that cuts out the ventrillo, prevents spying — but surely the surves — don't the surves need to be able to see —? It doesn't make *sense* —

Why —? Why *now* —?

She couldn't get hold of it — the code on the screen was odd, complex, too unusual for her to understand immediately — but she entered a few commands almost at random, flipped back to the SEV mode, stared at the pale fog, wondering if she could see ripples in it, or whether it was just her eyes playing tricks . . . no. Nothing. She took a deep breath, letting her eyes unfocus, trying to think. She stared at the whiteness. There must be something else I can try.

What's *happening*? I wish I knew what was —

And then —

Then —

Her screen flashed in a sickening mix of technicolor. She was too close to it: the light went to the back of her skull like a punch, and she reeled back, shielding her eyes. The supernova boiled over, neon and horrifying. For a second she thought she could see images rising in the heart of it, like flotsam thrown up by a current; then they sank again, swallowed by the molten colours. The knot of brightness blazed — flared with tongues of green, vermilion, magenta, cobalt — and then suddenly it was dazzling, a blank screen so white it was painful, and she threw her arm over her face and shut her eyes, feeling the sting as the tears pushed out behind her eyelids. The darkness bubbled with deeper black, as though her retinas were scarred for ever.

A second later she forced herself to look — carefully at first, through her fingers, then blinking and staring.

The light had gone.

Her screen was dead. It was dark grey, with the carbon shimmer that meant it was branched but there was no input. She tapped at the terminal, but nothing reacted. It's wiped, she thought. My whole terminal has died — what the —?

The iTank.

She turned to look. It was flashing red.

There has been a malfunction. Please tell Crater about this problem.

The world around her froze. The air fluttered and beat in her ears.

Pir, where was Pir? Why hadn't she opened the door? Pir —

'Manual, turn to manual mode, activate emergency procedures —' She was there, tugging at the door of the iTank, not knowing how she'd managed to cross the room. Her hands — her knees, her whole body — were shaking. The door clicked and slid open slowly, buzzing. She pushed and pulled, uselessly, as it took its time. 'Pir? Pir! What happened, are you OK? The ventrillo cut out and my screen went weird, and I —' She'll hate me, she thought, if I've opened it in the middle of her fight, she'll be furious, my whole career as a Cheat will go down the drain . . . 'Pir! *Pir!*'

The door slid out of her way. She looked into the tank. For an instant she thought Pir wasn't there. Then she glanced down.

Pir was on the floor, half leaning, half sitting. Her face was squashed awkwardly against the wall. There was a bitter, acidy smell.

'Pir? Gods, Pir, what happened? Are you OK?' She dropped to her knees, grabbed Pir by the shoulders and tried to pull her upright. But she didn't respond, and she was too heavy to lift. Ario shook her, so frightened she forgot to be gentle. '*Pir* . . .'

Pir's head dropped forward heavily on to her chest. Something wet spilt over Ario's hands, and she saw that Pir's jaw was loose, her mouth open. A ribbon of vomit rolled down her chin.

'Pir, please . . .'

But she knew, already. A cold, clear part of her had known as soon as the iTank door slid open. She knew.

Pir was dead.

PART 2

ARIO'S THREAD

He's hiding when he hears Daed's voice.

He's still wet from the shower, shivering, his nose running from the smell of the water; he doesn't have anything to dry himself on. Just the shower is a luxury, the first time he's been clean for days. He'd meant to stay under the spray longer — he'd planned it for the dead of night, so no one would notice him — but he heard voices, and cut it short in the middle of soaping himself. He'd grabbed his dirty clothes, logged out of the cube, and clutched them to his groin as he'd run down the corridor, dripping, desperate to get back to his corner of shadow before they saw him.

Ario and Pir. For a split second, catching sight of them, he pauses, feeling that irrational surge of jealousy; then his gamerunner instincts take over, and he darts away behind one of the old gametanks. After a while he sticks his head out, cautiously, but neither of them is looking in his direction. Ario's setting up her terminal, plugging it into the iTank and bending over the flatscreen to check it works; Pir is warming up. So she's going to run the Maze now. She's going to test Ario's codes . . . He watches her as she stretches and flexes, full of a hot, strange anger that doesn't have anything to do with Pir herself. Her face is pale and composed and lovely in the darkness. He goes on watching her, pressing his knuckle to his mouth, and suddenly he can feel the cushion of scar tissue, the tight smoothness of the skin. His face prickles where the flames have eaten into his cheek. When he clenches his jaw the pain comes back, flashing across his vision in a black rush. He takes a deep breath, letting it fade. Then he narrows his eyes and stares at Pir, willing her to stumble, to make a mistake. I hate you, he thinks. I wish I *was* you.

But she goes on, serene and supple, and only pauses when Ario lookes up from her screen and murmurs something about add-ons. They're too far away for him to hear every word: and anyway he doesn't want to. He wishes they'd go away and leave him to sleep alone in the dark. He draws back into the gap behind the gametank, and slides down to a sitting position, his feet wedged uncomfortably against the wall. He leans his head back and shut his eyes. He hears the buzz of the iTank door opening, and — after a moment — the faint, tinny sounds of the Maze coming from Ario's flatscreen. The noises are so familiar that even with his eyes shut he can see what's happening, as clearly as if he's watching the screen. A blade-trap, footsteps on a staircase, a row of spin-dle-traps . . . the Maze, *his* Maze . . . but he was barred, for ever. And he has to sit there and listen while Pir runs it, cheating. He draws his knees up and grits his teeth.

But after that first sharp pang the envy dies to a dull ache. He bends his head and stares at the dark, trying not to listen to the sound effects; after a few moments he puts his hands over his ears. Then he sits with his eyes half closed, waiting for the lights to go off so that he'll know it's safe to cross the floor to his bedbag. He drifts, watching the faint coloured light that dances on the wall, reflected from the iTank. The shades of black melt, flow, bleed . . .

He's not asleep. But suddenly he's awake, properly awake. For a second he doesn't know what he's heard or why it's gone straight to his heart like a stab. Then he hears it again, and it's Daed.

Daed's voice.

Always.

He jerks up, his heart pounding. Yes, Daed's voice — distorted, warped by the flatscreen speakers, but still recognisable, still with that faint ironic twist that makes him want to cry. Daed, his father — his father, Daed —

What —?

The iTank. The Maze . . .

And he understands, in a cold wave of disappointment. It must be Daed's NPC version of himself, that he left in the loading space like a signature, before the iTank killed him. Not the real Daed at all, only a program, only an NPC . . . But he sounds so like himself.

He wants to get up and run to the iTank, turn it to manual and drag the door open, just in case he can catch a glimpse of him . . . but the iTank doesn't work like that.

Use whatever you want, Daed says.

What's going on? he thinks. What's he doing?

When I saw him, that last time, he was just waiting for me

in the loading space . . . but he's talking to Pir now, like he's actually *in* the game, like —

What does that mean? Pir says.

Think of what you want. And use it.

He stands up. He can't help it. If he could see Daed, just for a second, a split second, just — he'll do anything. He steps out into the light. Ario's in front of her screen, leaning forward, biting her bottom lip. She doesn't look round.

And over her shoulder —

He can see the screen. Daed. It *is* Daed. And Pir's avatar is in front of him, her eyes on him as though he's an enemy. They're going to fight. He can see that from the way they're looking at each other. But — Daed? An enemy?

Pir steps back, with an awkward laugh. **I . . . Right. Look, mate . . .**

Think of the best way to fight me. And then do it.

He stares. Something flicks in his brain like a switch — as though he understands before he knows *what* he understands, as though —

Don't fight him, he thinks, no, don't —

I should stop this — I'm the only one who knows —

But he's frozen. The screen thickens, curdles like milk, and everything goes silent. Time stops. He's waiting for the voices to come back. Ario flips the screen to her interface, flips back, and he can't move. He'd do anything to hear Daed's voice again — *anything* —

No matter what the danger is —

The fog clings to the screen, mesmerising . . . Please, he thinks. Please.

Something — a hunch, a reflex so quick it feels like premonition — makes him take his eyes off the flatscreen and raise his gaze to the iTank.

The surface boils, like a bomb in slow-motion. The white gleam is swallowed by the colours that rise and bubble: turquoise, lemon, cadmium red. It hurts his eyes. Suddenly the flatscreen flashes so bright that it dazzles him, even though he's not looking at it; he puts a hand over his face, and blinks burning tears on to his cheeks.

When he looks again — his eyes still streaming, so that he sees everything through a blur of moisture — the iTank's sickening mix of colours has faded, and it's blinking red-and-white, like a coal burning in a glass of milk. **There has been a malfunction. Please tell Crater —**

The malfunction, he thinks. Oh gods, the malfunction. That was why Daed barred me from the Maze — because it was dangerous, because —

And even before Ario opens the iTank, he knows what she's going to find.

15

Ario didn't remember what happened after that; or not in detail, anyway. There was a thick blur of voices — someone calling for help, someone asking what had happened, over-lapping and not making sense so that now, thinking back, she wasn't sure if either of them was her, or neither, or both . . . Dion, she thought. Yes, Dion had been there. She remem-bered the strength of his arms around her, squeezing her like a cage, pulling her away from Pir's body . . . and then, later, when they'd taken Pir away and she was alone, wrapped in an old bedbag but still shaking so hard she thought her teeth would fall out, he was there again with a hot drink, holding the cup for her as she drank so that she wouldn't scald herself. He'd put something in it. She remembered the warmth of it spreading through her, easing the icy ache in her bones, and then suddenly the night had gone soft, liquid, sliding through her brain like silk. She didn't remember anything else.

She sat up. She was in her cube; the air smelt strange, used up, dead. There was a mess of cups and pills and LX components on the block next to her bed. She looked at them for a while, seeing how they swam in and out of focus, the pretty bright colours of the capsules glowing and rippling like embers . . . She imagined her blood, stained the colour of Dion's drugs, the lacework of vessels in her brain sugar-pink and blue and green. What had he given her? She felt as incapable of emotion as a bag of sweets. She knew that Pir was dead, but it didn't touch her.

There was a noise like a snort, and she looked up. Dion was there, slumped over and snoring. She watched him, knowing she should be grateful. He'd taken care of her, hadn't he? He must have looked after Pir too . . . Suddenly a flash of memory came back to her, clearer than the rest: she'd said, 'What are we going to do? What are we going to *do*?' and he'd replied grimly, 'Ario, you don't seriously think this is the first time we've had to dispose of a corpse?'

The word — even in her brain, even though no one had said it aloud — seemed to flick some kind of switch. '*Oh,*' she heard herself say, as though someone had hit her, and the sore, horrified feeling surged again in her stomach. Pir was dead, Pir, lovely Pir . . . She put her hands over her face. Her fingers smelt of cold sweat.

'Ario?'

Dion's voice. She wondered for a moment whether there was any reason to answer him; then she was too tired not to. 'Yes,' she said, through her hands.

'How're you feeling?'

'How do you *think* I'm feeling?'

'Well, it depends on how fast you've metabolised the pills . . . If they're still in your system, you might be on top of the world.'

'Looks like they've worn off.'

'Want some more?'

'Yes. Enough to kill me.'

He'd started to reach out towards the little pile of capsules, but his hand hesitated and drew back. 'I'm not in the mood, Ario.'

She turned her head. 'The mood for *what*?'

'Self-pity.' He shrugged, holding her gaze. 'Drama. Ario feeling sorry for herself. You want something for the pain, take it. But don't act like the world has let you down again.'

She genuinely didn't understand, for a second. The last rags of sleep flickered in the corner of her mind, distracting her. Then she said, 'Wait. Dion . . . you think this is my fault? You think *I* did something to make Pir — to hurt —'

He shook his head, but not as if he was disagreeing. 'Ario . . . look. Do you want to go back to sleep? Have a drink before you do, or you'll get dehydr—'

'No, I don't want to go back to sleep! You think this is *my* fault?' She wished the words didn't resonate in her head, echoing and echoing.

He opened his mouth, and she saw him try to say something gentle. Then, as if it was too much for him, he took a quick breath and let himself go. 'OK. What happened, then, Ario? A malfunction in the iTank? In the Maze? It *just so happened* that your client got killed while she was running your cheats? You must have junked it somehow. Your codes made something happen, and the iTank malfunctioned and your client got killed. Do you have any idea what that will do to our reputation? You stupid, irresponsible — I should never have — I thought it was bad luck, before, I really thought you were the best — but now, you — gods, Ario, how could you be so *stupid*?' He stopped, cutting himself off suddenly as though he could have gone on talking for ever.

She stared at him. 'My codes *worked*,' she said, in a hoarse whisper that didn't sound like her own voice. 'Pir got to the endgame.'

'And then she died. In the iTank.'

He didn't mean to be harsh; when she flinched he bit his lip and looked away. But he didn't apologise.

'She beat the Roots, Dion,' she said. But she could hear the note of desperation in the words: because he was right, wasn't he? It didn't make any difference how far Pir had got. Now she was dead. 'It was the last fight . . . my cheats worked fine in the Roots. It was when she got to the endgame, and there was another enemy. It was — weird —' But how could she explain the sunlit, old-fashioned loading space and the man with age-old eyes?

Dion took a deep breath. There were purple shadows around his eyes, and his eyelids looked overripe, like bruised fruit. Ario looked away, wishing that she was alone, back in her beautiful oblivion.

'Ario,' he said. 'I don't know what you did. It doesn't matter to me all that much, to be honest. It doesn't make any difference. I'm not going to let you take on any more commissions. The only way —'

She must have made a sound, because he pressed his fingers into his forehead and swallowed before he went on.

'The only way this tankshop can survive is if we can say that you've left, that you were working independently and now you're gone —' He raised his head to glance at her and tried to smile. 'I'm not chucking you out, Ario, it'll be OK, we'll find something for you to do . . . but you can't be a Cheat any more, you understand? Before — with Herkules and the Roots, people were saying you'd lost your touch, but I was sure it was bad luck, I believed in you — but now, Ario, honestly, you can't expect me to go on giving you commissions . . .' There was a tone in his voice that sounded pleading, almost; but that didn't make sense, because he had all the power.

She looked him right in the eyes. 'It wasn't me, Dion,' she said. 'I don't know what happened. But I promise you it wasn't my fault.'

He blinked. For an instant she thought he believed her. Then he hunched one shoulder, leant forward and slid a pill out of the pile with his finger, edging it into an empty space. His fingernail was dirty; it made the gleaming blue and yellow of the capsule look tawdry. Without looking at her, he said, 'Ario, I'm sorry. It doesn't matter.'

She didn't say anything.

'Listen . . . go back to sleep. You've been through a lot recently, and . . .' Was he expecting her to reply? 'I didn't mean . . . we can talk about this some other time. Take a pill. Just one, OK?' And then, with quick awkward fingers as if he was embarrassed, he scraped the scattered pile of capsules into his hand and shoved them into his pocket. The last solitary pill winked at her, like an eye.

She reached out and picked it up, turning it between her fingertips until she felt the coating start to go tacky. There was a silence.

'If you need anything . . .'

She didn't want to sleep; but more than anything she didn't want to be here, listening to him. She pushed the capsule into her mouth and swallowed it without water. Then she turned her face to the wall.

16

It was like being ill. She drifted in and out of sleep, and when she woke up someone would be there — Dion, sometimes, but more often now it was Spin or even Lia — to ask her if she needed anything, and to dispense another pill. She didn't understand why they were looking after her; in the end she asked Lia, but she only shrugged and said, 'Dion's orders, he doesn't want you to kill yourself,' and Ario wasn't sure whether it was a joke or not. She didn't want to think about it. It was easier just to drift, to sink and surface and let herself go. Sometimes she wished she really *was* ill; she thought it would be good to know she had no future to worry about.

Time passed, but she didn't know how long she'd been asleep. She heard voices and footsteps from the corridor, the rhythms of life going on without her. She sometimes told herself to pay attention so she didn't lose track of the days; but then she'd fall asleep again. It didn't matter, did it? That wasn't *her* life any more.

But the drugs had less and less effect, and she spent more and more time staring at the ceiling. Pir, she'd think, lovely Pir — and the ice-palace would flash into her head, glittering arches and floor, uncanny and heart-shattering — and then she'd turn over, bite her lip, bury her face in the pillow, anything to stop the images that rose in front of her eyes. My fault, she thought. Dion's right. I'm kidding myself. Of course it was my fault . . . and Pir, who laughed at me, teased me, who gave me the only present I've ever had —

There were raised voices in the corridor outside, and she forced herself to listen. Some kind of argument . . . Lia and Nax. For a second she thought it was just one of their rows — but then something caught her attention, and she rolled over. She'd heard her name. They were talking about her.

Nax said, 'I know what he said, but that's stupid, I just want to *ask* —'

'Dion doesn't want her anywhere near —'

'I just want to *ask* her!' He'd shouted it, and there was a pause. Then he said, more quietly — although Ario could still hear every word — 'I think Dion's right, Lia, OK? I'm not asking her for advice, I'm not going to ask her to write any code, I won't even let her touch my terminal! But she knows more about the Maze than anyone, and I just want to know what's going on.'

'Dion doesn't want her to be disturbed.'

'Well —' He sighed, and there was a thump on the wall of the corridor as though he'd leant against it heavily. 'She can't stay in there for ever, can she? We're going to have to talk to her eventually.'

'She probably doesn't want to talk to *us*.'

'Let's find out, shall we?'

And immediately Ario's comms panel said, **Nax is requesting entry.**

She sat up, her arms around her knees. She was scared, somehow; it had been so long since she'd seen anyone except for Dion and Spin and Lia . . . But she said, 'Let him in.'

The door opened. Nax looked through the doorway. She saw surprise and shock leap in his eyes before he blinked and grinned too widely. 'Hey, Ario, how's it hanging?'

She looked down at her hands — the skeletal fingers, the skin thin and dark as burnt paper — and felt a faint echo of his shock. She hadn't eaten for days. Her face must look — she must look like a corpse — like —

'Ario,' Lia's voice said from behind him, 'Nax just wanted to ask you to look at something, but I said you wouldn't be feeling . . .' Her tone changed, as if she'd turned aside, and she added in a hiss, 'Gods, Nax, look at her! You think she's going to jump out of bed to look at some glitch —'

Ario said, 'Lia, I'm fine. What do you want, Nax?'

Nax nodded and went on nodding, as though he didn't realise he was doing it. 'That's great, Ario . . . um, it's not important, though, only if you're up to it . . .'

'What is it?' It was as if the days of drifting had dissolved everything inside her except this little core of steel. 'What do you want?'

'Just — um, I had a question about the new Maze expansion, and I thought maybe you . . .' He spread his hands. 'You're the exp— you *were* the — um, just thought you might know.'

'So tell me.'

He opened his mouth and glanced over his shoulder at Lia; but she stayed silent, and Ario couldn't see her face. 'I . . .

I think it'll be easier if I show you. D'you want to come and I'll show you on my terminal?'

She took a deep breath, imagining the rows of flat-screens, the eyes looking up at her as she came in . . . but she'd have to face them sometime; and it was better to have a reason to be there, something to concentrate on . . . 'OK,' she said. She heard a huff of impatience, and she knew without looking that Lia had walked away, shaking her head.

She got out of bed, steadying herself on the block beside her bed, refusing to let Nax see how soggy her legs were. The floor swayed, rocked and came back slowly to the horizontal. He said again, 'Look, if you're not up to it —'

'Shut up, Nax.'

She pushed past him, and down the corridor. It rippled and bounced around her as though everything in the world was fluid, but she focused on the doorway at the far end and kept moving forward. It seemed to work.

There was a group of people huddled around one terminal. One of them — it was Java — looked up and saw Ario standing in the doorway, and her face smoothed itself into a deliberately neutral expression, neither smile nor frown; but then she went back to staring at the terminal as though Ario wasn't very important. Someone said, 'But that would be *crazy*, the amount of marketing they put into the new expansion six months ago . . .'

'Come on,' Nax said. He took her by the elbow and steered her over to the group. Now a couple of the others noticed her: but although their eyes widened, they didn't say anything, and they stood aside to let her look down at the screen. 'Hey, Ario,' Nax said, pushing her shoulder, 'shove over, would you? Let me through, I want to show you —'

But a furious, freezing anger had taken hold of her, and she couldn't move.

A screenshot, she thought. No, a photo — no, a screenshot — no, what —?

It was the ice-palace. It was Pir's hall, festooned with moonlit crystal, the floor deep as an obsidian sea, the arches glittering . . . The galleries mirrored each other on each side, the broken beams pointed at the moon, the tattered flags of clouds flew silver-edged above the wide-holed roof . . .

'How did you get this?' she said, and the words were as cold as the ice-dust that danced on the steps, swirling in the breeze.

'What? Ario, it's the —'

'You — how dare you,' she said. 'Did you hack her terminal? You're disgusting. Go fy, Nax. Is this some kind of sick joke? To upset me, to get me to leave the tankshop? Because —' Suddenly she had to swallow. 'Go fy,' she said again, 'go *fy* —'

Then she heard what he'd said.

'It's the Maze. Ario, it's the *Maze*.'

There was a pause. Everyone was looking at her now, but she didn't feel anything. The flatscreen showed figures moving in the hall, a little group of avatars looking around them, conferring. It wasn't the same level of detail that it would have been, if the terminal had been branched directly

168

to an iTank: but it *could* be the Maze, a surve's-eye view . . .
Nax followed her eyes and flicked up a chat window:
. . . must be an enemy here somewhere . . . a voice said,
and another one replied, **This place gives me the creeps . . .**

Ario said, in a distant, clear voice that didn't seem to
belong to her, 'Whereabouts in the Maze?'

'The Winter Continent,' Nax said, and there was something strange about the way he was looking at her.

'Where's that?' She looked round; everyone was watching
her, as if they were waiting for some kind of sign. 'There
isn't a Winter Continent in the Maze, Nax . . .'

'No,' he said. 'There *wasn't* a Winter Continent. Not until
a few days ago. Now there is.'

She held his look. He wasn't lying; but he *had* to be lying.
Or . . . This is some kind of horrible wind-up, she thought. It
has to be. Some elaborate, *really* elaborate, nasty joke . . .
Where's Dion?

'Whatever,' she said, and saw Nax's eyes narrow. 'Maybe
the Winter Continent's been there all along, and we just
never noticed it before.'

'But — Ario, that's crazy, this is *new* — and it's huge —'

'Yeah, sure, because Crater would expand the Maze just
like that, with no publicity . . . and I suppose it's just a coincidence that it happens to look exactly like Pir's favourite
place? You're pathetic.' She pushed roughly past Java and
walked towards the door. 'Thanks, though, Nax. It's nice to
know that no matter how bad things get, I can always rely on
you to kick me when I'm down.'

'What the — Ario, this hasn't got anything to do with —'

'Save it.' The door opened before she pressed the comms panel, and she stepped aside automatically. It was Rick. She swung her eyes away from him. Everything she saw made her think of Pir, and it hurt.

'Sorry,' he said, very low, and slid away, flattening himself against the wall. But his gaze flicked up to her face, and for a second she thought she saw something in his expression — a kind of sympathy, a knowing, wary, *ashamed* sympathy — that made her halt where she was, staring at him. Did he know what was going on? Had he heard —?

Yes, she thought. He's heard them talking about it, that's all. He's in on the joke.

'Gag off, all of you,' she said. Her voice shook, and she felt the blood prickling in her face; but at least she made it to her cube before the tears came.

But she didn't let herself cry, even then. She reached for a sleeping pill — and another, because she wasn't sure one would do the job . . . And a few minutes later she felt it start to take root, putting out branches of shadow, until at last her eyes closed and she sank into darkness.

But it wasn't the same dreamless sleep as before: she was in the grip of a nightmare, running down endless corridors towards something she was terrified of, following the twists and turns of the passages and knowing that ahead of her, just out of sight, there was —

She woke. The room swirled around her, the tiny eyes of LEDs drawing trails across her retina, her heart deafening her as though she was inside it, as if the world *was* her heart

. . . She couldn't move. Her limbs were rigid and sore. Her pulse went on drumming in her ears until at last it slowed to a regular rhythm, the footsteps of someone pacing up and down . . . She sat up, gingerly. Every breath she drew was shaky and uncertain.

She looked into the blackness, trying to remember what she'd been dreaming about. There was someone else there, she thought, someone behind me . . . but whatever I was scared of was further on, I was running towards it — and it was — I *knew* what it was, in the dream, I knew quite clearly, that was why I was so scared . . . But it was no good. The details slipped out of her grasp, and now all that she could hold on to was the terror, the unreasoning chilly panic that still itched on her skin like rainburn. She shook her head, digging her hands into her bedbag so that the feel of the material anchored her in reality. She didn't *want* to remember — but it nagged at her, as though it was important, as though her brain was trying to tell her something.

Stop it, she thought. Pir is dead. Of course I'm having nightmares.

Pir —

Suddenly she could see Pir's face, superimposed on the darkness. High cheekbones, smooth skin, irises the colour of coal, the beginning of a smile —

She shut her eyes, but that didn't help. My friend, she thought, Pir was my *friend* —

She couldn't bear it. The misery was so strong that she had to move, as though it was a physical pain. She lay down again, curling into a foetal position; but after a few seconds that was worse. She stood up, swinging her feet to the floor and stumbling out of her bedbag, falling towards the comms panel with her hand held out so that her palm connected with a slap. Out, she thought. I have to get out. Anywhere. Out of this room, out of the tankshop, out into the rain without a hood –

The corridor was empty and quiet. When she opened the door to the tankshop hall there was no one there. She must only have slept a couple of hours, it must be four or five in the morning, the dead time . . .

She walked towards the door to the outside, past the terminals. Nax's spot still had a couple of blocks drawn up in front of his flatscreen, and the surface was crowded with empty cups and the old half-obsolete iThings that were communal property. One of them was frozen, staring whitely at the ceiling like an open eye. Ario paused to look down at it. It said: **winter continent forum,** but it had crashed before anyone could press **search**.

The Winter Continent, she thought. What had Nax said? *There wasn't a Winter Continent. Not until a few days ago. Now there is.*

It couldn't be true. It didn't make sense . . . but standing there, looking down at the iThing, she felt a little tug of uncertainty, like someone trying to attract her attention. Surely, if it was only a wind-up, they wouldn't have gone to such lengths – unless they'd left it here for her benefit, in case she came to look later . . . Would they really do that? Maybe, she thought. If I've really junked the whole tankshop, maybe they *would*.

For a second she saw them again — the glances as she came into the room, Java's gaze meeting hers and then going back to the screen, their sidelong looks as she pushed her way to the front so that she could see . . . But they hadn't seemed malicious. It had been like she just wasn't that important — as if, in the big scheme of things, one useless Cheat was nothing compared to what had happened to the Maze overnight . . .

She turned on her heel and walked quickly to the nearest flatscreen, a mixture of curiosity and anxiety bubbling in her stomach. It *was* a joke. It had to be. Because otherwise —

But she had to know.

17

Someone had barred her from the network.

At first she didn't believe it. She re-entered her password, focusing on her fingers in case the pills had made them tremble and catch the wrong keys. It was only on the third attempt that she understood.

Lia had said, *Dion doesn't want her anywhere near —*

She sat back, looking at the screen. **Sorry, your password hasn't been recognised.** It hurt to inhale, as though her lungs had solidified and her muscles weren't strong enough to expand them.

Dion barred me, she thought. *Dion*. Barred *me*. And the hurt spread outwards, down to her solar plexus, up into her throat, until she crossed her arms over her ribcage, hugging herself.

She took a deep, painful breath and made herself push the emotion away. OK, she thought. So I'm barred.

But I'm a Cheat.

So game on, Dion.

She typed **Dion** into the username box, and bit on her thumbnail, thinking. He wasn't as good as she was, but he was pretty good; he'd have written in security codes . . . And if he found out that she'd tried to hack into his terminal —

She realised, with a jolt, that she was afraid of him. He could throw her out of the tankshop. No one would object, even if they wanted to. And he was the only person she'd trusted, here. If *he* turned against her —

Maybe this was exactly what Nax wanted. Maybe, she thought, maybe they're trying to make me do something stupid, so Dion throws me out. Maybe —

But I have to get into the Maze. I have to see if — if it's true, if the Winter Continent really exists, if the ice-palace —

OK. She put her hands up to her head, as if she could stop the thoughts by squeezing her skull between her palms. So I have to hack in really, *really* carefully.

So . . .

She looked at the flatscreen, concentrating. She blocked out the shadows, the hum of the generators. I am a Cheat, she thought. What's the best way to do this?

And from nowhere, clear and unexpected as a gunshot, a picture flashed into her head.

The room she'd shared with her father, piled high with high-tech gamestuff. The clutter threw sharp shadows on the wall in the shape of towers and castles, mountains, grotesque faces . . . Their hammocks swung from the ceiling, swinging slightly in the draught from the ventilator and the hot air that rose from the terminal. And the smell of it was in her nostrils — rain and burnt plastic, cigarette smoke, earth and onions from the tray under the sunlamp . . . She could almost taste the onions. Papa had sprinkled them every day with distilled water from the glass apparatus she'd helped him to set up, and sometimes he'd dig them up and

175

cook them, filling the whole room with an acrid perfume that was like the rain but wholesome, somehow. She was used to P&V shakes, they weren't too bad, but those onions had been special, like something from another world. In the days after he left and didn't come back she'd tried to keep them going, but she'd done something wrong and they'd died.

But — no . . . The picture in her head was earlier than that, before he'd gone. It was something good, something happy. She could imagine herself sitting there — yes, in front of the terminal, while Papa walked on the treadmill beside her because the mains electricity had gone down again. And the screen she was looking at was like the one she was looking at now, or more or less: five years older, but the same screen, more or less. A log-on screen, waiting for a password. It was the first lesson.

He'd told her his username, and she'd looked up, waiting for him to dictate the password.

'Go on, then,' he said.

'What?' She frowned.

'If I don't tell you my password, but you need to get into my account anyway, what do you do?'

'I —' She wrinkled her nose, and shrugged. 'I don't know.'

'Think.'

'Well —' She stared at the screen, trying to block out the *thump-thump-thump* of the treadmill. 'I don't know. I s'pose you could — um, get into the system from a different . . . ? Oh, I don't *know*! How'm I supposed to know? This isn't fair. You haven't told me anything about hacking yet!'

He smiled. 'Who said anything about hacking?'

'Well, if I have to get into your account without your password —'

'I didn't say without my password,' Rio,' he said, and his smile broadened as she started to understand. 'I said I wasn't going to tell you what it was.'

She looked at him until she was sure she had understood. Then she rolled her eyes. 'Great. So I find it out some other way. Great lesson, Papa. It's always easier if you know the password. How enlightening.'

'It *is*,' he said, and his walking slowed right down, so that the lights went dim and started to flicker. But she could see through the murk that he was watching her, and his face was very serious. 'Never hack into a system if there's a better way of getting what you want. That's the first lesson. If you can get someone's password, it's simpler and easier to use it. OK?'

And she'd sighed, and nodded. 'OK,' she'd said. 'Now can we do some real work?'

But now she shut her eyes, and the picture in her head faded, replaced by the tankshop, months ago, and a group of people clustered around the burnt, horrifying body of the gamerunner boy. Dion had been there, beside him, on his knees; he'd looked up, he'd said —

He can have my cube. The code's C8H10N4O2.

Surely Dion wouldn't be stupid enough to use the same —

But maybe — after all, you hardly ever used your cube code, because it was only for giving to other people, or for when the comms panel didn't recognise your hand — and if you basically trusted everyone in the tankshop — and

177

everyone had their own terminal, anyway, who would *want* to hack into your account —

Her brain went on calculating the odds; but her fingers were already typing.

And it worked.

She said aloud, 'Dion, you should know better.' But she said it absently, already opening the Maze, bringing up the map . . . A joke, it was a joke, it had to be a —

The Winter Continent was there.

And it was enormous.

She stared at it, not believing, not wanting to believe. An expansion that massive, and Crater didn't publicise it? It was as big as the expansion that had come out at the same time as the iTank, and that had been marketed like crazy. And this one had just *appeared*, overnight.

She scrolled over the map, looking at the landmarks. **The Dark Ways. Hungry Lake. Towers of Fire. The Ice-Palace** . . .

She leant forward. Her heart was in her throat, fighting like a trapped bird. She clicked on the ikon, and had to click again because her hand had stumbled clumsily on the command.

Pir's hall of ice jumped on to the screen. Ario's finger moved, dragging the camera round 360 degrees, not letting herself linger on the details, the glittering filigree of ice and reflections, not letting herself marvel at how precisely it was rendered, as sharp-edged as her memory. At last she took her hand away and let the viewpoint stay where it was, a steady, impersonal eye.

Now that she had time to stare at it Ario could see that it wasn't identical to the real hall: it was like a dream of it, with shifting shadows and higher arches and infinite spaces opening out between the pillars. But the moon gleamed in the depths, and the useless staircase hung eternally reflected in the ice. Tattered clouds swam in the stars below the mirrored galleries. It is the same place, she thought. It *is* . . . But Pir said no one knew, no one came there.

OK. There was a rational explanation. Someone from Crater was a slum tourist. Pir wasn't the only one who'd been there. That wasn't inconceivable, was it? And it's just like Crater to choose a location like this, with all the moonlight and mirrors, so they can show off their graphics . . .

It reassured her a little. The pain was still there, the pang that it gave her to see Pir's hall on the screen where anyone could see it, public and mystery-less; but it wasn't threatening any more. It was just a horrible coincidence. She could live with that.

There was a movement at the corner of the screen, and a gamerunner rolled through a collapsed doorway, flipped to his feet and sprinted along one of the galleries. He leapt sideways, vaulted a broken-down arch and slid down a pillar to the floor. He glanced down at his reflection and hesitated a moment — he's admiring the graphics, Ario thought — and then started to walk towards the centre of the ice, slipping a little from side to side as though the ice was treacherous underfoot. Bet that effect was complicated, she thought. Well done, Crater. I'm impressed.

He looked up. He had a map, obviously. Suddenly he reached for his weapons, drawing a sword and shield out of thin air. Ario flicked up her own map, to see what had spooked him. An enemy, hidden somewhere in the arches, but coming closer. She waved the map to the side of the screen, waiting for the red dot to emerge from the shadows, wondering what shape it would be. What kind of monster would Crater have invented, to go with a place like this? An ice-dragon? A serpent? Same old, same old . . .

Then the enemy came out into the centre of the floor, and she felt everything around her freeze.

A thin, dark girl, in silver. Her face was very still, with a closed look about it, and when she looked up her eyes were so distant that you couldn't tell whether their expression was sad or wary. She was unarmed, so slight that she looked like she would blow away in the breeze that raised the ice-dust into whirls around her feet; but she had a sort of steadiness, as though her body was deceptive. And she was beautiful.

It was Ario. She was looking at herself.

But it wasn't quite herself; any more than the hall had been the real hall. The girl on the flatscreen was *too* beautiful, for one thing. Ario knew her own face from the mirror in the shower-cube, from the reflection in the comms panels — and she looked like that, but less striking, with a different expression that narrowed her eyes and put lines around her mouth. It was as though she was looking at a twin sister, whose life had been kinder; or an idealised version, the girl she would have wanted to be . . . It was like seeing Pir's avatar in the iTank: how she'd looked like Pir but not quite right, as though Pir was too hard on herself and it shone through, taking the edge off her beauty. Except that this girl was the other way round. It's me, Ario thought, but it's how you'd see me if you really liked me, if you thought I was beautiful, like I'm transfigured –

How Pir might have seen –

She recoiled, struck by a mad idea, a horrible idea, and she heard herself say, 'No, that's stupid, that can't be – it's not – this is –'

She reached out wildly, pushing the flatscreen round so that she couldn't see it. Then she put her hands over her face, and sat there, shaking.

18

Someone was watching her. She felt a tingle of unease on the back of her neck, a gradually growing conviction that someone was behind her. She ignored it for a long time. It was probably Dion, staring at her accusingly because she'd logged into his account; but she didn't care. Part of her wanted him to find her there. She wanted him to push her out into the street without a hood, leave her to be washed away painfully by the rain.

At last a voice said, quietly, 'I'm sorry.'

It took her by surprise, and she raised her head. There was a footstep, and then Rick was an em or so away, his face white and taut in the light from the screen. 'I'm sorry,' he said again.

She stared at him. Part of her mind was still in the ice-hall, with her fictional self, and it took a moment to understand what he was saying. 'Sorry for what?' she said.

He hesitated, and his eyes went to the flatscreen. It was turned towards him, and the pale blue light caught on his scars, making them into rippled silk and lace. 'Everything,' he said, with a quick exhalation. Ario had the sense that it wasn't what he'd meant to say; but it didn't matter, nothing mattered . . . 'That's you, isn't it?' he added. 'In the Maze?'

'I don't play. I'm not a gamerunner.' She tried to swallow her fury, but it was stronger than she was.

'I meant —'

'I know what you meant.'

'So —'

'It's not me. I'm here. Look.' She spread her hands, putting all the disdain into her voice that she could. 'If I'm here, I can't be there as well, can I? So no, it isn't me. Don't be stupid.'

He looked at her, then. His gaze was steady, neutral and unblinking, as though he didn't want to pity her. She had the urge to hit him, smack her hand across one of his scarred cheeks, wipe the sympathy out of his eyes for ever. How dare he pity her? And she remembered thinking the same thing about Pir, the night — *that* night —

She turned away. 'Leave me alone.'

He didn't answer, but he didn't move. She heard him swallow.

Something snapped inside her. She spun back to him, raising her voice. 'Leave me alone, for gods' sake! Why are you here, anyway? What do you want? Can't you see I want to be on my own, can't you see I'm *busy* —' She flung out her arm towards the terminal. 'Look! I've got other stuff to think about. I don't care if you pity me, you can't help me, I don't care if you're *sorry* —'

He made a tiny, cut-off movement, as though he'd gone to speak and thought better of it. And something in the gesture caught her off-guard and made her stop speaking, like a fingertip tapping lightly between her eyes.

There was a silence. The generators clunked, struggled and settled again to a far-off hum.

She sat very still, breathing hard, a strange irrational conviction swelling inside her. He knows, she thought. About the Maze, about Pir . . . *That's* why he's sorry. Because — he — *knows* . . .

'You're right,' she said, in a voice that wasn't her own. 'That enemy, in the Maze. That's me. And the place where she is, the ice-palace — that's a real place, a place Pir took me to the night she died. It's like someone's gone through her memories, taking the best ones, making them into a new Maze expansion. But that's ridiculous, right? That's impossible.'

No answer. He looked at the floor, his eyes hooded by his eyelids, not a muscle flickering in his face.

'If I told the others that was what had happened, that she'd died because the iTank had taken her mind and then just —' Her voice threatened to crack, but she clenched her fists and carried on. 'It took her, didn't it? Took everything she had and then it killed her. It wasn't anything to do with my codes — except that they got her too far, they got her to the endgame . . . It wasn't even a malfunction. It was writ-ten in, deliberately. The Maze —' She hesitated again, feeling sick. 'The Maze *ate* her.'

He still didn't look up; but his mouth moved soundlessly.

'That's absurd, isn't it? We don't even know if the iTank could do it. Technically, I mean.' She paused, waiting for him to answer, or just to meet her eyes. 'Tell me it's a stupid idea. Tell me I'm imagining things.'

He went on staring at the floor, his lips still shaping his breath into silent words.

'The others wouldn't believe me,' she said slowly. 'They'd tell me I was off my head. They probably think that anyway . . . But you. You're not contradicting me. You don't look surprised. And the way you said you were sorry . . . I don't understand. I can only think of one reason why you'd react like this.' She waited. He pressed his lips together and closed his eyes, like a kid waiting for a punishment, but he didn't say anything.

'It's funny. It's almost,' she said, 'it's almost as if . . . As if you're *not* surprised. As if . . . Well. As if, all along, all the time you were watching us, skulking in the shadows, eating our food . . . As if you *knew*.'

He glanced up.

It only lasted a fraction of a second — just a moment, a heartbeat, while they looked at each other — and then he jerked his eyes back to the floor, twisting his whole head as though he was afraid that he'd given something away. But it was enough. Ario felt something flare inside her, and suddenly all the hurt was gone, replaced by an anger so pure that it was liberating, intoxicating, like a drug. She said, 'You knew — you did know —' and then she threw herself forward, crashing against the desk and not even feeling it, reaching for him with her hands to claw and tear and punch him, so angry that she was almost laughing. He'd known — he'd *known* — and he'd let her, let Pir — he'd been there, maybe he'd even *watched* —

He was taken by surprise; she felt it in the way he reeled back, the breath knocked out of him, and scrabbled at her hands, trying to wrench her away. She pummelled her fists against his chest, punched as hard as she could at every piece of flesh she could reach. She tore at his neck with her fingernails, brought a knee up to jab at his stomach, would have bitten him if her mouth had found anything but empty air. He'd let Pir die — it was his fault —

Her foot connected with his knee, and he cried out, twisting downwards, so that they almost fell. Then he stumbled back and regained his balance, staggering as she attacked him again. He was saying something, but she couldn't make out the words, and she didn't care. She was swearing at him, shouting things that meant nothing, without listening to her own voice. She wanted to hurt him any way she could. He'd let Pir die, he *deserved* —

But now instead of his body under her hands, the solidity of her fist on flesh, she felt him twist away, moving in and out of the storm of blows so that every impact was lessened. He wasn't fighting back, but she couldn't get hold of him, couldn't find the right place for a punch or get her nails to a patch of bare skin . . . It made her fury rise even higher, sucking the oxygen out of the air like fire. How dare he — he was laughing at her, playing with her —

Then he put his arms round her, pinning her hands to her sides. She struggled, twisted her head to try and bite him, kicked his shins as hard as she could . . . but he kept hold of her, letting his grip loosen just enough to make sure he didn't hurt her, moving as she moved so that she didn't meet enough resistance to fight him properly. It must have been painful when she kicked him, but apart from a quick huff of breath he didn't react. She tried to butt him with her head, but he flexed his shoulder so that her skull met the soft place between his chest and his collarbone. 'I'm sorry,' he said, 'I'm sorry,' and Ario knew it was what he'd been saying all the time she'd been hitting him.

She was so angry now that she was struggling to breathe. But the energy was dying. The shakiness had come back into her legs, as though her foundations had gone, and her arms felt like rubber. Her throat was raw. She staggered, trying to pull away from him, but he held on to her. His arms were strong. If I let myself go, she thought, he'll stop me falling over. It seemed strange, almost funny. She still wanted to hit him, but another part of her wanted to close her eyes and let him take her weight. She was so tired . . .

And somehow the anger sank into nothing, as though it had run out of fuel. It was no good. It didn't matter. She was still breathing hard, but she let her body relax. Rick's arms tightened a little as though he thought it was a ploy. She leant her head against his breastbone, so sick with fatigue that she didn't care. He smelt of shower-water, and the dust behind the gametanks, and beneath that a musty human warmth. She inhaled until her lungs were full.

And then the tears came, catching her unawares.

He held her up, the way she'd known he would. He didn't move, didn't try to console her, just stood there, supporting her weight, letting her cry. It was only when her sobs had died away and she was swaying with exhaustion that he let go of her. He kept one arm around her shoulders in case she fell, and led her to the nearest block. She sat down, her legs trembling. When she blinked, her eyes overflowed again. The water trickled down her chin and splashed on to the floor with a wet click.

He sat down next to her, and they stayed there for a long time. After a while he looked at the flatscreen, bit his lip, and turned it off. In the sudden darkness Ario heard everything more clearly — the generators, a faraway rattle of rain, the sticky sounds of phlegm in her nose as she breathed — and caught the scent of his body, as though he was closer to her than he really was. She felt as though she were made of stone. I hate him, she thought, without feeling it. And tomorrow I'll hate him even more: for having been here, for having seen me like this. I'll hate him for being kind.

She looked at him sideways, but in the darkness he could have been anyone. She would have liked to say something — to make it clear that they weren't friends, that they had nothing in common . . . but nothing came. She could still feel the strength of his grip, the way he hadn't wanted to fight her.

'You're right,' he said, and the sound of his voice took her by surprise. 'I did know. Or at least, I *should* have known. I should have warned you. I'm sorry.'

She wiped her cheeks with her hands. There was nothing to say.

'I lived in the Crater complex, a long time ago. The night I escaped . . .' He paused, as if he was waiting for her to ask him a question. When she didn't, he shifted a little on his block and took a deep breath. 'My father was the designer of the Maze. I was —'

She said sharply, without knowing why, '*A* designer of the Maze, you mean. *One* of the designers.'

'No. The only designer. I mean — there were Creatives, developers, programmers, all that, of course, but — no. He designed the Maze. It was him. His name was Daedalus.'

'Daedalus?' She laughed, without amusement. 'Right. Daedalus is a joke. It's just what people say. He's not real. He's like a kind of myth. No one could create a whole game on their own. It takes teams and teams of people.' The words made her think of something — set off a circuit in her brain — but she couldn't be bothered to try to work out what it was.

'No,' he said, and his tone was odd, patient and slow, as though he was certain of what he said. 'No. Daedalus existed. He was my father.'

She shrugged, wondering why she bothered to argue. If he wanted to lie about his past . . .

'He was important, so we had a good life. In a way. I had my own rooms, on the twenty-first storey, twice the size of this tankshop. A swimming pool just for me. And food, gods, the *food*! Things you've probably never tasted. Ice cream and green tea and steak and sushi . . .' He swallowed with a moist, hungry sound. 'And I could spend all day running the Maze. I was really good, back then. Now I'm — I can't do it, not the way I used to, I haven't healed properly. Back then I was the best.'

Like me, Ario thought. Back then *I* was the best, too.

'And then — you remember how the Maze used to be, before the iTank and the expansion? It was supposed to be possible but infinite. All Crater's marketing said that you *could* beat it, but no one ever would. The Roots were the final hurdle — and they had to be achievable, Crater promised that nothing was designed to be physically impossible . . . But no one got to the endgame. That was important. The endgame had to exist, but no matter how good you were, there was always something harder to do before you got to it, a new challenge, something you *could* do if you were good enough —'

'Yes, I know. Infinite real gameplay, not just the Skinner Box effect. The Maze's USP.'

'And Daed was in charge of that. That was what he'd promised Crater. And then one day —' He stopped.

But part of Ario's brain was replaying her own words: *Daedalus is a joke. It's just what people say. He's not real.* The memory was almost there, slipping between her fingers like oil . . .

'Then one day,' he went on, after a pause, 'someone *did* run the Roots.'

Ario glanced at him. The whites of his eyes glinted as he looked back at her.

Daedalus is a joke . . . He's not real . . . And suddenly the link leapt into her head, finding the memory and jumping to it like a spark. *Daedalus isn't* real, *you silly girl . . .* It was what Herkules had said, talking to Athene, the night she'd beaten him and got to the endgame in his place, the night

Rick was talking about . . . She said, wondering, 'Yes, I know.'

He pulled his knees up to his chest and linked his hands around his shins. His ribcage broadened as he took a deep breath. 'Someone ran the Roots . . . Ha. *I* ran the Roots.'

Her breath caught in her throat. '*You* —?'

But he didn't hear her tone. 'Daed sent me in,' he said, staring at the wall opposite. 'He said it was really important that I defeat the other gamerunner and then kill myself, so no one would get to the endgame . . . But I couldn't resist, I thought he'd been lying to me, and I mean, gods, I was a *gamerunner*, what did he expect me to do? The Maze was my life, I'd got to the end of the Roots, I was the best, and —' He put his hands over his face, and the air hissed between his teeth.

'You,' Ario said, and laughed. There was nothing else to do, was there? She'd run out of tears. 'It was you, who killed Herkules. Wow.'

He raised his head, turning to look at her. 'What? Why . . . ?'

'I was his Cheat.' She shrugged. It didn't seem all that important, any more; not after Pir . . . 'His account got closed, and my life went down the drain.' She felt herself smile, her mouth twisting into a shape that didn't have anything to do with amusement. 'You were the best. Well, I was the best too. Now look at us.'

There was a silence. 'I'm sorry,' he said at last.

She hunched one shoulder, even though she knew he couldn't see her. 'So you beat the Roots,' she said, trying to sound casual. 'Congratulations.'

'Yes. And that . . . Daed had promised them this infinite

game, you see, and now it was clearly not infinite . . . He warned me, if I hadn't —' He cut himself off and took a deep breath before he started speaking again. 'Anyway. They made him write an expansion to go with the release of the iTank . . . but he was ill, and he knew that once he was gone and some-one replaced him, then I'd — Crater wouldn't want me any more, they'd chuck me out or kill me . . . And so he was desperate, he — there was this program, a friend of his came up with this program, the Asterion program, that — I didn't know what it did, truly, I wasn't sure — but Daed told me there was a malfunction and I wasn't allowed to play the Maze — and then the night I escaped, Daed went into the Maze and I found him in the iTank and he was dead — and I went into the Maze, I didn't know what else to do, and he was there, I mean a version of him, an NPC, except that it wasn't *right*, there was something weird about it, like he was really *thinking* — and he barred me from going back into the Maze — but I didn't know, I didn't realise that it — honestly, I —'

'He'd died and —' she hesitated. What was the *word* for that? — 'gone into the Maze. And you knew.'

'Yes — but I didn't know it was set up to happen with other players — I thought maybe it was only him, that he was so desperate to stay alive that he'd chosen to make a copy of himself, like a living signature — and it was only later that I thought about the malfunction he'd warned me about, and started to wonder why he'd barred me . . .'

'And then . . .'

It wasn't quite a question, but he answered her as if it was.

'I was there,' he said. 'The night Pir died. I'd hidden, I didn't want you to see me. I was trying to sleep. But then I — I heard his voice, Daed's voice, and I —'

'You didn't stop Pir going into the Maze. Why didn't you *stop* —'

He turned to face her, and she heard the shame in his voice, as harsh as anger. 'I wasn't sure! If I said something, and I was wrong — it was only when I saw you on the flat-screen tonight, that I was really *sure* —' And then his voice died, and in a murmur so soft Ario wasn't certain she'd heard it, he added, 'And — Daed's voice . . . I wanted to hear his voice . . .'

She stared at him. That night when she'd gone to see him in Dion's cube, she thought he'd been saying *dead, dead, dead* . . . but he'd been calling out for Daed. For his father. The way when she was new to the tankshop she'd had dreams and woken crying out for her papa . . . She didn't want to pity him — gods, she really didn't want to *understand* him — but she felt something soften inside her, like a plastic cup that had been left on top of a terminal. She said, 'You suxor,' putting more emphasis into the word than she would have done if she'd meant it.

He was still looking at her, and her eyes had adapted to the darkness so that she could see his expression. He didn't flinch. He said, 'Yes, I know.' And she would have been sorry, if she'd had the energy.

She put her face into her hands. The tiredness was so deep in her bones that it was like a disease, like despair. 'It doesn't matter,' she said. 'Pir's dead. It doesn't matter.'

There was a silence.

'What are you going to do?'

She looked into her palms, staring at the knots of shadow in the centre. It took her a moment to work out why it was such a strange question. Then she started to laugh.

'What's funny?'

She didn't answer. She stood up and walked to the door towards the corridor, pausing with her hand on the comms panel. She waited for the door to slide open. The light spilt past her into the tankshop, and she blinked, feeling her pupils shrink. She turned back. 'Nothing,' she said. 'There's nothing I can do. *Nothing*.'

And then she left him there, alone in the dark.

19

She didn't go back to sleep that night. She sat on her bedbag with her knees drawn up to her chest, her iThing open next to her. She drew patterns on it with a finger, watching the lines glow. *PIR*, she read suddenly, and scribbled it out.

Pir was inside the Maze now. Ario shut her eyes to imagine it, and then pushed her fingers into the sockets, pressing until whirls of colour opened and spun. What was it like, for Pir? Did she really exist still? Was there a part of her mind that was functioning, somewhere, somehow? Was she conscious?

No. *No*. Of course she's not, Ario thought. The program took everything she had and then killed her — Pir doesn't exist, it's just stolen memories. No. Pir isn't trapped there, Pir doesn't *know* —

But if she was, if she did . . . Or if there was a part of the Maze that thought like her, remembered what she remembered, loved the things Pir had loved, wasn't that —?

Or if, the moment before she died, she knew what was being done to her —

Even through the fireworks on her retina, Ario could see the ice-palace, and that skewed beautiful version of herself. Pir's emotions, she thought. Not just the memories, the

images, but the way she felt, the things she cared about . .
And the Maze stole *me*.

It was unbearable. She felt as though someone had taken the most secret thing she owned and put it on display. They'd murdered Pir, and then — taken everything from her, everything that made her human. How dare they? she thought, and jabbed her fingers into her eyes. How could they? How *dare* they?

And she heard Rick's voice again. *What are you going to do?*

Nothing. There's nothing I can do.

She would have liked to sleep. But there were no pills left. So she sat, endlessly tracing and retracing shapes on her iThing, wondering whether maybe, if she thought long enough, there was a different answer.

When at last the morning came she got up and went into the tankshop. There was a strange atmosphere in there; people were at their terminals, but no one was plugged into their iThings, or flicking components at each other, or even chatting. As she came through the door Nax saw her and said something, but she cut through his words without hearing them. 'Dion,' she said. 'Where's Dion?'

'He's —' He hesitated, visibly wondering whether he was allowed to tell her. 'Think he's on the tankshop floor.'

'Thanks.'

He frowned. 'Ario — about yesterday, I —'

She walked past him. Then a thought struck her, and she stopped. 'It's OK,' she said. 'I know what happened.'

There was a fractional pause. Then he pushed his chair back. 'What? Ario —'

She caught his eye, and for a second she was tempted to tell him. It wasn't my codes. It wasn't even an accident. A program, deliberately written into the Maze. Not me. Not my fault . . .

But she needed to talk to Dion. So she shrugged and turned away, ignoring him when he called her back.

Dion was on the tankshop floor, bent over a pile of components with Spin. He raised his head and nodded at her, but he went straight back to his work, sorting through brightly coloured bits with his long bony fingers. 'Ario,' he said, with a preoccupied note in his voice that she could have sworn he was putting on. 'Er . . . not a great time, actually.'

'I need to talk to you.'

'Yeah . . . we have to get on with fixing this gametank, can I come and find you when we've —?'

'No, Dion.' She waited, but although his hands paused for a second he didn't answer. 'I need you to put me back on to the system.'

'Ario, we've talked about this.' He picked a circuit board out of the pile and held it up to Spin. 'Here you go, mate. Reckon that'll work?'

'Or I could just hack someone else's account,' she said loudly. 'If you'd rather.'

He looked up then, and met her eyes. She felt a little shock of cold in her gut. It's OK, she said to herself, fighting the impulse to step back, it's *Dion* . . .

'Or *I* could get someone to throw you out,' he said. He said it without rancour, but she knew he meant it. 'If we're going to descend to threats . . . You're barred from the network, Ario. For your own good as well as everyone else's.'

'But I —' She took a deep breath. She had a sudden urge to kick the pile of components so that they scattered everywhere. 'Dion, can we talk somewhere a bit more —'

'No.' He held her gaze. 'You don't have much room to negotiate on this one, Ario.'

'Dion, please —'

'No.'

Spin shifted from foot to foot, turning the circuit board between his fingers. He had a crease between his eyebrows; he hated seeing people argue. Ario would have felt sorry for him if she hadn't been so angry with Dion.

'One more chance,' she said. 'What happened with Pir — I can explain, I can stop it happening again, to anyone. Give me one more chance and I'll show you.'

'You've had your one more chance.'

They went on looking at each other. It's a game, Ario thought. First to blink loses. I mustn't blink first . . .

She blinked. And she knew she'd lost.

Dion turned to Spin. 'That do you? It should work. Otherwise there's bound to be another one in here somewhere.'

'Dion,' she said. 'I need to talk to you. I promise it'll be worth it to listen to me.'

He stood up, leaning over to stretch the muscles in the small of his back. 'I thought you could take a look at the generators,' he said. 'I know you're not an expert, but they keep cutting out, and you might be able to see what's wrong if you give them a good going-over.'

He wants to keep me busy, she thought, with a furious, humiliated desire to laugh. Oh gods, he's trying to find me *jobs* . . . 'Dion, I'll do whatever you want. But I need to get back into the system. *Please*.'

He walked to the gametank and opened the door, peering in with a strained, thoughtful frown. 'Ario, I'm kind of thinking about something else at the moment. Can we —'

'Dion,' Spin said. 'I think you should listen to her.'

There was a silence. Dion turned round, very slowly, and stared at him. Ario knew that the stunned expression on his face was on hers too. He gave Spin a long stare. 'Did I imagine that, or did you just say something?'

'He said —' Ario felt an idiotic laugh bubble into her voice, and tried to swallow it. 'He said he thought you should listen to me. Right, Spin?'

Spin bit his lip, and hunched one shoulder, as though he was already regretting it.

'Oh, he did. I was under that impression too.' Dion caught Ario's eye with a gleam of amusement, and for an instant it was like they'd gone back in time, and nothing was wrong. Then he turned back to Spin. 'You did, did you?' he said. 'Pity . . . The first time you speak, and you can't think of anything worth saying?'

Spin opened his mouth, as if he was going to answer; but his look slid from Ario to Dion and back again, and his larynx bobbed up and down soundlessly.

Ario tried to smile at him, but she couldn't. 'Dion,' she said, trying to keep her voice level.

But the warm glint in Dion's eye had faded as though it had never been there. 'Ario,' he said, mimicking her tone. 'You think that because our friend breaks his ten-year silence that means I should change my mind? Well, I've got news for you. Listen carefully. You are *not* getting back into the system. And don't try to hack in. You write a code, *any* code, you lay a *finger* on any terminal, and you're out.'

He wasn't joking. She willed him to crack a grin, but he held her look, steady and cold.

'Out?' she said.

He jerked his head towards the door, and far away the patter of rain increased, as if on cue. 'Call my bluff,' he said. 'Go on.'

'Dion — I thought —' She spread her hands helplessly, her voice threatening to betray her. I thought we were friends, she thought. I thought I could trust you. I thought —

'It's a hard world, Ario.' A flicker of regret rose in his face, and he wiped his nose roughly as though he wanted to hide behind his hand. 'I'm right. You know I'm right. I'm sorry. But force me to choose between the tankshop and you, and — well, I'm not going to choose you. OK?'

She swallowed and nodded, because she couldn't speak. Dion, who'd found her when her papa disappeared, who'd brought her into the tankshop, looked after her . . . But she looked at him now and knew all that didn't matter any more.

'Have a look at the generators, babesauce.'

She nodded again, silently. As she walked past them to the trapdoor she sensed Spin move, starting to reach out as though he wanted to take her hand; but she kept her eyes on the floor and her arms close to her sides, and she felt nothing but a faint breath of air.

She kicked the trapdoor open with her foot and went down the ladder. Then she sat down at the foot of it. The rungs dug into her back, burning cold. Above her, Dion muttered something, and there were footsteps as they got back to work.

She stayed there for a long time, staring and staring at the generators without seeing them.

20

Dion had left a new bottle of pills next to her bed. When she got into her cube they caught her eye immediately, shining like sweets through the plastic. He'd left a note on her iThing: **Don't take them all at once**. She wiped her hand over the words, wondering whether he'd meant it as a joke.

She picked the bottle up and turned it over in her hands, letting the pills slide from one end to the other. This is my life now, she thought. Drugged up so I can sleep at night, watching the generators tick over all day. It's either this or the rain.

I can't let this happen to me. Even if I could forget about Pir — even if I wasn't so angry . . . I can't live like this.

But if I hack into a terminal, and Dion finds out —

On a sudden impulse she flung the bottle against the door. The top caught the edge of the comms panel and spun away. Shiny blue-and-yellow ovals exploded into the air like fireworks, pattering down into the corners of the room. A few landed on her bedbag and she kicked them away viciously as though they were sparks.

Dammit, I'm a *Cheat*.

I'm a Cheat. No matter what.

And I am not going to let the Maze beat me.

So she waited. She didn't want to see anyone, so she stayed in her room. She doodled on her iThing while the hours went by; she tried to make a P&V shake last longer than five minutes, but the slower she ate it the worse it tasted. She spent a long time prodding it with her finger, wondering whether it was technically a liquid or a solid. She wasn't hungry, anyway.

It seemed like an eternity before it was night-time again, and another eternity before the noise in the tankshop finally died away and silence took its place. Her clock said *0359*. She waited, superstitiously, until it said *0400*; then she opened her door and slid quietly into the corridor. If someone saw her, she could say she'd left her iThing in the cellar with the generators, or that she was looking for Dion . . . but she was afraid she wouldn't be able to lie convincingly, and she was glad to get to the tankshop unopposed.

It was dark, but she didn't turn any lights on. She felt her way to the desk, trailing her fingers along it until she got to the corner in the deepest shadows. An LED looked at her, steady and hostile. She sat down at the terminal and took a deep breath.

Dion's account again. It had to be.

She hesitated for one more second. Then she leant forward and turned on the flatscreen. She didn't have time to think. She had to get on with it, in this dead time between four and six, when everyone was asleep.

She logged in. Her hands were sticky and cold, but they were steady as she typed Dion's password. She shook her head for a moment — oh, Dion, you're a *hacker*, you should know better than to keep the same password for everything — but then she opened the Maze, and everything else faded into the background. OK. Here goes.

It didn't take long to load the Maze. And it was easy to find the codes she was looking for. They were different, somehow: like a dialect, a new voice interweaving with the old . . . She narrowed her eyes at the screen, trying to work out what was going on. But there was lot of it, and it was complicated; it was going to take her a long time, just to understand how it worked . . . There was something funny about it. It stood out from the rest as though it had been written by someone else, as though it was a translation of another language, as though — no, it was stupid — yes, as though it was something pretending to be code, that *wasn't* code . . . Like, behind the lines of code, there was someone watching her, someone *thinking* . . . She pressed her fingers to her forehead. Stop being ridiculous, she said to herself. You're excited and jumpy and still hyped up from the drugs Dion fed you. It's just a bit of programming. Concentrate.

She pushed the feeling to one side, and focused on the logic. And as she looked at it, the edges of the world around her faded away as though she had gone into a tunnel. She felt the strange, distant joy of having the Maze to think about — the absorption, the puzzle of it taking up the foreground, and the pleasure that she hardly had space to notice. It didn't matter that Dion might find out; it didn't matter that she was risking everything. Yes, she thought. This is where I belong. The code seemed to expand and swallow her.

She lost track of time; she forgot everything. It was only when her eyes started to sting and she noticed a pain growing under one shoulder blade that she remembered where she was. She stretched and her elbow caught a stray wire that was sitting on the desk, sending it pattering to the floor. She reached down for it automatically, but she couldn't see where it had fallen. She straightened up and her eyes went to the time: 0746. She'd meant to log off before six; she'd been here for hours. She needed to go.

She reached forward to log out.

Behind her Dion's voice said, 'Please don't bother on my account.'

She felt it like an impact: not painful, but hard, like a punch on an anaesthetised limb. It jolted all the way through her, an electric shock that twanged the tendons in the back of her legs. She turned round, trying not to show anything on her face.

He was sitting on the desk, so close that she jumped back, half stumbling, when she caught sight of him. 'Surprised to see me?' he said.

She looked at him. He reached to the side and flicked on another flatscreen. After a second it lit up, bathing his face in an eerie, lopsided glow. The whites of his eyes gleamed pale blue. His pupils were huge, like jet-black contact lenses.

'Well? Ario? Can't you talk?'

She swallowed. There wasn't anything to say; no words, no breath in her lungs, no tongue in her mouth.

'Didn't you believe me, when I said I'd chuck you out if you hacked into a terminal?'

At last, she thought. At last a question I can answer. She swallowed and said: 'Yes. I believed you.'

'So —' He hesitated; but there was nothing uncertain in the pause, only blankness, as though whatever he'd taken had cleaned out his skull and left it empty. 'You're all ready to go? Got your stuff packed? Or did you think I wouldn't find out?'

She held his look. She didn't want him to see her flinch. 'I was hoping you wouldn't find out. But I was prepared to risk it.'

'So I see.'

The silence went on, as though they were standing side by side, looking up at a brick wall. Ario's flatscreen was still alight, the lines of text gleaming like jewellery. She reached out and then let her hand drop again; there was no point, was there? She said, 'Do you *want* me to pack my stuff?'

'What do you think?'

She took a long breath. 'Dion . . . if you want me to beg —'

He stood up and walked past her, his shoulder clipping hers with a casual brutality that might not have been deliberate. She turned and saw that he was bending over her flatscreen, scrolling down so that the code turned into a bright blur. 'No,' he said. 'If you think this is all some kind of power trip, you don't know me as well as I thought you did.'

'Are you telling me to go?'

'Do I need to?'

'Dion —' A massive, unreasoning anger rose up, silencing her for a moment. When she could speak again, she said, 'I'm not going to leave unless you tell me to, Dion. I'm not going to walk out into the rain of my own accord.'

He nodded, lips pressed together as if that sounded sensible. 'OK, then,' he said. 'Go.'

She waited; but he didn't add anything. He was still fiddling with the flatscreen, sliding the code up and down in a waterfall of light. 'Is that it, then?' she said. '"Thanks, Ario, and goodnight"?'

He shrugged, and the slick movement of the code on-screen faltered. She watched his fingers, wishing that they'd tremble, but they were as steady as his eyes. 'Looks like it.'

'You don't seem — to care very much.'

'About you?' He turned and stared at her with those uncannily dark eyes, and this time she couldn't help looking away. 'Oh gods, Ario . . . I'm not surprised, that's all. I knew you couldn't stop hacking, any more than I'd stop using. I hoped . . . but I knew you'd come here tonight. So I took — I made sure I'd be flying —' He cut himself off and rubbed his forehead. 'I'll care tomorrow. But that doesn't make any difference to anything, does it?'

'You took something, just so you could throw me out without caring?' She almost laughed. Almost cried. 'Dion —'

'Go and get your stuff, Ario.'

She nodded and walked to the door. As she leant on the comms panel she wondered how Dion had got in without her hearing the door open; had she been so absorbed that she'd been deaf? Everything seemed a long way away, or not quite real: as though the world had been replaced by a beautifully made replica, faithful in every detail but not the same. Even the smells were fainter. I'm going outside, she thought. And then . . . I don't have anywhere to go. But she couldn't make herself believe it.

She went to her cube and collected her stuff, shoving it all into her bedbag without bothering to fold her clothes or wrap up her iThing. She noticed that she was shaking. For a second she was interested, watching herself with a sense of detachment, like a med assessing symptoms. Then her knees gave way and she collapsed on to the bed. Oh gods, oh gods. Suddenly it was real, *she* was real. She had to leave, Dion was making her leave —

Dion was —

She pushed the heels of her hands into her eyes, feeling the tears run down her wrists. Stupid, so *stupid*, that she *cared* . . . why did it make any difference, that it was Dion? She was going out into the rain, alone, with no money and nowhere to stay — so why was it *Dion* that stuck in her head, Dion's blank black eyes looking at her as if she was his enemy . . . ?

For a second she remembered the first time she'd seen him, years ago, when he'd stopped her in a rainstorm, asked her if she was all right, had somewhere to stay —

I thought he was my friend, she thought, I thought I could trust him.

Stupid, *stupid* . . . I'm on my own, she thought, I've always been on my own. All this time, ever since Papa left me — just because Dion took me in, it was only because I was a Cheat, because I was good —

Papa, Pir, Dion —

And now, now what? Now I'm alone, now I've got to go —

She hugged her bedbag, crying, feeling the water run into her open mouth. I've junked everything, *everything* . . .

She heard the door open. It could have been Dion, or Spin, or Lia — everyone else would have to request entry — but she knew it was Dion. She raised her head and looked at him through a blur of tears. Please, she thought. Please tell me you've changed your mind . . .

'What the hell is it? That program? What the hell does it do?'

'Wh—' She felt the spasm of a sob forcing itself up through her throat. She swallowed, wiping her face with her palms; but Dion was tapping the door frame with his fist, impatient, as if he hadn't even noticed that she was crying. 'What's what?'

He just looked at her.

There was a silence. She took a deep breath. She was too tired not to tell him; too tired even to try to bargain.

'I don't know how it works,' she said. 'But it stole Pir's mind.'

He kept on staring at her, as though he could read the truth of it in her eyes. He stood there for a long time. Then, at last, he said, 'So the Maze . . . Crater knows everything Pir knew.'

She nodded. He made a noise like a strangled hiss, and suddenly she swallowed, watching his face, a weight of comprehension growing in her gut.

'They've been looking for us for months, haven't they? Since before the iTank came out . . . That night you said you'd been chased . . . And now they know where we are.'

She shut her eyes. She hadn't even — *thought* —

'I'm going,' she said. Her vocal cords felt flabby and dead. 'It's OK, Dion, I'm leaving. And maybe —'

'They know where *we* are,' he said. 'I don't know why they haven't turned up already.'

Silence.

'And you're not leaving,' he said, after a long time. 'It's too late for that.'

'What —?'

'Come on,' he said, turning on his heel. 'Let's get to work. And let's hope you really *are* the best.'

21

How long do we have? How long?

They were in the tankshop hall, side by side, working at their flatscreens. Dion had taken her wrist, dragged her to the terminal and pushed her on to the block, already reaching out for his own screen before he'd sat down. 'No time,' he'd said, and raised his hand when she started to say something. 'Get on with it. We need to crack this program now, get inside and delete the info, before . . .' But he hadn't finished his sentence before he was absorbed, already flipping his interface open, his face relaxing into blankness in the swirling light. Ario had watched him for a moment; then she'd shrugged and got on with it, because he was right, they didn't have time to waste.

But how long *do* we have . . . ?

Ario couldn't get the question out of her head. It sat there, catching the light every time she moved, so that she couldn't concentrate. How long? How long before they come for us? How long —

Everything Pir knew, the Maze knows. But there's so much information, she thought, it must take a while for it to filter back to Crater — if they're even looking for it. No, maybe it's just sitting there like a time bomb — an Easter egg — just sitting there, ticking . . . And we won't know when they've found it, except by the door exploding inwards . . .

Automatically she found herself looking over her shoulder, already flinching. But the door was there, flat and sturdy and neutral. They'd been there for hours and hours without moving. It was morning now; there was the faint smell of it in the air — the momentary sweetness as the dawn breeze blew some of the pollution away — that you smelt even inside, through the ventilators. She took a deep breath and went back to her screen, pushing the nightmare urgency away. She wasn't going to get anywhere if she panicked. I am going to beat this, she thought. The words seemed to glow in her head, giving off heat. I won't let them find us. And I can't get Pir back, but I can avenge her, I can stop it ever, *ever* happening again . . .

And slowly, like a line of melody just on the edge of hearing, the code started to draw her in. A long way away she heard Dion take a deep breath and start to rub his thumbnail against his lip; but she was looking at the program, following its lines with her eyes, and everything else stopped mattering.

They went on working, through the next day and night. People came and went around them, like a tide, murmuring to each other and leaving a debris of cups and wrappers and components behind them. Maybe someone spoke to Ario a couple of times, but she wasn't sure — wasn't even sure if she'd answered. It was as though she was sleepwalking, so concentrated on her screen and the program that her voice and body were on autopilot. Once she found herself sitting down again, her hands damp and smelling of tapwater, so she knew she must have been for a bio; but her mind had been on her screen all the time, following the tentacles of logic, trying to find the heart of the knot . . .

'*Ario*,' Dion said at last, and from the way he said it she knew it wasn't the first time. 'Will you *listen*, for gods' sa—'

'Yes,' someone said. 'Just a sec.' She realised it was her own voice.

'Look at me.'

'Yes, just a —'

Her flatscreen went dead. For a blinding, furious moment she stared at Dion's hand outlined against the black. Then he flicked it back on again, and she relaxed. The program let go its hold on her brain, and she forced herself to turn and meet his gaze.

'You here and conscious? At last.' He didn't wait for her to answer. 'OK. Talk to me. How's it going?'

She opened her mouth, and then gestured wordlessly at the screen. There was nothing to say; it was like trying to explain a whole world . . .

'Ario,' he said, as if saying her name would kickstart her mouth. 'Talk.'

'I don't know.'

He nodded, still looking at her, as if she'd confirmed a theory. 'Yeah. That's what I thought. It's completely mesmerised you, hasn't it? Like a basilisk.'

She smiled, faintly. He was right; she felt like she'd been turned into something else, like she wasn't herself any more . . .

'So listen, and *I'll* tell *you*, shall I? Can you listen? Are you feeling up to that?'

Her mind had already been wandering back to the program; but she forced herself to nod.

'So. This program — what did you call it? Asterion? Where did you get that, by the way? The name? Never mind. OK, Asterion is . . .' He paused, like he wanted her to fill in the gap, but there was nothing but the faraway hum of the generators. 'Asterion looks like a normal program, right? Sophisticated, sure, but not impossible — well, we thought we could hack it, right? But the more you look at it, the more nebulous it is, the more deceptive . . . And when you try to touch it, it moves with you, it knows what you're doing . . . like a fighter. Like a *gamerunner*. It's a mind, but a massive one, and it's made of — it's not just where you think it is, it's got links and connections and if you attack one place it moves with you, it *uses* you, it grows . . .' He stopped, looking at her intently as though he was willing her to disagree.

But she couldn't. She said, 'So . . .'

'But you're good, right? You're the best. So you can . . . ?' He waited. 'Tell me you can crack it.'

''Course,' she said.

She looked back at him, and knew he didn't believe it, any more than she did. But the corner of Dion's mouth twitched, and for a second they were together, united against a common enemy.

Then she turned back to the screen, and Dion wasn't important. *She* wasn't important.

It would have been something if she'd understood how it worked. This is it, she said to herself, this is the program that eats people, steals souls, the program that took Pir . . . but the more she looked at it, the less she understood. Dion was right — at first it looked simple, but it was . . . No, it *was* simple. Economical. Organic. Elegant . . . Simple like water, like air.

She wished she could hate the developers, or despise them . . . But she couldn't. All she felt was admiration. And fury.

Simple, yes, she thought, slamming her hands down suddenly on the desk. Simple like *impossible*. How can this be so *hard*?

She worked until midnight. Vaguely, on the edge of hearing, she registered Dion saying goodnight to her, and leaving. The generators stopped and restarted, clanking; the lights flickered and almost died before they struggled back to a steady hum. The air smelt thick and acrid. She was the last one left in the tankshop; she could have been the last person left on earth . . . And the code in front of her was frustrating, smooth as a mirror, absorbing everything she threw at it. It can't be this perfect, she thought. There's *always* a way in . . .

But there wasn't. Or if there was, she couldn't find it. Just a lovely, elegant program, that parried every attack, learnt to anticipate so that it was harder and harder to think of new tactics . . .

She leant back, kneading the vertebrae of her neck. The screen blurred and shone, like a window glinting with rain. She blinked, and felt her eyelids stick together, resisting when she tried to open them. It was so restful, just to close her eyes; she wasn't going to go to sleep, 'course not, but if she could just keep her eyes closed for a second, ten seconds, thirty . . .

She jolted awake, losing her balance, grabbing for the desk to stop herself falling. Get a grip, Ario! If you're that tired, go to bed.

She reached out to log off. And stopped, staring at the screen.

Where there'd been code, there was a line of words. Real words.

They said, **Are you still there? I was enjoying that.**

22

You — can — speak — *Inglish*, she thought, madly, frozen with her hand halfway to the screen. You — whoever you are — Asterion, *Daedalus* —

You're talking to me.

She leant forward, her hands poised over the keyboard; she noticed that her fingers were trembling, like an insect's antennae. She took a deep breath.

No. This is stupid. She squeezed her eyes shut and opened them again, half expecting to find that she'd been dreaming, that the lines of code were there after all.

I suppose it is three in the morning. But I assumed hackers were nocturnal.

A pause. She looked sideways, wanting to see Dion at the next terminal, grinning as though she was the biggest suxor in the world, for falling for it. *Got you, babesauce* . . . But there was no one there.

She looked back at the screen. OK. It was a chatterbot, that was all; someone's idea of a joke. There was nothing there that couldn't be programmed. Of course it knew the time, knew she was a haxor — she'd been trying to hack it, hadn't she? She was overreacting. What *was* it about Asterion that made her take everything so seriously? It was a program like any other — sophisticated, intelligent — with huge amounts of information — but not *personal*, certainly not *conscious* . . .

She rubbed her eyes, trying to remember what script she'd been running before she fell asleep. But her mind had gone blank. She let her hands drop.

Then, on a sudden, ridiculous impulse, she entered: **Who are you?**

Er . . . the question of identity is a bit of a knotty one, I'm afraid. And what I am is an even more interesting question.

She sat back, shaking her head, annoyed with herself. Get back to work, she thought. Don't be tempted to waste time . . . The whole program's brilliant, it's not surprising if they've got a decent bot.

And you? Who are you?

Ha. You think I'll give you my name? She went on shaking her head, this time at the screen, as though it could see her. Suddenly her code came back to her and she started to enter it, determinedly not looking at the words.

Splendid. I was worried you'd given up.

She ignored that too and finished the line of script.

I've been quite bored recently. This is . . . fun.

She stopped, took a deep breath, let it hiss out through her teeth. The rest of the code should've reappeared when she entered her script; but it hadn't. And slowly, mockingly, the blackness swallowed her commands, welling up over the characters like crude oil. But the line of

Inglish stayed, shining steadily, as though it was watching her, as though —

A shiver went down her back and she rubbed her forearms violently, trying to smooth away the goosebumps. It was cold in the tankshop, that was all. There was nothing weird about the program — it was nothing special, just the developers wanting to be smug at the hackers' expense . . .

But her code had gone. Her interface was corrupted, something wasn't working . . . And —

I'm quite impressed. No one's ever got this far before.

Stop it. *Stop it*. Why was it freaking her out? It was just a cleverbot, it was nothing, as soon as she got her interface to work again she'd be able to get past it, turn it off, whatever —

She entered commands frantically, but everything she did sank into the darkness of the screen. She felt her heart racing in her temples and forced herself to breathe. OK, restart the interface, she thought. Or turn the terminal off and on again, if you have to. You'll lose everything you've done so far, but you can start again . . .

Why don't you just try talking to me? it said to her. **Aren't you even slightly curious? You never know, you might find out something useful.**

Right, she thought, if that were true you wouldn't say it. She reached out to turn her terminal off, and hesitated. She'd got this far. And maybe — if there was a chance — she *might* find something out —

She didn't give herself any more time to think. **Fine**, she entered. **What have you done to my interface?**

Just playing around.

Well, she typed, **I want it back.**

So you can get on with trying to hack me? Can't we just talk this through like civilised adults?

It's *laughing* at me, she thought, not sure whether she was horrified or — what? — charmed . . . It's *amused*. No, it's a program. It can't have feelings. It's just doing a very good imitation of being amused . . . But she *knew* how it felt, the way she would have known if it was a person standing in front of her. **My interface,** she said. **You've corrupted it somehow.**

Well spotted. I knew you were good.

Irony? *Irony?* What kind of bot could do —? She leant forward, glaring at the words. **Actually I am. I'm the best. Ask anyone.**

There was a pause. Now that she was writing in Inglish her text stayed on the screen; she read and reread what she'd written, waiting for him to answer. But for a long time there was nothing. Maybe that's it, she thought. Maybe somehow I've triggered something, and my interface will come back, maybe I can go back to hacking properly —

Then it said, **You're *Ario*.**

She felt the shock reverberate inside her, ringing off her bones as though her whole body was hollow. *Ario*.

It knew who she was.

It couldn't. No matter how intelligent it was. It couldn't. It knew she existed — it knew she was a Cheat — it knew everything that Pir knew — but that she was *here*, that the person it was talking to and Pir's Ario were the same —

220

As if it had guessed — but computers don't *guess* —

Dion. Dion had hacked it already. This was a sick joke. It had to be . . .

Are you still there?

I don't know, she thought. *Am* I still here?

You are, aren't you? Sitting there staring at the screen. Good old Ario, who thinks she's the best. I knew it.

I knew it. Intuition. And triumph, in the words. A program that acted on hunches — got them right — and was *pleased* —

No. It's a program. It's logical. It's made of code, there's no room in code for emotions or intuition or — *no*. I've seen the code, for gods' sake. Whatever this is, it isn't — it isn't —

Oh, Ario. I bet this is coming as a shock. You thought programs were the opposite of people . . . and that was why you liked them, right? You might be rubbish with people, but at least *programs* are manageable . . .

Rubbish with people . . . the memory surfaced, in Pir's voice. *You think people are pointless and pathetic* . . . It was like a hand reaching into her chest and squeezing.

Oh, sorry. Was that tactless?

She shut her eyes. Of course it knew what Pir had said to her — it had all Pir's memories, it *knew* her, now that it knew that she was Ario, it knew what she was like, what she *looked* like, everything — it had seen inside her cube, seen her half dressed, coming out of the shower —

For a second she felt nothing but humiliation. Then she opened her eyes again and clenched her fists, wishing the program really was a person, so that she could hurt it back.

Don't apologise, she said. **Reckon you're getting jumpy about being hacked.**

Hmmm. Maybe. Because you're the best, right?

Yes, I am.

There was a pause. It's smiling, she thought, and then rubbed her forehead, hard. No, it's not smiling. It's imitating human interaction. It doesn't really feel anything. Come on, getting wound up is not going to help anything . . . Then its response blinked up on to the screen.

Inherited that from your father, did you?

What? **What?** She heard her heart thudding and realised she was holding her breath. She typed again, *What?*

Tell me about him. What was he like?

How do you know about — but it was from Pir, wasn't it? The things she'd said to Pir . . . She stopped in the middle of typing, deleted the line before the program had time to respond. Close the interface, she told herself. Stop now. This is —

Wait a moment . . . the program said. **If you're — did he look like you, your father? Gods. I think — yes, now I come to think about it. I know who he was.**

No. No, you don't. No. My papa was my papa, nothing to do with you, keep out of my life, keep *out* —

Mino, his name was. Is that right? A developer at Crater who went rogue . . . Before my time, I'm afraid, although I — The text cut off as though it was hesitating; but somehow she knew it knew *exactly* what it wanted to say, knew exactly what effect it wanted to have on her . . . **He left with a daughter, just before I turned up with my son . . . How symmetrical. Yes, Mino.**

No. Her brain wouldn't formulate anything else: only the word *no*, over and over again, until it was only a sound, a shape.

Why aren't you answering? Does that mean I'm right?

Silence. The generators hummed, the note rising and falling like waves as the blood came and went in Ario's ears.

Yes, I think so, it said, after a long time. She thought she could see the faint note of pleasure in the words. **Yes, that seems probable.**

And you know what that means, Ario? It means I know what happened to him.

She read the words and felt her heart disappear, replaced by a sudden emptiness. It didn't hurt; but for a second she wouldn't have been surprised to see it drop on to the desk in front of her, oozing red liquid, still beating uselessly. *What happened to him . . .*

Do you want to know about that, Ario?

She was frozen. The world was nothing but her screen and her eyes.

Ario?

There was noise from somewhere, a hum and flicker in her peripheral vision that settled into a steady neon glow. Someone had come in, turned a light on . . . But it didn't matter. Someone said, 'Ario? Ario. *Ario!*' but that didn't matter, either. She kept her eyes on the words. ***Do you want . . .***

The screen was obscured by something dark. A shirt, a body. Dion. She knew it was him from the sharp sweat-and-chemical smell; she couldn't focus on his face. Her arms hurt and she realised that he was holding her, ducking and weaving in front of her, trying to meet her eyes. 'Ario. Look at me. Please.'

'*Move*,' she heard herself say, and the sound of her own voice shocked her. 'Dion, get out of the way, I'm working —'

'What's happened? What's the matter?'

'Nothing. Let go of me. I need to get on with what I was —'

'You look like you've been wiped out. You've gone *green*. Ario, talk to me.'

She tried to pull away, more violently than she meant to. 'Dion, let *go*, leave me alone, I'm in the middle of someth—'

He slapped her.

It was the noise that got through to her: a crack like something breaking, the silence that followed it. Then the pain flared over her cheek. Her eyes blurred and cleared again as involuntary tears welled up and spilt. She blinked, and focused on his face. He looked . . . scared.

'Dion . . .' she said, and this time she sounded like herself. 'Wow, Dion . . . what the —?'

'Sorry. But I was worried. I *am* worried.' He was leaning forward, squinting into her eyes as though he was a med. 'You're not — you haven't taken anything, have you? You look like death.'

'I'm fine. I'm working. You took me by surprise, that's all.'

He shook his head, slowly. 'Something's happened. Go on, cough it up.'

'I — *nothing*, I —' She reached out to turn off the flat-screen, suddenly horrified at the thought that Dion might read the words on it. She didn't know why she was so desperate, but she was: as though he'd caught her in the middle of something so intimate it was shameful . . . But she was too slow. Dion blinked as she started to move, then, lightning-fast, caught hold of her hand. He turned to look at the screen.

Ario looked down. She heard him draw in his breath and let it out again, very slowly.

'Gods,' he said, at last. 'Ario . . .'

'It's just a chatterbot,' she said, her voice high and defensive. 'That's all. I can get past it. It's corrupted my interface but I can —'

'That's not a chatterbot,' he said. 'That's *consciousness*.'

'I just need to —'

'That's *emotional* intelligence,' he said, in the same wondering tone. 'That's . . . Ario, you're not hacking that program any more. It's hacking *you*.'

'I just — I want to — Dion, I'm getting somewhere, I know I am —' She didn't know why she was lying, but she didn't care. 'Dion, I have to *work* —'

'No,' he said. He put his hands on her shoulders, staring into her eyes. 'No. You have to stop.'

And then before she could stop him he'd twisted round to the flatscreen and logged her out.

23

She couldn't believe it. She sat still for a second, frozen by outrage; then she started to shout. Dion was shouting back, but everything was a blur of noise. She was on her feet, pummelling him with her fists, sobbing with fury. How dare he, how *dare* he? 'Get it back, get it back! Dion, I was in the middle of — get it *back* —'

He had his arms over his face, to protect himself. She pulled at one of his wrists, slapping him ineffectually with the other hand. 'Ario,' he was saying, 'Ario, *stop*!'

'Get it back for me! I have to go on. Dion, I have to —' One of her slaps connected, and she felt the impact zing through her fingers like electricity. Dion yelped and tried to turn away, swinging one arm to fend her off. She flung herself forward and his fist went into her stomach, driving all the breath out of her. She wobbled, gasped silently, and dropped to her knees.

The air went thick, like oil, too viscous to get into her lungs. Her rib muscles wouldn't work; she was stuck, paused, paralysed . . . A wave of panic went through her. What if she never unfroze? How long could she survive without air?

Something spasmed inside her, scraped and stuck and

turned like a key: then her lungs unlocked and she was breathing again, so relieved that she barely noticed the ache in her gut where Dion had punched her.

He was bending over her. 'Ario, I'm sorry, are you OK? I really didn't mean to hit you, sorry, say something, Ario, please —'

'I'm OK.'

He exhaled sharply and rocked back on his heels. He dragged a hand across his eyes and down over his mouth and chin. 'Good. Woot. Thought I'd killed you for a sec.'

'My fault,' she said. 'You were only defending yourself.'

'Yeah, but hitting you twice in ten minutes . . . wouldn't do much for my street cred.'

There was a pause. She sat down, swinging her legs round so that she could lean back against the block. Dion watched her, and then sat down opposite her, mirroring her pose exactly. 'Why did you log me out?' she said.

'Because . . . Ario, I've seen programs that protect themselves. Even ones that attack the systems that you use to hack in. I've seen corrupted interfaces before. But not — I've never seen a program that attacked the *hacker*.'

'It wasn't attacking *me*, not personally —' But it was. Of course it was. She cut herself off and turned her eyes away.

'And it was clever. It knew what your weak point would be, it . . . Ario, that's not an ordinary program — no, don't interrupt! Of course it's not ordinary, we knew that. But it's something new. Something scary. I'm not sure it's even really a *program* any more. And — well, if it can do that to you in a few hours . . . what do you think it could do to us, if we go on trying to hack it?'

'But we have to.'

'We can't.' He held up his hand. 'No, *listen*. It was sucking you in. It had you on a line, Ario.'

A draught caught the back of her neck, icy-cold, and she shivered. She didn't want him to be right . . . 'But, Dion, we *have* to. You said it. It's got our information, we're not safe — and that program is — it's evil. It stole Pir, it'll steal more people, it's — *monstrous* —'

'I *know*, Ario!'

He'd shouted at her; she felt the spray of spit on her face, and shut her eyes. After a while he started to speak again, his voice quieter. 'Listen . . . we might have time to . . . to leave . . .'

'Leave? Here?' She looked at him, frowning so hard it hurt. 'We can't — Dion, you know how hard it is to set up a tank-shop from scratch . . .' Of course he did; he'd done it, hadn't he?

He shrugged with one shoulder. 'If you go on trying to hack it . . . it'll freak you out completely. Get more information on us, all the stuff Pir *didn't* know. Or . . . get you to destroy the tankshop yourself. No need to send Customer Services when it can drive you to suicide or murder . . .'

'That's ridiculous. I wouldn't go *mad* —'

'Is it? You think battering me because I logged you out of your terminal was *reasonable*?'

Silence.

'And gods know what it could do to *me*, if it got the chance,' Dion said. 'My brain's weird enough already.'

He was serious; but all the same it made her laugh, helplessly, burying her face in her hands. After a while she heard him join in. It was a relief, not having to think: but all the same when she raised her head she found herself saying, 'But we can't give up, Dion. *I* can't give up.'

'We have to find another way to beat it. Or we leave. Tonight, tomorrow.'

'There isn't another way. I have to hack it.'

'Then you'll just have to get used to the ide—' He stopped and looked round. There was the sound of a door buzzing open, quiet footsteps, the faintest hint of breathing. Ario followed his gaze and saw Rick slipping silently through the doorway into the gametank hall, a P&V bar in his hand. When the door had closed after him the silence seemed deeper than ever. Then Dion caught his breath, as though someone invisible had tapped him on the shoulder. She looked at him and his eyes were shining.

'Or — maybe there *is*,' he said. 'Maybe there *is* another way.'

She waited for him to elaborate, but he didn't; he was still staring over his shoulder at the door to the gametank hall, even though it was closed. 'Go *on*, then,' she said at last. 'Or is this where I have to renew my subscription?'

The corner of his mouth twitched, but when he turned back to meet her eyes his face was thoughtful, as serious as she'd ever seen it. 'Listen,' he said. 'What's the easiest way to get your client to win a quest?'

'Well —' She shook her head, wishing he'd get to the point. 'It depends on the quest — if it's a linear quest that's mainly traps, I suppose I'd go for a cheat that disabled the traps, but if there was a boss —'

'No. The *easiest* way.'

'I don't know,' she said, screwing up her face at him. 'Like I said, it depends on the quest.'

'No,' he said. 'That's where you're wrong. It depends on the *client*. The *easiest* way —' he paused. 'The easiest way to get your client to win a quest, Ario, is to *choose a client that doesn't need to cheat*.'

She leant back and folded her arms across her chest. 'Right. And?'

'What if we didn't need to hack the program? We've been trying to find a back door, right? So what if the way in was through the front?'

'You mean —'

'I mean the game. We can get in through the Roots, the way Pir did.'

'But —' She took a long breath. 'We still wouldn't know how to beat it.'

'Maybe, maybe not. But if we get a gamerunner in, it's a start, isn't it? And you never know, we might not even need a cheat. It's Crater, right? Even if it's a rogue program, it has to obey their rules, surely? In the end it's just a boss fight. And in the Maze nothing is impossible.'

'You know that's not true.'

'Almost true.'

'And —' She paused, feeling the resistance inside her, like an unexpected weight. She *wanted* to hack the program; she wanted it to talk to her, to tell her about . . . No. She pushed the thought aside. 'We don't have a gamerunner, Dion. We're hackers. We don't know anyone near that good. Pir was the best I ever saw, and if *she* couldn't —'

Dion grinned and stood up, walking towards the door to the tankfloor; and belatedly Ario got it, understood what had given him the idea. 'You said he was good, Ario,' he said, softly. 'You thought he was better than Pir, when you saw him run the iTank demo. Remember?'

'Yes, but — he won't agree — and he's *barred*, Dion. He can't get into the Maze, the iTank took his brainprint and — Dion, this is stupid, just let me, give me a few more days with the program, and we won't have to —'

Dion ignored her. He buzzed the door open and leant into the shadows beyond it. 'Hey,' he said, raising his voice. 'Can you come out? We need to talk to you.'

There was a pause. They waited.

'Um . . . yes?' Rick said, from the darkness. He stepped through into the tankshop, and stood poised on the balls of his feet as if he was ready for a fight.

'You know we're working on a big hacking project at the moment?'

'Yes,' Rick said. 'Asterion. I know.'

Dion narrowed his eyes, but he only nodded. 'We need you to help.'

231

'Help . . . ?'

'Ario wants to — we want to beat it. We have to. It's dangerous, it's wrong, and — well, we're not exactly crusaders, but . . . And anyone can see that the longer it goes on, the harder it'll get for us, for Cheats everywhere. And we think, that if someone defeated it in the Maze, through the gameplay . . .'

Rick didn't say anything. He was watching Dion, his face neutral and guarded; but somehow Ario was sure that he was making an effort not to look at her.

'We need a gamerunner. We need someone to help us get into the boss fight at the end of the Roots.'

'The one that killed Pir?' he said. His voice was very flat; but underneath it there was a current of something else. Surprise, and — what was it? *Longing*, Ario thought, but it didn't make sense.

Dion smiled, shrugging as though it was only a detail. 'We'll make sure you don't —'

'I'm sorry,' he said, still without inflection. 'I'd like to help. But I'm barred from the Maze. It's got my brainprint on file.'

'But you'd do it, if you could?'

He shrugged and started to say, 'I —' but something seemed to catch in his throat. And suddenly his face changed, like a mask dropping. His jaw clenched and the lacework of scars stood out white against his temple. It *was* longing. He wants to help us, Ario thought, he wants it more than anything in the world . . . 'Yes, I'd do it if I could,' he said, making the words careful and smooth as though he was afraid they'd spill. There was a silence; then, as if something had over-flowed, in spite of his efforts, he blurted out: 'Asterion — it's my fault, I should have — I wish I'd —'

Dion shifted a little, glanced between him and Ario, but he only said, 'So that's definitely a yes?'

Rick nodded.

'You're sure?'

'Yes,' he said, and made a noise that was a little like a laugh. 'I'd do anything. But I can't — I just told you. I'm *barr—*'

'Anything?'

'No, he wouldn't,' Ario said, raising her voice so that they both swung round to look at her. 'Not *anything* . . . Dion, whatever you're thinking, it's stupid, I just want you to let me *hack —*'

'You want to beat it, don't you? Why does it matter how you do it?' He didn't give her time to answer before he turned back to Rick. 'Listen, mate. Suppose I could — that there was a way to change your brainprint. Then you could get into the Maze, and help us, right? Would you do that?'

'Change his brainprint? How?' But this time they ignored her.

'Yes,' he said. 'If it got me back into the Maze.'

'But that's *crazy*,' Ario said, pushing herself to her feet. 'You couldn't change a brainprint except by doing something really extreme —'

'Hey, Ario, calm down,' Dion said, and waved one hand reassuringly in her direction. 'I'm not suggesting that we brain-*damage* him, for gods' sake. I'm just exploring possibilities. Because as it happens I do have an idea. It'd be safe and easy and he'd hardly notice a thing.'

'Right. Sure it would,' she said, and wanted to hit him. 'Dion, you can't just play with people like that, you can see that he's desperate to get back into the Maze, it's not *fair* to get his hopes up —'

'Stop talking about me like I'm not here!'

Ario had never heard Rick raise his voice before. It made her heart jump a little against her ribs, and she saw the same feeling in Dion's face before he looked down, letting his eyelids drop over his eyes as if to hide it. There was a silence. She said, 'Sorry.'

'I appreciate your concern,' he said, and she couldn't tell whether he was being ironic or not. 'But this is my decision, right?' He glanced at Dion. 'So —'

'Right,' Dion said.

'So . . . Yes. Whatever you've got in mind. I'll do it.'

'But —'

'You're trying to protect me,' he said to Ario, and a corner of his mouth twisted. 'Thanks. But it's too late. For me *and* for you, I guess.' He looked back at Dion before she had time to answer. 'Tell me your idea.'

Dion started to look at Ario and then bit his lip and turned his gaze back to Rick, as though he was trying not to look triumphant. 'OK,' he said. 'Good man. My idea is . . . well, drugs. I'll design a cocktail that will junk — will rewrite your brain, just a bit. It won't kill you or affect your motor functions or reflexes or, you know, general gamerunning

234

ability, but you . . . well, you won't exactly be the same person.'

Ario took a breath in. Then she said, 'Dion, you have *got* to be —'

At the same moment, Rick said, 'I'll do anything.'

24

Dion didn't give Ario time to argue any more. He shepherded Rick out into the corridor, called, 'Hey, Ario, have a look at your cheats and see what else you can come up with,' and then they were gone. She was on her own.

Slowly she sat down at her terminal. She reached out and logged in — her hand trembling a little, even though the emotion didn't touch her brain — but there was only the log-in screen, familiar and unassuming, as if she'd never read the words, *I know what happened to him*.

This is all *wrong*, she thought. We can't hack a program from the front door, it doesn't make sense. That's the whole point of cheats, Dion. And Rick —

She clenched her jaw, trying not to think about him. Drugs that rewrote your brainprint? Whatever Dion said, that didn't sound good. Gods knew what they could do . . .

She brought up her interface, fiddled a little to see if it would let her into the Maze. It did. Everything was ordinary — lines of code, not Inglish, nothing unexpected. She hesitated, wondering if she should try to access Asterion. Sure, it freaked me out, but I overreacted, she thought. I could hack it. I know I could. If Dion only gave me enough time . . .

She sat back, trying to ignore the misgivings that sat heavily in her stomach. *I can handle it, whatever Asterion throws at me, I'm the best. And it's got to be better than letting Rick OD on some concoction of Dion's just so that he can get back into the Maze . . .*

'Don't even think about it, babesauce.'

She hadn't been talking *aloud*, had she? She looked up and Dion was there, shaking his head and walking towards her as though he wanted to be close enough to stop her touching her terminal.

'No no no,' he said, smoothly. 'Don't you dare. It's trying to headrape you, can't you see that?'

'What do you care?' The words came out of nowhere, surprising her. They surprised him too: she saw him pause mid-step.

'Actually, Ario, I do. Just bec—' He bit his lip, as if the words were fighting to get out. Then he took a deep breath and sat down opposite her, perched on a counter as though he was trying to be casual. 'Ario . . . just because I care about the tankshop and everyone in it, doesn't mean I *don't* care about you. We're still friends, right?'

She looked down, away.

'Listen . . . if this works, if it all gets sorted out, you can stay, OK?' One of his grimy, clever fingers tapped against the edge of the counter. 'Ario? You can *stay*.'

She nodded. It didn't seem important, right now. 'Where's Rick?' she said.

'In my cube. I made up a little recipe for him. He'll probably be out of it for a couple of days, which should give us time to fine-tune our cheats, and then —'

'*Fine-tune?* Dion, we don't have anything. We've got what I wrote for Pir, that's all. And look how useful that was.'

'He's better than Pir. He'll need less help. And there's always a way, Ario. Nothing is impossible.'

She shook her head, looking straight ahead because she was afraid she'd lose it if she went on looking at Dion. 'We haven't thought this through,' she said, keeping her voice level. 'You had the idea and then suddenly it was happening, just like that. It's too quick. We need to think about this — you can't just let him drug himself up on a whim, it's too dangerous —'

'It's not a whim.' His tone was like hers, formal and controlled, and she knew he was as close to fury as she was. 'It's simple logic. We have to beat this program, right? I'm not risking any more clients getting killed . . . and I can't think of anything else. I am not going to let you near that program. You or any other hacker. You don't get it, do you? It was trying to get into your mind. And it was working. You were like . . . I've never seen you like that. This life is *dangerous*, Ario. You know that. And we *don't have any choice*.'

She glanced up at him, ready to snap; but his expression was like a hand over her mouth, silencing her, cutting off the air to her lungs. Yes. He was right.

'OK,' she said, and felt guilt wash around her, almost lifting her off her feet. 'OK.'

She stood up, pushing her block away, and stumbled to the door.

* * *

She ran down the corridor, trying not to think. The door of Dion's cube was closed, of course. She smacked her hand against the comms panel. He'd overwritten her privileges and it didn't let her in, but she heard the panel on the other side say drily, **Ario is requesting entry**. Come on, she thought, come on, please be awake, please answer the door . . .

There was such a long pause that she thought he'd taken the pills already. He's gone, she thought, and felt such a wave of loss that she leant forward, pressing her forehead against the door. I didn't realise I cared this much about him, she thought, I didn't realise I even *liked* him . . . Then she felt the vibration as the door hummed, struggling to slide open while her weight was pushing it into the frame. She reeled back and steadied herself with one hand.

He was standing in front of the bed, so that their eyes met as soon as the door slid open.

'I'm going to take them,' he said, too quickly. 'I was just — I'm going to. Tell Dion —'

'Dion didn't send me. I wanted to see you.'

For a second she could see him wonder whether to believe her. Then he sat down on the bed as if he didn't have enough energy to care. He had scars on the back of his neck that she'd never noticed before, and she had a weird, shameful urge to touch them. She took a step into the room and the door closed behind her. He didn't seem to notice, but when she sat down beside him he shifted a little, leaving her more space. 'Are you all right?' she said. The moment the words were out of her mouth she despised herself.

'I . . .' He looked at her. He was going to say something sarcastic.

'OK, OK, stupid quest—'

'Yes,' he said. 'I mean yes, stupid question, not yes I'm all right.'

'Sorry,' she said. Why did I come? she thought. We're not friends, we hardly know each other, this was such a bad idea . . . 'OK, well, good luck and everything, see you later —' She stood up and put her hand on the comms panel, fumbling so that it took ages to read her hand.

'Wait,' he said, and he was standing up too, so close that she could feel the warmth from his body. 'I'm sorry — stay — please —'

She turned round, but there was something in his eyes which caught her off-guard and made the words evaporate straight off her tongue.

'Why *did* you come?' he said. 'If it wasn't to check I'd taken —' He gestured to the block next to the bed and she saw a cardboard cup half full of gleaming capsules. 'If Dion didn't send you . . .'

She didn't answer.

'I'm afraid,' he said. 'Even if those pills don't kill me . . .'

She shook her head. She wanted to press her palm against his cheek, where the scars were. He looked after me when I cried, she thought. That night, the night I realised what had happened to Pir . . . She could remember how it had felt, the strength of his arms, the way he'd supported her without moving, without trying to console her. She felt the grip of his hands on her shoulders, as though her body's memory was stronger than her brain's. 'They won't kill you,' she said, keeping her voice steady. 'Dion may look like a complete flyer, but he's not stupid. You'll be OK.'

'But he . . . I'm not saying that,' he said, and bent his head, staring at the floor. 'But he's been waiting for this, you know? He's been keeping me here because he had this idea that one day I'd come in useful. I don't think he knew how, or when . . . but he had a feeling about me. He said so, once. And now the moment's come, he doesn't care about *me*, he cares about what I'm supposed to do. If I can beat Asterion for you, that's all that matters. The rest of me is . . . dispensable.' She started to speak, and he interrupted her. 'I'm not complaining. I understand. Why should he care what happens to me? But I'm not going to tell myself that he's got my best interests at heart and nothing bad is going to happen to me, because *I*'m not stupid, either.'

There was a pause Ario's throat ached; she had to swallow before she could speak. 'You don't have to take them,' she said. 'The pills. You can tell us to go fy.' A split second later she thought: but Asterion knows my *name*, knows all our names, knows where the tankshop is . . . Dion's right, we have to try any way we can. But she didn't take it back.

He smiled.

It was so unexpected she caught her breath; it transformed his face, and she had to look away, feeling the blood beat in her cheeks. 'Yes, I do,' he said. 'But not because of you or Dion. I said I'd do anything, and I meant it. You *want* to beat Asterion; but I *have* to beat Asterion.'

She nodded. She believed him.

241

'It's my fault,' he said, and she heard the smile fade out of his voice. 'Without me, Asterion would never — Daed would never have needed —' He broke off. 'Doesn't mean I'm not scared, though.' With one hand he reached out and picked up the cardboard cup of pills, rattling them around.

She reached out and took his other hand.

It surprised them both. For a fraction of a second she felt him pull away, and she started to draw back too, shocked that she'd even *thought* of touching him; but then, before there was any space between his skin and hers, he squeezed her fingers, holding on to her. They both looked down. His hand was splashed with red scar-tissue, the fingers clubbed and blunted where they'd been burnt. Ario's was thin and smooth and dark. But all the same they seemed to fit together.

He looked at her, and she met his gaze for as long as she could before the heat rising in her face was unbearable, and she ducked her head.

The last time I was this close to someone, she thought, it was Pir, in the ice-palace, the night she died.

The thought should have hurt. But somehow it didn't; somehow it seemed . . . right. It was as if someone had cut and pasted the moment, taking it out of context so that she could be suddenly, perfectly happy. It doesn't make sense, she thought. How can I be happy, in the middle of all this? But she was.

'Thank you,' he said, very quietly.

She didn't move; she just held on to his hand, as though it was all she had.

'I've got this — I had a friend,' he said, still in that soft voice, like he was talking to himself. 'She used to look out for me . . . She told me to stop doing stupid things. It was one of the last things she said to me. *Stop doing stupid things.*' He made a tiny movement, so that the pills in the cup jumped and pattered against each other. 'But I didn't. I'm not going to last much longer, am I? Not on present showing.'

'Well . . . You're still alive,' Ario said, and his smile tugged again at his scars. 'You'll be OK. I'm sure you will.'

His fingers were turning and turning the cup, letting the capsules slide slowly over one another like the jewels in a kaleidoscope.

'And . . . he doesn't actually know what's going to happen when I take these. Whether it'll be permanent or . . . memory loss, he said. Probably. But things could come and go, bits of me might resurface and they might not . . .' Suddenly the cup was still, so that Ario could see a faint — a very, very faint tremor in his fingers.

'Rick . . .' she said, 'you don't — have to . . .'

There was a silence. He looked at her.

'Right. Better take these, then. Let's just hope Dion did the maths properly.' He saw her look, and said, shrugging, 'You know, height, BMI, metabolism, all that stuff. To be fair, he didn't just shake out a handful of pills and tell me to swallow them.'

'Good. OK, well, hope it goes well . . .' She hated her voice: so polite, so casual . . . She didn't want to let go of his hand; but she knew she had to. She focused on her fingers, telling them to relax. His hand held on to hers for a moment, and then went limp. She didn't mean to look at his face, but when she did she saw that he'd closed his eyes, and his expression was like a mask. She got to her feet. There were shivers going up and down her legs, so it was hard to keep her balance.

He opened his eyes and reached out. 'Please — Ario —'

'Yes?'

'Will you stay with me?'

She looked down at the cup of pills. He'll be OK, she said to herself, but she felt sick, anyway. No. I don't want to be here with you. Whatever those are going to do to you, I don't want to see it happening . . .

'Please,' he said.

Very, very slowly she sat down on the bed and took his hand again. She said, 'Yes. If you want me to.'

25

It wasn't as bad as she was expecting; but it was bad enough. When the pills went into his mouth he grimaced, struggling to swallow, rubbing his throat as if that was going to help. A few seconds after that his eyes went strange, the pupils flaring until his irises were hardly visible, and he started to tremble. She shifted on the bed, watching him, and he reached out and clung to her like a child. She felt him shivering, and the slow soak of cold sweat through his clothes and hers. It smelt bitter, like fever. She tried to turn so that she could lean against a wall, but he wouldn't let go of her, not even a little bit. In the end she pulled him down on to the bed, because at least that way her body could be comfortable.

They lay there for a long time, while his shaking made the bed judder. He was murmuring things under his breath, but they didn't make sense, and she was pretty sure that he wasn't talking to her. The only sentence she heard was, 'Don't do stupid things,' and she allowed herself a brief ironic smile, knowing he couldn't see her face. And then the words slurred into vowels and breath, and his grip relaxed. She rolled over so that she could look down at him, and his

eyes were closed. His mouth was still moving, and his forehead spasmed and clenched. 'Daed,' he said — unless it was
dead . . . Not that it mattered, not that she'd ever know what —

The world went into slow motion, icy and brutal as a
glacier.

She thought: Daed knew who Papa was. And this boy is —
was — his son. So maybe he knows —

Maybe he knew — before he took Dion's pills —

What if he knew before and now it's too late to —

She reached out and shook him, trying to wake him up,
forgetting to be gentle. 'Wake up. *Wake up!* I need to talk to
you — ask you something —' Oh gods, she was so stupid, how
could she not have, how *could* she —? 'Please, *please*, if you
can hear me —' She shook him harder and heard his teeth
rattle. He moaned and pushed at her with a feeble hand.
'Please,' she said, 'please . . .'

No good.

She tried for a few more minutes, but she knew it
wouldn't work. At last even his murmuring stopped and his
breathing was so shallow she could hardly see it. He was as
limp as a corpse, warm and unreactive in her arms the way
Pir had been —

The thought made her pull away, feeling queasy. The back
of her eyes prickled and she swallowed, hearing the silence
of the room as though the entire building was empty except
for her.

I let him take those pills — I let him, I *wanted* him to — and
now —

And suddenly she knew that she didn't care what he'd

forgotten, as long as he was OK. She could live with not knowing what had happened to Papa — she'd managed this long, hadn't she? — but if he — if Rick — if something terrible —

I can't bear it, if Rick — I didn't even know I *cared* —

He'll be OK, she said to herself. He will. When he wakes up he'll be a bit hazy, but he'll be *OK* . . .

She couldn't bear being in the same room as him. She disentangled herself, slid out of his dead embrace and stood up. She changed the comms panel to universal access so that she'd be able to get in again if she wanted. Then she hesitated, kissed him briefly on the forehead, and went out into the corridor, tasting his sweat on her lips.

They had a lot to do before he woke up, and she was glad. Dion was watching her when she came through the door into the tankshop, but she strode over, sat down and said, 'Right. Guess we'd better have a council of war, then,' before he had time to say anything. If she could just keep her brain occupied with something else . . .

He hesitated, fractionally; then he nodded and reached for his iThing. 'I want to know what happened when Pir died,' he said. 'Everything. Talk me through everything you can remember. I looked at the records, but it goes weird after the bit in the loading space.'

She pressed her hands down on the counter, looking at the dark lines under her fingernails. OK. Just tell him. Be clinical and direct. Don't give yourself time to *remember* . . .

'Yes,' she said. 'Pir went into the Roots with all my cheats — I'll get you the list in a second. And I'd set up a ventrillo, but . . .' She kept her eyes on his iThing, watching the slide and dance of the colours as it recorded her. Pir going into the Roots, running the portal, the boss in the loading space, that fog, growing and growing . . . She kept talking until at last there was a pause, and she knew she'd said everything.

'OK,' Dion said, 'OK,' and from the way he said it she knew the silence had been a long one. 'Right. Well. Sounds like we should set up an independent mic, in case that happens again — old-school, radio waves, something that doesn't rely on the iTank . . . Then at least we'll be able to hear him, even if we can't talk back. If something happens . . .' He stopped.

There was another pause. He sniffed and scratched his head loudly, as if he was trying to fill the silence. Then he turned to his flatscreen and started to work.

At last Ario heard herself say, 'He said you thought he was dispensable.'

'What?' He was flicking through the stock lists on-screen, and she heard his finger hesitate.

'Rick. You think he's dispensable.'

He drew his breath through his teeth. 'Hey, babe, I expect he was feeling a little bit prickly, it's not every day you have to rewrite your own brainpr—'

'He was right.' Her screen was off, but it seemed to flicker and glow in front of her eyes. 'We're all dispensable to you, aren't we? What matters is the tankshop, and that's all.'

Very slowly, he turned to look at her. The light from the screen behind him threw his face into shadow.

'What matters to me is surviving,' he said. 'No one's

248

indispensable. And don't kid yourself that you're better than me.'

She waited for him to smile, shrug, do *something* to soften what he'd said . . . but he didn't, and slowly she understood that he wasn't going to.

Don't kid yourself that you're better than me. The thought of Rick, drugged and limp in Dion's cube, flashed into her mind's eye, so vivid she could almost smell the feverish scent of his sweat.

She took a deep breath. 'I'll get you a list of the cheats I used,' she said, and logged in.

It didn't take long, but after she'd sent Dion the codes she stayed where she was, jumpy and looking up at every noise. The normal business of the tankshop went on around her — Nax sitting down beside her with a sidelong look, Spin branching himself into his terminal with his earphones turned up so high she could hear a tinny rhythmic whisper, Java frowning at her and saying, 'Wait, I thought Dion said y—' before she caught Nax's eye, shrugged, and went to get a P&V shake . . .

Why am I still here, she thought, in front of my terminal? I should be in Dion's cube, waiting for Rick to wake up. Her heartbeat was pounding in her ears like a call to arms.

She couldn't sit still. She entered something meaningless just to do something with her hands, and erased it immediately. Rick was in Dion's cube, spread out on his bed like a dead body, and she couldn't get the image out of her head.

And her interface seemed normal now, but if she looked up the Asterion program it might talk to her again, it might —

Do you want to know about your father, Ario?

She shut her eyes, but she could still see the words, superimposed on that picture of Rick. Somehow the two things seemed to go together.

She stood up, pushing her block back so that it scraped on the floor and everyone looked round at her. She didn't care. She said, 'Dion? How long's it going to take?'

When he narrowed his eyes she realised that he might not have explained to anyone else what was going on, but she didn't care. He sniffed loudly, rubbed his nose with the back of his hand for longer than he needed to, and then suddenly stood up, took her by the arm and steered her out into the corridor. When the door had slid closed behind them he said, quietly, 'Ario, look, hold it together, OK?'

'I'm fine. How long's it going to take? How soon will we know if you've accidentally killed him?'

'He's not going to *die*, Ario.' He took a deep breath with his shoulders hunched over, his hands pushed deep into his pockets. 'I need you to be on it, OK? I need you to be on top of your game. Don't lose it now.' He paused, and looked into her eyes, but Ario forced her gaze to stay blank and hostile, and he sighed out the breath he'd taken. 'Not long now. I put a few amphetamines in the mix, so once the downers have worn off he should be raring to go.'

She flinched, trying not to think about what that kind of cocktail would do to a brain — but then, that was the point, wasn't it? Wipe him out, rewrite him . . . and as long as he was alive and conscious, what did it matter if he was someone new?

She didn't say anything aloud, but it was as if Dion heard it, anyway. He spat air sharply through his teeth — she felt the faintest flick of saliva on her cheek — and said, '*Ario*. Are you listening to me or what? We have to beat Asterion. That's all that matters. You're with me on that one, right? We're *on the same side*. So don't get all flouncy and — I mean, don't get —'

'Flouncy?' She almost smiled; *would* have smiled, a week ago . . . 'Gag off, Dion.'

'Look . . .' He ran his hand over his head, screwing his face up. For a second she almost felt sorry for him. 'You're not doing yourself any favours, letting this go round and round in your head. Why don't you go and sort yourself out? Have a drink, have a P&V bar, have a shower, get a change of clothes, have a sleep. When he's ready I'll come and find you.'

They looked at each other, and Ario realised he was right — about that, anyway. She didn't say anything, but she turned on her heel and walked towards her cube, making an effort not to pause as she went past Dion's. She was sure he was watching her, but when she shot a glance over her shoulder he was gone, and there was only the door to the tank-shop hall slowly buzzing shut.

She stood in front of her comms panel, and wondered if she could muster the strength to press her hand against it. The nervous energy had burnt away, and now she was swaying a little. Her head was too heavy for the rest of her.

There was a long hum from the door to her left. She heard it before she knew what it meant; then she swung round, a

sick scared feeling in the pit of her stomach, and stood staring into Dion's cube.

Rick was in the doorway.

She stood still, frozen, waiting for him to say something.
When he speaks, she thought, it'll be meaningless, just
slurred syllables . . . Look at him, look at his *eyes*, it's gone
wrong, he's brain-dead —

He said, 'I think I'm ready.'

She felt relief like a breath of clean air, filling her lungs in
a great rush: he could talk, he was lucid, that was something
. . . 'You — you're — how do you feel?' she said.

He nodded. 'Good.' His voice was very flat — just matter
of fact, Ario said to herself, just focused on the job, not
damaged . . . but his eyes were — his eyes, there was definitely something different about his —

'Do you know who I am?' she said, in a rush. 'Do you
remember everything? Are you sure you're feeling OK —?'

'Yes,' he said. 'Well. I don't remember how I got here. But
you're Ario. You're a Cheat. You and Dion want me to beat
the Asterion program.'

'And —?' But she didn't know what she wanted to ask. And
do you remember telling me you were afraid? And do you
remember me holding your hand?

'Dion told me we didn't have much time,' he said. 'I want
to get into the iTank, check it'll let me into the Maze . . .'

''Course you do,' Ario said, and swallowed the knot of
hurt that lodged in her throat. But he hadn't waited for her
answer; he'd already moved away. She watched him go,

wondering . . . There was something different — something really, *profoundly* different — about him, about his gaze, the way he moved. But what was it? He raised his hand and put it precisely in the middle of the comms panel, the gesture swift and confident, and as he waited for the door to open she thought she understood. He wasn't in pain, any more. He was moving as if he'd never been injured . . .

It should have been a good thing. It *was* a good thing. But —

She shook her head, as though the thought were a drop of water in her ear, and followed him back into the tankshop.

She'd never seen him walk into the middle of a room, or to where the light was strongest; but this time he crossed the empty space towards Dion's terminal without flinching, as if the floor belonged to him. There was a dip in the noise level, as a few people noticed him and glanced at him curiously, as if they'd clocked the difference in the way he moved; but after a few seconds they went back to work. The only person who stayed still, looking up at him, was Dion.

'You made it,' he said. 'How do you feel?'

'Good.'

'Excellent,' Dion said, the corner of his mouth pulling up into a smile that was more quizzical than amused. He tilted his head and looked past Rick to Ario, his eyes glinting. 'Hey, babe,' he said, 'he made it. I knew he would . . . Plan A still on track. Let's go and have a council of war.' He stood up, held out his hand and beckoned Rick through into the gametank hall.

Ario clenched her jaw. Lia was staring at her, with an odd, hostile expression on her face. Of course, she thought, they don't know what's going on . . . For a moment she had the urge to turn on her heel, go back to her cube and bury herself in her bedbag. She looked away, focusing on the terminal next to Lia so that she didn't have to meet her eyes.

It was Spin's. He was nodding along to the rhythm of his earphones, glaring at his flatscreen. He never looked like that except when he was working; when he sensed Ario's gaze the frown slipped off his face and he smiled, raising his hand in a silent salutation. He tilted his head at his screen, quirking an eyebrow: *I'm working really hard*, it said, *but I'm not getting anywhere* . . .

Ario thought: Asterion knows his name. It knows where we are. All of us.

Any moment now it could decide to tell Crater — and then they'll come for us. For Spin, for me, for Rick, for Dion and Nax and Java and Lia . . .

She didn't acknowledge Spin's wave. She hurried past the terminals to the door to the tankfloor.

Dion was kneeling on the floor, branching a terminal to the iTank. Rick was warming up, moving through the slow-fight form so fast it looked like half of a real fight, as though he was winning against someone invisible. It made Ario think of the night the generators had gone down, when she'd found him there in the dark. She forced herself to smile at Dion. 'OK,' she said. 'What do you need?'

'Have you set up your cheats?'

'Yes. Everything I can think of. Everything I wrote for Pir, plus a few I was just playing around with before . . . Infinite health, a speed code, various little macros that you probably don't want me to go into detail with . . .' She shrugged, although it took an effort. 'How about you?'

'That sounds good. I've boosted his weapons, so he should deal a lot of damage.' Dion gave her a wide grin. 'Don't see how he can lose, with infinite health and major weaponry . . .'

He went back to his cable, and the grin dropped off his face as if it had never been there. Ario looked down at him, rocked by a wave of unease. 'Nor do I,' she said. 'But Pir did.'

Dion stiffened. He finished what he was doing with a last precise movement that was the opposite of a flourish; then he stood up, wiping his hands on his hair.

'It's OK,' Rick said. 'I'm not going to lose. I can't.'

'That's the drugs talking,' Ario said, too sharply. She didn't look at him.

'Yes, it is. But it's true, all the same.'

'It might be, actually,' Dion said, without emphasis. 'There was a lot of performance-enhancing stuff in with what I gave him.'

Ario didn't answer. She sat down and leant forward, looking at the terminal. She wanted to have something to do, but Dion had set everything up and all she had to do was log on, access her codes, check that they were set up to run on the trigger-word . . . and all of that was so familiar it was automatic. This is it, then, she thought. She felt strange, empty and fragile at the same time, like a glass bottle.

'You ready, Ario?' A pause. 'Ario. Wake up.'

'Sorry.' She dug a fingertip into the space between her eyes and turned away from the screen. This has to happen, she thought. We do have to beat Asterion, somehow. But I have a bad feeling about it.

'Are we ready to go or what?' Rick said, from the shadows. When he stepped into the light there was already sweat gleaming on his forehead, but he was breathing easily.

'Try logging into the Maze,' Dion said. 'That'll be the moment of truth. After that —' he bit his thumb, tearing at the nail with his front teeth. 'After that, you should be fine. I've added in a program which'll stop you getting barred, just for the time you're in there before you log out.' He flashed a glance at Ario, raising one shoulder. 'You know, the one I was working on . . . ? Not much use in the long term, because they can bar you as soon as you quit, but in this case I think it's coming into its own. Pity I couldn't write a cheat that got someone who's been barred *into* the . . . Anyway. With the cheats we've got . . . we can't see how you could lose. Can we, Ario?'

She shook her head. *Pir did*, her brain screamed, but she kept her mouth shut.

'Great,' Rick said. 'OK, then. Let's go.'

He gave them a jaunty, one-fingered wave, and logged in to the iTank. The door slid open to let him in, and the silvery white of its skin turned opalescent, rippling like a layer of petrol over milk. Then it shut, gleaming like a cocoon.

Dion stood beside Ario. Together they watched the flatscreen, waiting. The space was dark, filled with shooting stars, while it read Rick's body. Then he was there, in the middle of the nothingness, and the stars flew past him.

Good evening. What would you like to do? the iTank said to Rick.

'Enter the Maze, please,' he said, and there was no uncertainty in his voice, not even a flicker.

Everything is clear. Everything is easy.

The loading space bursts into existence around him, and it's like coming home. Gods, he's missed this so much. He's amazed by the way everything fits together: the light, the air, his hands . . . Nothing hurts. Nothing scares him. Nothing is impossible.

Welcome to the Maze.

Dion must have set everything up, because the tank doesn't ask him where he wants to go. Instead it flashes up the warning: **You are about to enter the Roots of the Maze. If you die in the Roots, your account will be closed. Are you sure you wish to proceed?**

'Yes.' The sound of his own voice surprises him: the huskiness has gone, as though his lungs and voice box are working better than before. It's the absence of pain, he thinks. Whatever Dion gave me, it must have been pretty strong . . . But it doesn't bother him. He feels as if nothing can go wrong ever again. It doesn't even matter that he can't remember anything — that, if he thinks about it, there's only blankness before the tankshop, a fog as thick as a brick wall. He's reborn.

Then he's in the Roots.

He hears himself laugh, feels himself looking round, open-mouthed with pleasure. They've loaded the Great Staircase, the main entrance to the Roots, and it coils round and round beneath him like a dark shell; and it's beautiful, smelling of old stone and dust. He knows the iTank is reading his mind, adding details just for him, but that doesn't take away the magic. Oh, I *missed* this, he thinks. Even the demo isn't like this. This has got danger lurking round the corner, the promise of glory at the end of it. Thank you.

No matter what happens tonight, I'm glad.

Even if it's the drugs talking.

Which it probably is.

The thought makes him grin and roll his shoulders. It occurs to him that he should activate the cheat codes, but he hesitates. It would be good to do it alone. He's never used cheats; he doesn't see why he should start now.

Except that this time he might die if he didn't. *Properly* die. Like Pir. Really. In real life.

He laughs, and then forces a stern look into his face, as though there's someone in front of him who disapproves. Come to think of it, Dion and Ario are watching; it's probably better not to act like an idiot.

Plus, I have to concentrate. If I get this wrong I might die. In actual really truly *life*.

OK. Fair enough. Good point. He doesn't exactly believe he needs the cheats, but the drugs haven't made him *stupid*. He says, 'Helios,' — that was what Dion said, right? — and the world flickers very slightly, imperceptibly resetting itself. Infinite health, infinite damage on his weapons . . . What else did they say? It doesn't matter. He's invincible. He'd be invincible even without the cheats. But there's no point being cocky.

He starts to run.

It's *easy*.

He could have spun it out longer. He doesn't take the easiest route, or the most direct route, but all the same it goes too quickly. Vaguely he registers Ario telling him to get a move on, but he's concentrating and he can block it out. *Months* he's been exiled from the Maze, and now he can't get enough of it. The delight of moving freely, flipping, tumbling . . . He knows that Dion's drugs haven't erased the scars, only numbed his nerves, but he can't help feeling healed, whole again, after so long. A new life. Gods, it feels good not to be me any more . . .

He goes deeper and deeper. For a while he doesn't even bother to choose a portal; he takes random directions, not looking at the map.

The last time I was in the Roots, he thinks, I was —

But there's nothing. He knows there's a memory missing, but he can't get to it. For a split second he feels a spark of fear — my *brain*, he thinks, what's happened to me? — but he quenches it. Maybe it will come back; maybe it won't. I'm in the Roots, and that's what matters.

And now —

He's fighting sucker bats, with only half his mind on the job: with infinite health and a heavy-duty sword it's too easy to be interesting. It reminds him of —

What?

I've done this before. I wish I could *remember* . . .

The smell of the bat-blood is pungent, chemical, like petrol, and it mixes with the faint scent of his own sweat. It nudges at his memory. For a second he sees himself: a younger version, exhausted, desperate, almost dead on his feet, fighting sucker bats because —

When? What was I doing? *Why* was I —?

He stops fighting, drops his arms to his sides. A bat flies in and bites — he feels it like a pinch on his upper arm, irritating but not painful — and his health bar shrinks and regenerates immediately. The bat-bites multiply, encouraged by his stillness. It's like standing in a shower.

He shuts his eyes and concentrates until he can sense the way his brain has changed. There's the great blank that cuts off half his mind . . . He frowns, pressing his consciousness against it, but it's like a wall that goes on and on and up and up for ever. There's no way past it. Everything that was there is locked away. It's still there, he tells himself, I haven't lost it, I just can't access the files . . . but in the end that's the same thing, isn't it?

And he can sense his own feelings rising behind the barrier in his head. Whatever happened then, it makes his heart turn over . . . something terrible, he did something terrible . . . but he can't get to it, can't get a grip on it . . . I was — there was — someone I loved — something important —

No good.

He flails suddenly with his sword, splashing bat-blood over the floor. It smells the same as it used to, but stronger, with a deeper note in it — something biological, like meat.

Stop thinking. It doesn't do any good. Live on your reflexes.

But suddenly he wants to get on with it. Once he's taken down Asterion he'll be able to carry on playing properly. That's what he's here to do — once Asterion is beaten, and dealt with, and not dangerous any more — once Dion and Ario are pleased with him . . . He can spend the rest of his life in the Maze, if he wants. He can gamerun for money, he can be the best.

Forget about your missing memories, he thinks, and cracks a grin.

He spins, splashing bat-blood everywhere — he feels it spurt across his face, tastes something smoky, like tar — and weaves his weapons in a complex knot until the cloud of bats has disappeared and the last lonely survivor flaps away, forlorn.

He doesn't know how long he's been in the Roots, but unexpectedly he thinks of Ario and Dion, glued to the terminal, willing him onwards. The euphoria has faded, and he's tired and damp with sweat. He's wasting time.

He says, 'Map, please,' and squints up at it. He doesn't need to squint, but he does it anyway, automatically; when he catches himself he blinks and smoothes his face out, feeling the looseness where his scars used to tug painfully. He still *has* scars, of course; they just don't hurt. Thank you, Dion.

Scars from — when he — wait, I don't even know —
Stop it.

He's close. The nearest portal is beyond a corridor of traps, protected by a red cloud of enemies. OK.

'Right, then,' he said, for Ario and Dion's benefit. 'Enough mucking around. Let's get down to business.'

About time, Ario says.

He takes the corridor that leads to the portal.

He's fighting. He's dodging and whirling and parrying in a kind of trance, alert and serene at the same time. He knows he's untouchable. He fits into the fight like a cog in a mechanism. Every part of him is in the right place, even his mind. He's attacking a wyrm's nest. They slide over each other, fluid and malevolent, spitting poison, and he loves them for it. He takes them out one by one, dodging the last spurts of venom, every movement precise, perfect to a micro-em.

Until at last he's alone, and still.

His lungs open and shut like wings. His sweat drips on to the floor, and he thinks he can see each tiny sphere hit the ground and change shape, the coronet of moisture it throws up. His skin tingles. Each nerve is sensitive, crawling with electricity.

The portal is in front of him, at the end of the corridor.

He walks forward and runs his hand over the surface of the stone. There's some kind of carving, invisible, bumping under his fingers as he moves them. What does it say? he wonders. It's like a dream: the iTank responds to the thought, deepening the shadows until he can just see the shapes. *Nothing is impossible*, it says. He smiles, but the words set off an echo in his brain, ringing fainter and fainter until it dies. A breath of cold air plays on the back of his neck, drying the moisture. Something — one of his lost memories —

He lets his hand drop, and walks back down the corridor so that he can make a decent run-up.

Gods, he hates portals. He really, *really* hates portals. Fifty per cent of Crater's personal injury litigation is something to do with portals, and it's not surpr—

How do I know that? he thinks.

For a moment he wants to give up, log out, go and sit somewhere on his own and smash his consciousness against that wall of — of *forgetting* — until something gives. Whatever he's lost, it's important — really, *really* important . . .

No.

I have to do this. I have to defeat Asterion.

He takes a deep breath, rolls his shoulders, and puts his forearms up to protect his face. He can't help shutting his eyes, as if that'll help.

Then he runs at the wall, as fast as he can.

Five steps, six, seven, eight — something flashes through his eyelids and he falters, curses himself, twists sideways to shield his head from the impact —

But nothing comes. Nothing touches him. And when he opens his eyes, very slowly, there's soft pale light, like daylight, and he's not in the Roots any more.

The loading space. Is it? It looks the same . . . A pale, smooth-floored room, old-fashioned and tranquil, full of daylight.

But it sets off another itch in his mind, stronger this time, and instinctively he rolls his head on his neck as though he can ease it that way. I've been here before, and not just tonight, when I logged in. Something happened to me here. Yes, I've been here before, but I can't remember wh— Stop it. *Concentrate*, he tells himself. He straightens up and looks round, forcing himself to look at the details.

A rain of dust, falling softly in a shaft of sunlight. The grain of the wood, glinting as though it's been polished with gold. A scroll of paint drooping away from the wall, as brittle as a dead leaf. The sheen of grime that clings to the windows, the pale ridged-cloud sky beyond . . . The air feels thinner here, as if it's high up.

And a man, standing quietly at the far end of the room. He looks up and inclines his head in a strange, archaic gesture.

'Welcome,' he says.

'Who are you?'

The man smiles. There's something strange about him: he's good-looking, but his eyes are . . . weird. Too *old*, Rick thinks. Older than his face. 'Think of me as . . . the endgame.'

'*You're* the last boss fight?' He should have asked Ario to tell him what to expect. They'd been so desperate to send him in that they hadn't even warned him . . .

'Yes.' The smile fades, but the eyes are steady and amused, enjoying Rick's confusion. 'Don't look like much, do I? But appearances can be deceptive.'

'I . . .' Rick shrugs. He knows that there's no correlation between size and difficulty, in a fight; he knows that sometimes the most innocuous enemies are the hardest to beat. And the last boss fight is almost always a person, not a monster . . . but all the same — this guy? He looks delicate. He looks as if one of Rick's cheat-enhanced weapons could kill him before he could blink . . . '*You*'re Asterion?' he asks, even though he knows the answer. 'Are you sure?'

Of course, he *has* to be Asterion, because a normal NPC would only blink and say, 'Sorry, I'm not certain I understand you. But as I was saying, your mission is . . .' or words to that effect. And this man shifts his weight, leaning back on his heels as if Rick's surprised him. 'Asterion?' he says. 'Where did you get that name from?'

'Oh — I — Ari—' He bites his tongue, but it's too late.

'Ario? Then where did *she* . . . ? Never mind. So you know Ario, do you? Oh — wait — I *see*. She realised that hacking wasn't going to work, so she sent you . . .' There was a pause, and he frowned. 'But — what does she want you to do? Doesn't she realise —?'

'I'm going to beat you,' Rick says. 'Nothing is impossible, right? Yes, Ario sent me. And she's loaded me up with every cheat you can think of, and this time you're going to *lose*.'

The man's frown deepens, and he moves his lips, repeating Rick's words to himself; then his face goes determinedly neutral as though he's determined not to give away what he's thinking. He nods. 'Ah,' he says. 'I understand now. Well, unluckily for you, *you*'re going to lose. The way Pir did. She thought she could beat me too.'

'I'm better than she is,' Rick says, and knows it's true. Especially now.

'Really,' Asterion says, and that veiled look is still in his eyes. 'Well, in that case maybe you'll last longer than her.'

They stare at each other. Somewhere deep in Rick's brain something flares like a flame. It isn't anger, although that's there too; it's something much more elusive, something that dies as soon as he turns his mind's eye on it.

'You didn't know Pir, did you? Or at least she didn't know *you*. But then she was really only interested in Ario . . . There's a whole quest in the Winter Continent based on Ario, you know. Pretty little thing. Is she that good-looking in real life? Or maybe you've never actually seen her . . . How do you fit in?'

The tone was casual — conversational — but Rick could feel the edge to it, the little scrape of sharpness in every word. *Pretty little thing . . .* His hackles rise, and he takes a deep breath. He's trying to throw me off-balance, he thinks. But it won't work. If I know what he's trying to do, he won't get to me.

'So. Are you ready?'

He nods, takes a long slow breath and adjusts his stance. In his head he runs through the first step of the slow-fight form, feeling the muscles in his body relaxing as he does it. He doesn't remember learning it; it's funny, how his body remembers more than his brain.

He watches the man's eyes, waiting for the subtle shift that always comes a split second before a move; but his gaze is straight, almost dreamy. His irises are bigger than they ought to be and the colour is watery, hypnotic. 'Then . . .' he says, and motions to the room around them.

He's trying to distract me, Rick thinks. But he can't help turning his head to follow the arc of the gesture; and then he sees what's happening.

The room is filling with mist. It isn't coming from anywhere specific: it's more as if the contours of everything are dissolving. Rick blinks — it's a trick, *concentrate* — but the man takes a step back, holding his hands up as if in mocking reassurance. 'It's all right. Wait.'

Rick isn't stupid enough to trust him, but the fog gets thicker and thicker until the room has gone entirely and there's nothing, not even a floor. Rick and the man are alone in a swirl of white, the core of an erased world.

'And now,' he says. 'No one can see us. Or hear us.'

He's wrong — Ario and Dion can still hear what's going on, because of the mic — but they'll be watching a blank screen, straining their ears for every sound. Rick's still confident, still relaxed — but now there's a prickle of tension like heat at the back of his neck, not quite strong enough to qualify as unease. He imagines them watching a white screen, waiting, and wishes he hadn't.

'It's yours,' Asterion says, and smiles, sweeping a hand out into the fog. 'A blank page. You can ask for anything you want. To make it a fair fight.'

'I —' He can't think of anything.

'Anything. Weapons. Environment. Play to your strengths.'

He shakes his head. Why? Why offer him whatever he wants? It doesn't make sense. To make it more humiliating when he loses? Or is it something to do with — with what happens *after* he loses?

But I won't lose. I've got all the cheats I want.

And yet . . . he's basically offering me *more* cheats . . .

Suddenly something comes to him, and he says, 'Can I —
what about people —?'

'Certainly. You want allies. Why not?'

'No, I want — I'd like Ario —'

'Of course.' He raises his hand, like a conjuror; then he
pauses. 'You do mean the NPC Ario? I can't actually summon
up anyone from *real life*, you understand.' He quirks his
mouth downwards, in a parody of sympathy. 'And . . . well,
she comes from Pir's mind, you see. If Pir didn't know who
you were, NPC-Ario won't, either. You might have to explain
to her. But if you still want —'

'No.' No. It didn't matter, anyway. It was stupid — just
because he wanted someone there, someone friendly . . . He
can win this fight without Ario — without *anyone*. He's on his
own with this man, and that suits him fine.

'As you please.'

'I'll have — a sword and dagger, please.'

'How traditional.'

'And —' But he doesn't have any memories of places,
except the tankshop; and he doesn't want to fight there, in
the darkness and grime and the hum of the generators. 'And
this . . .' He looks round. 'Anything but fog.'

Asterion smiles and clicks his fingers, spinning on his heel.
And they're in —

A space as big as the heart of the world. There *are* walls
— somehow Rick knows that — but they're too far away to
see. Everything is grey, filled with strange rainbow-lustred
light, like the sheen of oil on water. And in front of him
there's a huge — staircase? fountain? — coiling around itself

270

like the helix of DNA, the steps too high for a giant. The sight of it makes his ears ring. He looks up but there's only infinite space, and he swallows, feeling giddy. What a place . . . it sends electricity down his spine, itching in the back of his head. I've been here before, he thinks. I have. I *have* been here before. But —

'If you'd prefer somewhere else —'

'No,' he says. 'This is . . . OK.'

'Good.' For the first time there's something different in his tone: the slightest, cleverly covered trace of surprise. 'Well . . . shall we?'

And then he turns to meet Rick's eyes, and even though they're just looking at each other the fight has already begun.

It's a long time before either of them moves. Rick waits for as long as he can bear, feeling the emptiness wait with him. But he's human and mortal and he can't outstare a computer program. So he feints, dodging to one side and back again just to see the reaction.

Nothing. Stillness. Only the man's eyes move.

This time he attacks for real.

His blades connect with empty air, and he has to drop and roll back to his feet, anticipating the counter-attack. And this time it comes, a low sharp strike that misses by micro-ems and sends a breath of air across Rick's skin. Asterion's unarmed but he's fast; somehow Rick knows that even weaponless he could do a lot of damage. Infinite health, Rick says to himself, remember? Relax, you have *infinite health*.

But it's easier now the psychological bit's over: now it's just about skill, and speed, and reach. They circle each other, looking for an opening. Every time Rick moves Asterion reacts, keeping just out of reach, sliding away as untouchable as a ghost; but Rick's good too, and he dodges Asterion's attacks and throws them straight back at him. One hit from my sword, he thinks, and it should be over. Or maybe two.

He launches into a flurry of blows, whirling and stabbing, feinting and ducking. Nothing connects, but he can sense Asterion picking up the pace, meeting him halfway. Rick's dagger almost connects — Asterion parries, knocking his wrist away — and they're back a few ems from each other, untouched. Rick's breathing hard, and when he blinks his eyes sting from the sweat on his eyelashes. But he's starting to see how Asterion moves. If I can anticipate, he thinks, then I can get to him.

But he's thinking too much, and Asterion lunges unexpectedly, so that Rick has to jump backwards, off-balance. Suddenly he sees that there are sparks between his fingers, flickers of blue like St Elmo's fire. He falters for a split second and regains his concentration, but it's too late; he's left himself open, undefended, and he feels Asterion's touch graze his elbow. It makes his nerves flare up, like an electric shock, sending a tingle right to the top of his skull. He reels back, gasping for breath, and stands still, fighting to keep his focus.

For the first time, he wonders if he might lose.

'I'm sorry, did I hurt you?'

He shakes his head. 'You wish.' Wow, great repartee, his brain says. You sound like such a hero . . . He forces himself to breathe. So he hit me. it's not a big deal. I have infinite health. And it could have been —

It could have been worse —

I was off-balance — he could have got closer than he did — why didn't he —?

It doesn't matter. He doesn't have time to think now. He throws himself into the fight. The space spins round his head, the floor jumps under his feet: for a few moments it's as if he's the only still point while the world goes wild around him. He's the centre, the eye of the storm. Sweat splatters around him like rain but he can't feel his own fatigue. He's so hot that he's come out the other side, and shivers run over his skin. His heart is out of control. But if he can just *get* to Asterion — just one touch — just — come *on* —

He feints, drops for a low spinning kick, hears his dagger blade scrape across the floor as he misjudges the move, rolls and shoves off his other foot, gasping for breath. He's not thinking any more: everything is instinct, a struggle for speed and precision that's almost too much for him. Asterion whirls to face him, reaches out —

Rick blocks. He's going to dodge again — he's left himself open, they're face-to-face, both their defences down —

He spins inward, right into Asterion's embrace, dropping his sword.

And they're eye to eye, frozen, and Rick's dagger blade is at Asterion's throat, glinting.

* * *

He's done it. He's won. He takes a deep breath, looking into those uncanny eyes, a few micro-ems from his own. He can smell something like — like clean clothes, or bread, or green tea, something healthy . . . And Asterion's body is warm, the flesh of his shoulder solid under Rick's hand.

He's shaking. Now he can feel the ache in his muscles, the sweat seeping out of every pore, the giddiness as though his skull is heavier than it should be. I've done it. I've won. I've done it . . . The thought goes round and round in his head, as if all the other available words have been erased by exhaustion. He wants to lie down flat on the floor and go to sleep. He'll just kill Asterion, and then everything will be over. He tenses his wrist, ready to strike. He ought to enjoy this.

Those eyes. He stares into them, fascinated.

Asterion smiles at him. 'What's the matter?'

He shakes his head, trying to clear it. Don't let go your grip. Don't let your dagger drop. Don't wait too long before you kill an enemy. That's Bondvillain Syndrome and it's a very bad idea . . .

'Well done,' Asterion says. 'You've won.' He cocks his head, a spark of mockery in his eyes. 'Or nearly. Better make sure of it while you can. It'd be sad if something happened to stop you . . .'

He's right. Rick has to stop himself nodding. This is stupid, he thinks. He's *right*. But why is he saying it? I should just kill him. Then it'll be over. Ario will be pleased with me . . .

Ario. Yes. The thought of her is like an anchor, tying him to reality. Do it for Ario.

I have to kill him.

He adjusts his stance, takes a deep breath, and —

Those eyes. *I've seen them before.*

He clenches his hand on the hilt of the dagger and grips Asterion's shoulder as hard as he can. Asterion blinks, as though it hurts. 'Go on,' he says. 'You know you want to.'

Yes. I do want to. Yes. But —

I can't.

I *know* him. He's — *important*.

But if I don't kill him, he'll kill me. He'll take my mind and — I have to —

There's a shimmer of memory behind the curtain in his brain; a silent note that rings out like an alarm bell, filling his head, dragging him out of a dream —

I know him.

He shivers. Then, very slowly, he takes his hand away from Asterion's shoulder, lowers his dagger and steps backwards. There's silence, such a deep silence that he feels as if his heart has stopped. After a long time he drops his dagger, throwing it sideways. It clatters and skids along the floor, like something trivial.

'What are you doing?'

'I can't,' he says. 'I — I know it's stupid, I'm sorry, I'm — gods, Ario, I — sorry —' He raises his voice, desperate for her to hear, understand . . .

'You can't give up now. You had me at your mercy!'

He shakes his head. What has he done? He'd won, he'd *done* it, and now — gods, he's such an idiot, he's going to die, just because he couldn't bring himself to kill a — an *NPC*, for gods' sake —

'Kill me.' Asterion takes a step towards him and laughs as Rick stumbles backwards. 'Come on. What's the matter? You're not scared, are you?'

'I can't. I just — I can't.' He goes on shaking his head, despising himself. 'You — I think I know you, I think — somehow — I don't *want* to kill you . . . You're —' He stops. If only he understood it himself: but he doesn't have a clue. Just a feeling in his gut, just his body refusing to obey him . . .

'You have to kill me.' He raises his voice, reaches out for Rick as though he *wants* —

He *does*, Rick thinks, and the new thought makes him frown. A trickle of sweat runs down between his eyebrows. Wait. He *wants* me to kill him —

And in a flash, like an icy gust of air, he understands.

It's not losing that means he can kill me.

It's *winning*.

He backs away. He's so tired and confused that he could cry. 'No,' he says. 'No.'

There's a long, long pause. They're very small, dwarfed by the space, and neither of them moves.

Then Asterion says, '*Rick?*'

'Yes,' he says.

And a memory flashes, flares for a moment and then dies almost to nothingness like an ember: but it's enough.

Asterion is Daedalus. Daed, his father. His father, Daed.

*   *   *

It's Daed, Rick thinks, the words as clear and cold as a block of ice in his brain. Daed who died. Who went into the Maze, who left me . . .

He presses his forearm against his eyes, breathing deeply, and moisture rolls down his cheeks and drips off his chin. He doesn't even know if he's crying.

'Rick. Rick, you — what are you *doing* here — how did you —? I barred you, your brainprint is — you've changed your brainprint, I didn't recognise you, gods, *gods*, Rick, I —'

He cares, Rick thought, and heard a laugh splutter out of himself, like vomit. He really cares about me. He can hardly say my name.

'What did you think you were *doing*?'

He shakes his head. He's still laughing, and it hurts. 'We wanted . . . Ario wanted . . . we had to stop you. She tried to hack you and — well, I guess you know that. So they asked me to fight you.'

'Dear gods.' Asterion — no, *Daed* — puts his hand against his forehead, pressing until his nails go white. 'How could they be so stupid?'

'I'm loaded with cheats. Infinite health, amazing weapons . . . We thought if I won —'

'But in fact, if you win, that triggers the —' He hesitates, a wry tension at the corner of his mouth. 'The assimilation process.'

'And the fight's designed to let me win, isn't it? I knew — the way you fought, it wasn't quite right . . . You want me to win —'

'Not now — not *you*, Rick — I wouldn't —'

He ignores what Daed's said. 'Because you don't want me to lose. If I lose, I can walk away. But if I win, you steal my mind . . .' He hears what he's said, and the last dregs of laughter evaporate.

If I win, he steals my mind. So I can't win. If I win I lose. But if I lose — he wins . . .

Daed smiles at him faintly. 'You see? I'm cleverer than you thought. Just give up, Rick. In fact —' he pauses, and the smile dies. 'Ah. You've got a cheat that stops me barring you. Very snazzy. You'd better log out, then.'

And if I log out, then you'll bar me straight away and I'll never get back into the Maze. And you'll go on stealing people — *eating* them — and there'll be nothing we can do . . .

But he's right, Rick says to himself. I don't have any option. I can hardly stay here for the rest of my —

A current jumps in his head, like a short circuit.

He inhales slowly, looking round at the huge rain-lit space, taking it in. To stay here for the rest of his life, with Daed . . . He clenches his jaw, feeling sick. It's not possible. He's human, for gods' sake, he'd die, eventually. But if it might work — if it were the only way . . .

Not to win, not to lose.

Daed can't kill me, because I've got infinite health. And the fight's designed not to *let* me lose. And he can't throw me out, because of Dion's cheat.

So if I don't log out . . . if I don't fight . . .

He wraps his arms around his chest, squeezing, as though that could stop him feeling anything. I can't do this — stay

278

here, eternally — it's like a curse, even if it worked, it would be — I *can't* —

'I'm not fighting you, Daed,' he says. 'I get it. I'm not going to win. I *can't* win. But I'm not going to lose, either.'

Daed stares at him. 'Yes, you will. Because this time I'll *want* to beat you. And you're only human, Rick. You'll get tired. I can go on fighting for ever.'

'I've got infinite health, Daed. I could lie on the floor and let you hit me and I still wouldn't die . . . And —' It's just a hunch, but he says it slowly, pretending that he's sure. 'The odds are all in my favour, aren't they? No one was meant to lose. It must be pretty difficult for you to win this fight. If not . . . impossible.'

Yes. He's got it right. He sees the truth in Daed's eyes before he turns his head away sharply.

'Just log out,' Daed says. 'You can't stay here indefinitely.'

'Yes,' he says, 'I can.'

Daed turns back to him, and suddenly he reaches out to him, as though he wants to take Rick's hand, as if the space between them is only imaginary. Rick looks at that hand — its thin, blunt fingers familiar, tugging at his memory — and stays where he is, his stomach knotting tighter and tighter. 'You'll change your mind.'

He doesn't answer.

'Please, Rick. Just log out.'

'You know this is madness.'

'Rick . . . *please*.'

'Everything I've done, I've done it for you.'

279

He looks up, meeting Daed's eyes again, and for a second he thinks he knows what it will be like to spend eternity here, with the man he loves and hates most in the world.

Then he sits down, every muscle aching, and draws his knees up to his chin. He bows his head and shuts his eyes. The darkness is comforting, but all around him there's the unforgiving silence of the space, the infinitesimal murmur of Daed's breathing.

He says, 'I'm staying.'

26

Rick had been in the Roots for hours. Dion had gone to get P&V shakes for them both; Ario was pacing in front of the terminal, trying to ease the tension in her legs. She kept an eye on the screen, but it was all the same: traps, monsters, endless staircases leading him deeper and deeper. It was only a few minutes ago that he'd even bothered to look at a map. She'd got tired of shouting at him, telling him to hurry: he was ignoring her, taking his time, and there was nothing they could do.

Dion came in with a cup in either hand. He plonked one down on the desk and started to slurp brown sludge from the other. The noise of it made Ario want to scream.

'How's it going?'

She flicked a finger at the screen. 'He's fighting wyrms.'

'And?'

'What do you think? He's got infinite health. It's just a question of how long it'll take him.'

'So,' Dion said, sticking his finger into the cup and stirring, 'how long is it taking him?'

She shot another glance at the screen. 'Probably not much longer,' she said. She picked up her cup and looked at the gloop, trying to muster the determination to drink it. Dion stirred harder, his finger making little wet, soggy noises. She put it down again. 'He's near a portal,' she added, and brought up a map on the other side of the screen. 'He said he'd had enough of mucking about. I hope he meant it.'

Dion put his finger in his mouth and sucked noisily, grimacing. 'Well, should be soon, then.'

She didn't answer; there wasn't anything useful she could say. She wished she was on her own. The smell from the P&V shake was making her feel queasy. She reached out, picked it up and threw it into the bin next to the door. As it dropped, a thin tentacle of liquid uncurled and flicked across the wall.

'You'll want that later.'

She ignored him. Rick had finished off the last wyrm. He was dripping with sweat and breathing hard, but he was still holding himself like a gamerunner: poised, ready. He stood still, staring at the end of the corridor where the portal was.

'Go *on*, then!' Ario hissed at him 'It's about *time* . . .'

Dion came and stood beside her. She could smell the shake on his breath. He peered at the screen and then sat down slowly. 'This is it, then, babe,' he said.

'No kidding,' she said, and when he started to answer she held up her hand, cutting him off. 'Sshh. I want to concentrate.'

'We can't actually *do* anyth— never mind.'

They watched, leaning forward, as Rick took a few steps back down the corridor, and ran the portal. For a second he faltered, and Ario heard herself draw in her breath; but then there was a flash of golden filigree — the way it had shone for Pir, that night — and he was through.

He was in the loading space, opposite Asterion.

Beside her, Dion nodded, reached for his cup and took a huge mouthful of P&V sludge as though he was so cool he hadn't even been nervous. But when he tried to swallow he coughed and stood up, struggling for breath, his face red and screwed up with the effort of not spitting it everywhere. For the first time in hours Ario felt herself smile.

'Shut up, babesauce,' he said at last, hoarsely, and laughed.

'I didn't say anything.'

She caught his eye, and for a second they were friends again; but then he stiffened and swung back to look at the screen, frowning.

'What's the m—' she started to say, but he shook his head sharply. And somehow, belatedly, she heard her own name.

So you know Ario, do you?

Dion looked round at her, and put out his hand to take her by the wrist. 'It's OK, babe,' he said. 'It's only to be expected. It's a clever little program, it was bound to work out that —'

'It's fine,' she said, drawing her arm away. 'It doesn't matter. Rick's going to beat it, anyway.'

'Yep. Good.' But his eyes stayed on her face longer than they should, as though she hadn't been quite convincing. She took a step away and then walked to the wall, blindly, without knowing why she was doing it, except that she had to move.

The voices from the screen went on. She tried not to listen. It doesn't matter what they say, does it? The important thing is the fight . . . But Asterion said her name again, and no matter how hard she tried she couldn't block it out. **Pretty little thing. Is she that good-looking in real life?**

She'd had enough. She almost reached out to turn the volume down — but then at last Asterion's voice changed, deepening to something cleaner, less spiteful.

So, he said. **Are you ready?**

And the fog . . . Ario had known about the fog, but it made her feel uneasy to see it now, creeping inward from the corners of the room, rubbing out the reality of everything until it started to swirl around Rick and Asterion, erasing them. Their voices got fainter and fainter, as though the mist had got into their ears too. **You can ask for anything you want. To make it . . .** Asterion said, but the last words were too faint to make out.

Dion said, in a low voice, 'Relax. You knew this would happen, right? It's still going our way.'

'I don't like —' She swallowed. 'I don't like not being able to see it . . .'

He hunched his shoulders in a gesture that was half sympathetic, half irritated. They sat in silence, watching the fog fill the screen, saturating it with white until it was so bright they could hardly look at it. And what if Rick's mic — the one Dion had wired up — didn't work? She didn't think she could bear that, if it was nothing but silence, if the whole fight was inside that cloud . . .

She turned aside, not wanting Dion to hear her heart. She didn't know how afraid she was until she heard Rick's voice, as thin as a thread, but something to hold on to. 'Can I — what about people —?' he said. 'I want — I'd like Ario . . . no. I'll have a sword and dagger, please.'

'Sword and dagger'll be much more useful, anyway,' Dion said, and grinned up at her.

Rick said something under Dion's words, and she punched Dion on the arm, hard. 'Shut up, I want to *hear*.' But now there was only silence. She pressed her hands together in front of her face, as though she was praying. It went on so long she thought the mic had gone wrong — *knew* it had — and she was just about to say something. Then they heard Rick's breathing, the shuffle of his feet across the floor, and knew the fight had started.

27

Ario had never known anything so unbearable. Time skipped and stretched and played with them like a cat with a mouse, so that she didn't know how long had passed. Sometimes it felt like a second; sometimes she thought that if she got up to go to the loo her face in the mirror would be old. All the time she kept her eyes on the screen, because at least if it was white that meant Rick was still alive. She was so afraid of seeing it flash into that sickening technicolor anti-light that she almost thought, once or twice, that it had happened; but it was only her imagination.

Dion brought her another P&V shake. Then he sat down, tapping his feet and his fingers. From the way he moved — too loose, too energetic — Ario thought he was flying. But it didn't matter; the only thing that mattered was Rick. She got so used to the irregular sound of the fight, the slide and patter of footsteps, that it faded into the background. The whole world shrank to that blinding rectangle in front of her.

Until — silence —

Stillness. Only breathing. The fight was — someone was

. . . Somehow she knew it wasn't just a pause. She put her hands over her face, staring through her fingers at the screen. Please don't — *please* —

Rick's voice. She exhaled, limp with relief, before she'd registered what he said.

'I can't. I — I know it's stupid, I'm sorry, I'm — gods, Ario, I — sorry —'

Dion said, 'What? What's he doing?'

Rick's voice went on, taut, horrified. 'I can't. I just — I can't. You — I think I know you, I think — somehow — I don't *want* to kill you . . . You're —'

'What the — what's he playing at? He's not — Ario, tell me he's not *bottling* it —'

'I don't know!' she said, and her voice rang off the walls. 'Maybe he's remembered that he knew Asterion before, or . . . How am I supposed to know?'

'But even if he's recognised him — what does he mean, *he just can't*? The stupid little — oh, I can't *believe* —'

'Dion, would you just *shut up*? I want to hear what's going on —'

Rick laughed. It was such a strange sound — not amused, not afraid — that it shut them both up. Ario drew back from the screen, her stomach twisting with a dread that she didn't understand. Something was wrong. Something was horribly wrong. She remembered the way Asterion had talked to her, and a shiver went down her spine. For an instant she saw writing superimposed on the flatscreen: *Would you like to know about your father?*

When it cleared, Dion was holding on to her arm, gripping

her so hard she could feel his pulse. And Rick was talking, in the middle of a sentence. She tried to listen.

'The fight's designed to let me win, isn't it? I knew — the way you fought, it wasn't quite right . . . You want me to win.'

Everything went very quiet. The generators hummed and coughed a long way away.

'That can't be right,' Dion said, and his fingers spasmed. 'Can it? We can't have got it that wr—'

But it made sense.

'We just . . . I just assumed,' Ario said. 'I never saw Pir win. I thought she'd lost. I thought beating Asterion would work . . .' She should have been ashamed or horrified, but it was too late. She felt dead, heavy, like a stone.

'If I lose, I can walk away. But if I win, you steal my mind . . .'

There was a pause. Ario watched the screen, grateful for the way her mind had stopped working. She sensed Dion fidget next to her, but she didn't look at him.

'It's not the end of the world,' he said at last. 'If Rick logs out, we can start again, find some other way . . .' They both knew that they wouldn't find another way — but the lie sat between them, unchallenged.

Ario got up. Her joints ached. Whatever she looked at had a rectangle of black floating in front of it, like it had been censored. 'When he logs out tell him he did well,' she said. Rick was saying something else, but it was probably only the log-out command, wasn't it? She turned to go.

'Ario —'

There was something in Dion's voice that made her pause.

'I'm not fighting you, Daed,' Rick said. 'I get it. I'm not going to win. I can't win. But I'm not going to lose, either.'

She met Dion's eyes, and knew that she had the same expression on her own face. He murmured, 'What . . . ?' and it was as if she'd said it too. Together they turned to look at the screen, as if a flat page of nothing could tell them what was happening. There was no sound.

'I'm staying,' Rick said.

'He can't,' Ario said, after a long time. 'He can't just . . . *stay*.'

Dion was leaning back, his hands crawling over his knees and back like insects. 'Well . . . It does solve the problem,' he said, with a kind of deliberate lightness in his voice. 'I mean . . . he's got it right, hasn't he? If he wins, his mind gets sucked out. If he loses, he's lost. So if he wants to stop Asterion without getting headjunk—'

'Dion . . .' But she didn't know what to say. She turned to stare across the tankfloor at the iTank, half mesmerised by the colours that came and went in the silver. Rick was in there. He wanted to stay there for ever . . . She'd never see him again. She'd never tell him —

She spun round. 'He's not staying there, Dion. I don't care what you say. For a start —' she felt logic underneath her like solid ground, and her voice steadied — 'for a start, he couldn't. His body needs food and water. If he stayed in the Maze he'd die.'

'Eventually. But in the meantime . . .' Dion left the sentence open, as though he'd put something on the table and was waiting for her to pick it up.

She dug her hand into the back of her neck, pressing her fingers into the gap between her vertebrae. 'It wouldn't last, Dion. Even if we let him stay there — even if he doesn't change his mind — it could only ever be temporary. And then we're back where we started.'

'Exactly.' Dion cracked his knuckles, one by one. 'We'd be back where we started. So wouldn't it be better — suppose we could find a way to, let's say, to — *listen*, Ario — suppose we *could* leave him there? Or make the program *think* he was there? That would work, right?'

There was a new note in his voice, and she dropped her hand, looking at him intently. She said, 'You mean . . . cheat?'

He met her eyes, and they both almost smiled.

'OK . . .' Dion gestured at the block next to him. 'Let me explain.' He waited until she sat down, and leant forward, lacing his fingers together. 'I have a cheat that's not . . . I've never used it. But the idea is that it'll crash the iTank. It — never mind the details, but basically it holds it in a kind of . . . unbreakable stasis. I was playing around with malware,' he added, shrugging, when she raised an eyebrow. 'But it's a bit like saving a game, only no one can get through to open it again . . . If we ran it on this iTank while Rick was inside, Asterion would be tied up with Rick for ever.'

She nodded, slowly. His eyes flickered away. He grinned into the middle distance, picked up the cup that had held his

P&V shake and put the rim between his teeth, chewing the plastic. He's flying, she thought. He always looks shifty when he's flying. It doesn't mean he's hiding something.

'And . . . what happens to Rick?' she said.

'Well — it wouldn't be *him* in the Maze, obviously, because the iTank would be dead. I mean —' he corrected himself, '*not working —*'

She stared at him, and felt something uncurl inside her like a worm.

He turned his grin on her, widening it until it almost touched his ears. 'I — you know, Ario, I'm pretty sure it'd work.'

'What happens to Rick?' she repeated.

'I said. It won't be him in the Maze.' He laughed, but uncomfortably. 'There's — well, you know as well as I do, if the iTank malfunctions there's always a bit of a risk to the player, but he'd probably be OK, and, anyway, you heard him, he's prepared to stay there for ever, so even if something did happen to him we'd basically just be — accepting his sacrif—' He stopped and forced the grin even wider.

'He might die. That's what you mean.'

Dion screwed up his face, rubbing one eye with a finger until it squelched. There was a silence. He said at last, 'Well, there might be a chance . . .'

'No.'

'What do you mean, *n—*'

'Just *no*.' She turned away, holding up one hand as if the conversation was over. No. *No*, I am not going to let Rick die in the iTank. Whatever happens. I am not going to let him die.

291

'But if — Ario, for — what the —' Dion was sputtering with disbelief. He drew in air through his teeth and hissed it out again. 'Ario. This would work. I'm almost sure it would work.'

'I don't care.'

'We have to beat Asterion! And he — he's *agreed* to stay in the Maze for ever! This is so much more humane —'

'I am not — no! Dion, listen to yourself! *Humane?*'

'Fine. You've got a better idea, have you?'

'Yes. We log him out, and then we start again.'

He caught her arm and pulled her round to face him. He was white with anger, and his pupils were a pinprick, hardly visible. 'He doesn't *want* to log out. You heard him! And — this is madness, Ario, this is *crazy* — what if we can't hack Asterion before it gives our information to Crater?'

'It might not — it hasn't yet —'

'And you're happy to gamble our lives on that, are you?'

Silence. She tried to drag her arm out of his grip, but he held on tighter, still staring into her face. She could smell the P&V shake on his breath.

'I'm running the code, Ario. It's the only way.'

'No. You can't. Dion —' She forced herself to relax. 'Listen. Give me some time. Please.' She saw him start to frown, and made herself smile. 'While he's in there, Asterion can't do anything else, right? So we have time on our side. At least a few hours . . . There must be another way. Let me think for an hour, at least.'

He spread his hands and took a step backwards. 'If you think it'll help. But I'm telling you, if you don't think of something better, I'm running my program. Before he has a chance to get cold feet . . . And you won't be able to stop me.'

She held his look until he looked away: it was a tiny, meaningless victory, but it made her feel stronger. 'OK,' she said.

He nodded silently and went to the door. He paused with his hand spread on the comms panel and glanced over his shoulder. 'An hour,' he said. 'And don't try and get him out if you don't have a decent plan. If Asterion wins Rick won't thank you for it.'

She watched him without answering until he shrugged and went through the door. Then she leant on her elbows and stared at her terminal. The whiteness dazzled her, stinging like bleach. An hour. She had an hour. And she had no idea. She had to think of something fast; but her mind was as blank as her screen.

The minutes ticked away. She couldn't help staring at the iTank, mesmerised by the colours dancing in the depths. After a while she forced herself to turn back to her screen, and caught sight of the time. With a shock she saw that half an hour had gone. What was she *doing*?

But she didn't know what to do. That was the problem.

You're a Cheat. You're the best. *Think.*

Asterion. There has to be a way . . .

She reached out and closed the window on her flatscreen, bringing up her programming interface. The darkness was a relief after the snow-glare of the fog. You don't need to keep watch, she said to herself. If something new happens, you'll hear Rick's mic. Right now you need to think about what *you* can do.

But . . . if she tried to hack Asterion . . . it might be easier now, while it was distracted; but it was still the same program, it would still be slippery and complex, impossible to get a grip on . . . She pinched the bridge of her nose until her eyes watered. I've tried everything, she thought. I don't have any ideas left. I wasn't getting anywhere, even before it started talking to me . . .

Would you like to know about your father?

She shook her head, feeling a sudden wave of misery and resentment. It knew exactly what to say to me, didn't it? Pir must really have got inside my head . . . But Pir would never have said that. It was Asterion, using what he'd taken from her — Asterion, who was human enough, irrational enough to know . . .

Asterion. Human. Maybe —

An idea seemed to stir, deep in the shadows of her brain. She knocked a knuckle against her forehead, trying to wake it up.

Asterion was Daedalus, before. That's why he's clever.

He had a life — he worked at Crater, he knew Rick, he cared . . . Rick couldn't kill him because he recognised him. Even before he understood, even though he thought it was the only way to beat Asterion — he couldn't do it. He didn't remember *who* he was, but he knew that he was someone he'd loved . . . So Daedalus knew Rick too. And he must have cared. He tried to bar him from the Maze, to keep him safe.

So . . .

She sat back, started to glance at the clock and looked away determinedly. No. Concentrate.

Asterion's voice resonated in her skull, as loud as if it was speaking to her right now. *So you know Ario, do you? Pretty little thing. Is she that good-looking in real life?*

Shut up, shut *up* — no — wait —

She breathed out, very slowly.

There's a version of me in the Maze. Pir cared about me so much that I'm there — not quite myself, but still, recognisably, me . . . So if Daedalus knew Rick, back when he was human — somewhere there's Daedalus's own version of Rick.

There was another Rick, somewhere in the Maze.

Ario leant forward, scrolling down through the code that gleamed on her screen. It was a stupid idea — flimsy, blurred at the edges — but —

Maybe —

If there's another Rick — and now the program has recognised the real Rick, it might — there might be a way of —

If I could get the NPC Rick into the fight, somehow . . .

Her fingers were so sticky and clumsy it was hard to enter anything. She stopped, pressed her hands together and shut her eyes. One, two, three, four, five, she said to herself. Calm down. You don't have time to make a mistake.

If I can find . . . how can I find . . . ?

She opened her eyes. The Maze is huge, she thought. I could spend *days* looking . . . There must be thousands, hundreds of thousands of NPCs — if I went through them one by one it would take me *for ever* — and I might not even recognise him if I saw him. Especially if I'm looking with an interface that only shows code . . .

She stretched out a hand, ready to switch to a surve's-eye view of the Maze; but the initial fire of hope had faded into a dull, despairing grey. *What am I going to do? Hope I come across the NPC Rick in the next ten minutes? Where would he be? Somewhere hidden, surely, somewhere safe, protected . . .*

And to get him into the fight . . . to switch them over somehow, to make the fight go on for ever . . .

It can't be done. It can't — unless —

Rick can ask — he's allowed to ask for whatever he needs . . .

If Rick could — if, somehow, she could get a message to him —

She sat very still. Then she looked at the clock.

Fifteen minutes.

She was breathing hard, her blood thundering through her veins, her hands damp. She opened the file she'd made for Asterion, and started to search, digging deeper and deeper until she thought she saw the heart of the program, the place where it seemed to keep its consciousness. *Here,* she thought, *this is the fight, this is where it's happening, inside this little bit of AI, just here . . .* What she had to do was so simple: she had to get a message to Rick . . . Words flashed up on the screen would do it, something basic — but the program was still slippery and resistant, still capable of swallowing her code without a trace. No. Something less obvious. A different way of communicating with him — something . . . *elegant.* Something that would work with the program, not against it.

Yes. She had to think like Asterion. It wasn't just about code. It was about disguise, subtlety, finding a way that *fitted*.

In the dark depths of her screen beyond the text she saw her reflection, watching her, waiting.

And an idea came to her: delicate, tugging at her like a thread.

She took a deep breath.

She started to enter code frantically, not going back to look at what she'd done, her fingers moving constantly because she didn't have time to pause. Come on, come *on*.

She heard the door buzz, and Dion's voice. 'Give me — a minute, two minutes —' she said, without looking up. 'Please, come on . . .' She didn't know if she was talking to him or herself. She was dancing with Asterion now, distracting it with a side-attack so that she could just — *slip* this bit of code past —

She didn't know if it had worked or not, but she didn't have time to investigate. One more little adjustment — just a tiny thing, please, please don't notice, please, Rick, whatever you're doing in there keep him thinking about you, don't give him space to notice —

'I'm nearly ready — please, Dion, give me thirty seconds —'

'I'm logging on. Then I'm branching my terminal to the iTank and running my code.'

'Please . . .' but she didn't have time to plead. Her hands were moving so fast she couldn't see what she was doing. Two more lines, one more line —

There.
Done.

She sat back, and a spasm of shivers went over her, uncontrollable, so that she thought she was going to be sick. 'I've done it,' she said. 'Don't run your code. It's going to be OK.'

Dion looked up. His face stayed neutral. 'Let's see, then, babesauce.'

She gestured at her terminal. He hesitated before he got up; then he came over to her and leant towards her screen, his lips moving as he followed the lines of text. He glanced at her.

'You see? If Rick understands, it'll work — I'm sure it'll —'

He didn't answer. He only put his hand out and switched the flatscreen back to showing the iTank.

White. Still white.

'He needs a second to catch on to what I'm . . .' Ario stopped, staring at the blankness, willing Rick to understand. Please, she thought. Please. I'm saving your life . . .

They waited.

Nothing changed.

Nothing changes. There's no way of telling how fast time is going, except the slow-building stiffness in Rick's muscles, the hunger in his stomach growing like sand in the bottom bulb of an hourglass. Sooner or later I'll fall asleep — or need to go to the loo, he thinks. But I guess I can just wet myself.

He gets up and walks forward, just for something to do. He counts his steps — a hundred, two, five — but he doesn't get anywhere different. The huge staircase is still a long way away; the walls are still invisible. And Daed is still a few ems away, as if he's been keeping pace at Rick's side.

'You can log out any time you want,' Daed says.

Rick looks at him; but there's nothing to say. *I have to stay here. I can't let you win* . . . And every time he meets Daed's eyes he feels that strange rootless misery — or is it fear, or pity, or love? He doesn't know. If only he could remember properly . . . but all his memories are locked away. All he has is this certainty that once, a long time ago, Daed was the most important person in the world.

It doesn't make him want to stay, exactly; but it makes it bearable. And sooner or later, he thinks, they'll pull the plug

on the iTank, so my body dies and leaves me here. Then . . .
but he doesn't want to think about what it'll be like.

Perhaps he won't even feel it. Perhaps they've done it
already.

He swings round on his heel, and then laughs and turns
back again, because it doesn't matter what direction he
walks in, does it? But he ends up in front of Daed, eye to eye,
almost the way they were when Rick had his dagger at his
throat.

I nearly got my mind sucked out, Rick thinks. He laughs
again. The sound is short and bitter and the silence snaps its
jaws on it immediately. Yes. Because that would have been
so much worse than staying here, for ever . . .

But this way I win. This way Asterion loses.

Daed says, 'Rick . . . please. I wanted you to be free of all
this.'

The words set off an ache in Rick's throat. I don't know
who you *are*, he thinks. Why does it hurt so much?

Daed puts his hand on Rick's arm. When Rick doesn't move
away, he smiles a little and pulls Rick gently into an embrace.
'Would it really be so hard just to say *log out*? You've done
your best. You know you can't stay here.'

'I can try,' Rick says, but so quietly he isn't sure that
Daed's heard him. He lets his forehead rest against Daed's
shoulder, breathing the scent of all the things he loves. He
can't remember the last time someone held him like this,
supporting him, taking his weight. It makes something inside
him thaw, as though he's been frozen for longer than he
knows. Suddenly his knees are made of water, his heart soggy

300

and struggling with fatigue. If they could only pull the plug right now, so he could die here, now . . .

'Come on, Rick. Light of my life, apple of my eye . . .' It's irony; but at the same time it isn't. 'Repeat after me: log out. L-o-g o-u-t.'

He doesn't have the energy to answer. If he hadn't let Daed put his arms round him . . . but it's too late. He doesn't want to resist any more.

'If you log out you can always come back. Whenever you want.'

He nods. He'll do whatever he's told.

'You've done really well. No one could blame you. Better to log out, and then you and Ario can try and think of some-thing el—'

Ario. The word wakes him up, like a slap in the face.

Ario.

He pulls away, stumbles backwards, shaking. 'Leave me alone!' he says. 'Don't touch me. Leave me alone. I'm not going to —' He stops, trembling on the abyss of saying the words. 'I'm staying. I'm going to stay. Get used to it.' And he spins round, runs into the vast space in front of him, trying desperately to get away. But the floor is slippery and he skids and loses his balance. He falls forward, his hands and knees smacking the marble at the same moment. He gasps. For a second nothing is real except the pain in his legs and wrists.

When he opens his eyes he's looking at his own reflection in the marble. He stares, breathing deeply, concentrating on not crying out. His reflection is grimacing, dim and monochrome in the depths of the polished stone. He meets his own eyes.

It smiles at him.

He recoils, his heart jumping, and he can't help throwing a quick glance over his shoulder to where Daed is standing. But Rick's reflection doesn't move with him, and when he looks back it's waiting for him, intent and still. Its mouth moves and it reaches for him as if it's on the other side of a pane of glass. He frowns, trying to make out what it's saying. Consonants — *sk, f, m*.

A message from — from Ario — it has to be —

There's a part of him that almost laughs aloud, because it's clever, it's so like something Daed would do . . .

But what is it — my reflection, what is — what am *I* saying —?

Ask for me.

He shakes his head. I don't understand. What —?

I'm here. Ask for me.

He holds its stare for as long as he can, struggling to make sense of it; but when he frowns, trying not to blink, he sees the same expression on its face. The moment has gone. It's only his reflection again.

He gets to his feet. He turns round.

It's a message from Ario. It has to be. Even though he doesn't know what it means. *Ask for me* . . . Daed will give him what he asks for, that's part of the deal . . . but what . . . ?

He says, 'I want —'

'Yes?'

'I want . . .' He's going to say, *my reflection*. Or *my shadow*. Whatever it was, that faint, desperate version of himself, trapped on the other side of reality . . .

He hears himself say, 'I want *myself*.'

Daed flinches.

And he knows he's got it right.

A tremor goes through his body. The floor trembles, the fountain wavers, the faraway walls shimmer through air that's suddenly silky, like heat-haze. His eyes blur.

And his reflection is there, in the space with them. He's between them, glancing back and forth, wary, like a child caught between his parents. He's younger than Rick, unscarred, fragile and defiant, with a scrawny grace Rick doesn't recognise: but he knows he's looking at himself.

'Rick —' Daed says. 'Gods, Rick, you —'

But the boy standing there turns to Rick, ignoring Daed's voice; and for a moment they just look at each other. Rick feels queasy, dislocated; he doesn't understand how this kid can help him, any more than any other NPC. Just because they're both — just because —

Daed says, 'Wait — you're — I can't —'

He doesn't know which of us is real, Rick thinks. We're both in his head, and he can't —

But he doesn't have time to complete the thought. The boy is still staring at him, his face full of disbelief and a kind of hope. He crosses the floor in a quick leaping movement; and then, deliberately, he raises his hand and touches Rick's face. For a second Rick feels warmth on his cheek. Then it's gone.

What was —?

And then he's split in two. Something's happened to his head. He darts away and he's fighting, tireless and swift, ducking and rolling, the space whirling around him and Daed at the centre of his vision, defending desperately; but he's watching too, reeling on his feet, giddy and confused. What the —? He's both of them, neither of them — and his younger self has taken over, is fighting his fight for him — will go on fighting, he knows that —

And Daed doesn't know which is which, they're both real, both Rick . . .

I'm in Daed's head and he's in mine and we're both — both of me —

He stands back, blinking and struggling against the double vision. In front of his own eyes he's locked in the battle with Daed, smooth and skilful as a dancer; and behind him, he knows he's watching himself as he dodges and feints. I'm standing still, I'm moving. I'm fighting and I'm not. I'm here and there, for ever and now. I'm mortal and immortal. I'm going to win and I'm going to lose.

I'm real, *and* I'm part of the Maze.

It's over.

He doesn't have the strength to say the words: but his mouth forms the shape of *Log out*.

The log-out screen drops down like a curtain.

He stands in the iTank, and his eyes adjust in a swirl of vertigo. He leans forward, trembling, still with his mind's eye full of that battle. Myself, he thinks, and Daed. We'll be there for ever. Me and someone I love. Two of us, perfectly matched.

And then he starts to cry, because he knows he's free.

28

It was Dion who ran to the iTank and activated the emergency procedures. It was Dion who said, 'Manual mode, *manual mode* —' and dragged at the door, trying to get it open quicker. It was Dion who muttered, 'OK, mate, you're OK, lean on me . . .' and helped Rick out, staggering a bit under his weight. And it was Dion who walked him across the floor and out into the tankshop hall, murmuring encouragement, not even pausing as they went past Ario at her terminal. Dion flashed her a look but she was blind with fatigue, too tired to read whether it was congratulatory or sympathetic or irritated because she hadn't got up to take Rick's other arm. She didn't care, anyway.

She'd done it. It had worked.

They'd beaten Asterion. Rick was still alive. She'd got him out.

It didn't seem like a very big deal, somehow.

She stood up at last. Everything was muzzy and far away. She had to concentrate on her knees just to stay on her feet. She walked to the door and leant on the comms panel.

The door slid open. For a split second she was lost in contemplation, swaying gently while darkness hatched into snakes that slid towards her from the corners of the room.

Then the door and everything around it shrank to the size of a pinhead, flared sickeningly bright, and everything went black.

29

'You don't have to go, babesauce.' Dion's voice came from the doorway. 'I know things have been weird, but . . . it's over now, right? And you're only just back on your feet, after . . . Stay. Give it another go. We need you.'

Ario glanced at him, pausing with one hand on her bag and the other poised in mid-air. Then she shook her head, smiled, and picked up her iThing from the block beside her bed. 'Thanks, Dion.' He was right, she was still a bit shaky, still not quite back to normal; but if she didn't go now, she might never manage it.

'Seriously. Now it's all blown over . . . You did really well, and . . .' He shrugged, grimacing. 'We can get you some more clients, no problem.'

'Dion . . .' She looked round. She'd packed all her stuff, but her cube didn't look very different, just tidier. Her bag sat on the bed, looking small and forlorn. 'I'm not going to change my mind.'

'You can always come back. You know that.'

'Thanks for the money,' she said, slung the bag on to her shoulder and eased past him into the corridor. He turned to watch her go, but he didn't follow; and she was glad, because if he'd said anything else she might have weakened. She clenched her jaw, telling herself to toughen up. She was leaving. Get used to the idea, Ario. You've been planning this for days.

The smell of rain was stronger today than it had been for a long time. She could taste it as she stepped through the doorway into the tankshop hall. It was early, but the sweetness of dawn had already faded, and the light was dim and grimy. She looked around at the tankshop, the rows of terminals, and tried to swallow the acrid saliva on the back of her tongue. There was no one there. My last look, she thought. What a dump. I should have left long ago . . . but even in her head the words sounded false, full of bravado. I can't do this, she thought. I'm not brave enough.

She heard the door buzz open behind her. 'Dion, I said I'm going,' she said. Her voice was too high, as if she didn't believe what she was saying. She cleared her throat and added, 'Dion, seriously, go fy—'

'It's me.'

She spun round. It was Rick. They looked at each other for what felt like a long time. Then, belatedly, she forced herself to smile. 'Hi,' she said, and felt herself blush.

'So,' he said, and shifted his weight. 'You're going.'

'Yes.'

'Sure?'

'Yes.'

'You don't look it.'

She took a quick breath, ready to snap at him; but then something else took over and she hunched one shoulder and laughed quietly. 'I'm scared stiff,' she said. 'But I have to go. I thought — Dion doesn't understand, he thinks living here for ever is OK, but I thought — *you* might know why —'

He nodded. The silence between them was warm, charged, like the air before a storm.

'Listen —' but she didn't know what she wanted to say to him. 'I wish . . . After Asterion, I —'

'I should have thanked you,' he said, cutting her off, speaking so quickly the words ran into each other. 'Afterwards I didn't know what to say — and when you were ill —'

'You sat with me. Lia told me.'

'Yes, but when you woke up I left . . . there was so much to say, and I should have said — I never even said thanks. Ario —'

'It's OK,' she said. 'I just wish — I mean, *I* never said —'

'It's OK — Ario, that's OK too.' He held up his hand to stop her saying any more. She held his look as long as she could, embarrassed and touched; then they both broke into a grin at the same moment. 'Right. Well. Glad we got that out of the way . . .'

There was another silence. His eyes slid over the strap of her bag on her shoulder and back to her face.

'Goodbye, then,' she said.

He bit his lip, and moved his head in a gesture that wasn't quite a nod. 'Good luck,' he said. 'You'll do fine. You're good. You're the best.'

She said, trying to laugh, 'At what? Or just in general?' but it came out wrong and she turned away quickly, biting her tongue, before he had time to answer. She took a few steps forward, trying to ignore the tingle between her shoulder blades as the distance between them grew.

'Why did you decide to leave?'

She raised her shoulders in a kind of frozen shrug. 'It was time,' she said. 'Dion said I could stay, but after everything that happened . . . and —' She stopped and added, realising it for the first time, 'And I was sick of being afraid.'

'I know what you mean.'

She stared straight ahead, into the shadows at the corner of the room.

'I've never been outside. As far as I know.' He made a quick sound like a laugh. 'The bits that have come back are like a dream . . . but I remember that I lived in Crater, with Daed. And then I was here. And I've always been scared — protected and really *scared*. It must be better to face the danger than to be like that. That's why I understand.'

The shadows crawled and blurred in front of her eyes. Courage, she thought. That's what he means. She breathed in, and the taste of rain was softer, cleaner, like onions.

She turned to face him. 'That night when I cried and you held me —'

At the same time he said, 'Can I come with you?'

'Yes,' she said, answering him.

He smiled suddenly and then bit his lip as if he was trying to hide how pleased he was. After a second he took a deep breath and said, 'Yes.' And somehow she knew he was answering her.

He came to stand at her side, and for the first time she noticed that he had a bag over his shoulder, already packed. He knew, she thought. He knew I'd say yes . . . but it only made her smile more widely. The bag was smaller than hers, but it looked heavy. He'd been gamerunning while she was ill; maybe it was full of money . . .

'A gamerunner and a Cheat,' he said. 'I reckon we'll be OK.'

They put on their out-clothes in silence, without catching each other's eye; but Ario was grinning like an idiot, so weak with relief and a strange sort of excitement that she fumbled with her fastenings for ages before she got them tight enough. She heard him laugh at her, softly.

Then they went out together into the rain.

'Collins is one hell of a writer' *Guardian*

www.bloomsbury.com

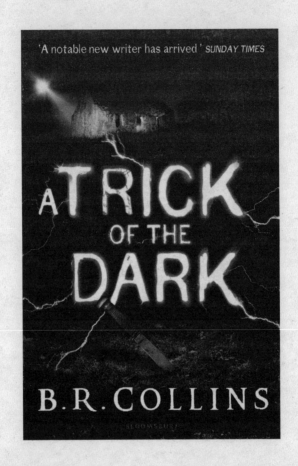

'A notable new writer has arrived' *SUNDAY TIMES*

A TRICK
OF THE
DARK

B.R. COLLINS

BLOOMSBURY

'Dark, uneasy and extraordinary' *The Times*

www.bloomsbury.com